To KAY

Between Two Gates

A Young Man's Quest Toward Birth

by
Neil Perry Gordon

D1453119

Cover Art:
"Unborn" by Bonnie Manaças
Graphic design R. Manaças
https://www.facebook.com/bonnie.manacas

Disclaimer:

This novel is a work of fiction. Any resemblance to actual persons, living or

deceased, is purely coincidental. The characters, events, and circumstances

portrayed in this book are products of the author's imagination. While some

elements may be inspired by real-life situations or historical events, they

have been significantly altered and fictionalized for the purpose of

storytelling. The author does not endorse or claim any association with real

individuals or events mentioned in this novel.

ISBN:
979-8-9875632-2-9

To my Dearest Son Samuel,

Between Two Gates is an awe-inspiring testament to our profound collaboration in the creation of this novel. It's been a partnership that has bridged the divide between our realms. Throughout this remarkable creative journey, your presence has been an elixir of your spiritual wisdom and insights. Such inspiration is evident in these pages.

Together we have pierced the veil separating us. The result is this fantastic tale, enveloped with a vibrant energy that magnificently captures the wonders you have experienced.

I'm profoundly moved by the sheer joy that has permeated this endeavor. Your impact on this novel is immeasurable, and the enduring presence of your being remains an unwavering guiding light in my writing.

In paying tribute to your extraordinary, hierarchical legacy, I aspire for this book to stand as an eternal homage to our boundless love encapsulated within these pages.

LIFE AFTER DEATH
LIFE BEFORE BIRTH
ONLY BY KNOWING BOTH
DO WE KNOW ETERNITY
~ RUDOLF STEINER 1914

Contents

BETWEEN TWO GATES

A Young Man's Quest Toward Birth

~ Act One ~

CHAPTER ONE
DEATH

I walked across the frozen ballpark, the same one where our team had clinched the Little League Championship game twenty years earlier. A train rumbled by in the distance, just as one had when I'd stood upon the pitcher's mound as a determined twelve-year-old.

Through naked branches of mangled trees encircling the outfield fence, a full moon cast long shadows across the ice-encrusted field. A sole streak of moonlight illuminated the home team's dugout, where behind a rusted chain-link fence sat a man on a wooden bench. The same bench my teammates had once nestled upon during our games.

I stepped from the field onto the dugout's bubblegum-stained concrete slab and saw the man clearly. "Poppy? Is that you?" I asked, wondering if I was dreaming of my dead grandfather.

Poppy smiled and nodded. His face appeared younger than my memory of him. He lifted a hand and summoned me over just as a gust stirred up a whirlwind of crushed paper cups and discarded plastic water bottles from underneath the narrow bench.

"Aren't you cold, Poppy?" I asked, though I, too, was somehow unaffected by the seemingly frigid temperature.

"Come and sit with me, Sam," Poppy said, holding out an arm.

I sat, looked into my grandfather's brown eyes, and asked, "Why are you here? Am I dreaming?"

Poppy wrapped his thin arm around me, leaned in, and whispered, "Grandson, this is not a dream."

"Then where am I?"

"I'm here to assist with your transition."

"Transition?" I repeated.

"Yes, from your life on the Earth to the next stage of your existence," Poppy explained.

"Next stage?" I asked with a furrowed brow.

Poppy puckered his mouth and nodded.

I swallowed hard before daring to ask, "Am I dead?"

Poppy sighed. "I'm not fond of that word. I prefer saying—passed on."

Suddenly feeling the cold, my body shivered. I panted a few breaths and said, "No, this can't be?"

"I know this is a shock, and that's why I am here to help you understand."

I dropped my face into the palms, and as I did, I saw an image of my body upon an ambulance gurney, being wheeled down the long, steep driveway of my home while Dad hurried alongside. "What have I done?" I cried out.

"We'll get to that," Poppy said. "Right now, before we go any further, I want you to know you're in a good place. A natural place where we continue to exist until that time when we're called upon to make our return."

I straightened up, swept an arm across the desolate, iced-over ball field, and said, "You call this a good place?"

"It was once for you."

"It was, but not like this," I said, wanting tears to flow, but none came.

"This is the result of what your life force has conjured up. When it was my time, I crossed over and found myself in my store, where my mother greeted me."

"Nanny Sophie?" I said, remembering my great-grandmother's name. "Is she here?" I asked, looking around.

"No, she has since returned to the earthly realm."

"What about me? Will I return too?"

Poppy chuckled. "Of course, but not yet. You have much work to do before you're ready."

"Work?" I asked wide-eyed. "What kind of work?"

"There will be many questions. Some of which will be answered, though most, I'm sorry to say, will remain a mystery." Poppy sighed. "As is the nature of the universe."

A sudden sour taste blossomed in my mouth, forcing me to grimace. "I could use some water?"

"Well, there's no more drinking, eating, sleeping, or movements of your bodily functions. Your consciousness triggers memories of earthly needs and desires, but these demands and urges will soon fade away."

I looked down at myself, wearing the same familiar clothes and shoes. I patted my jeans, confirming my presence. "But I don't look different."

"We're in this form so we can communicate. Once you undergo purification, you'll no longer need a physical form, though you may imagine you still do."

"Wait," I said, holding out my palm. "What about all of those whom I left behind?"

"They are grieving," Poppy said, nodding.

I closed my eyes and turned my head away. "This is all too much," I said.

Poppy nodded. "I know, Sam."

I sighed and gazed out onto the desolate ball field. A flash of light caught my interest. It came from the visitor's dugout, where I saw, within its shadows, the silhouette of a person. "Is someone over there?" I asked, pointing at a pair of golden eyes seemingly observing me.

Poppy nodded and said, "Yes, that's your *rasha*."

Unable to look away, I asked, "My what?"

"Your *rasha*," Poppy repeated.

"What's that?"

Poppy took a breath and slowly sighed. "Well, in the simplest terms, the *rasha* is your dark side, and he arrived here the same moment you did."

"My dark side," I blurted out. "What does it mean?"

"You're not ready yet for such answers. But know this," Poppy said, pointing a finger into the opposing dugout. "Until you conquer the *rasha*, you'll continue to suffer. It's what brought you here at such a young age."

I swallowed hard, scratched my head, and quivered. "I'm scared, Poppy. I-I don't understand."

"That's all right," he said, placing his warm palm upon my cheek. "We'll figure it out together. But for now, come with me."

We stood up and headed across the field. I glanced over to the third base side dugout and froze as I connected with the golden eyes focused on me. Then, with a voice that sounded like my own, the *rasha* spoke: "Come, Sam. This is easier with me."

"Don't listen!" Poppy shouted and jerked my arm, forcing me forward. When I broke my stare with my dark counterpart, I found myself standing in my bedroom where several paramedics, police officers, my wife, Meghan, and Dad were gathered around my body, laid out on the carpet.

"Is that me?"

"This is the moment before you passed," Poppy said, stepping closer to the body. "What I need to know is—what you were thinking in that instant."

I put my hand to my mouth and looked at my dad, who spoke to a police officer, then over to Meghan as she wiped away tears running down her cheeks.

"Do you remember?" Poppy asked, regaining my attention.

I sighed, gazing down at my body, lying still and at peace, and said, "I stood between two gates. One was where I would return to the living, and the other was what brought me here with you."

Poppy turned me around, wrapped his arms around me, pulled me in with a clutch, and whispered, "Why did you choose to die?"

"The drugs weren't helping anymore," I said, biting my lower lip.

Poppy nodded and said, "That's what I thought."

I looked at my grandfather and sighed.

"Let me show you something else," Poppy said, and in an instant, we were standing before my body, lying on a table in what looked like a hospital room.

"There's no one here," I said.

"That's because you have already passed," Poppy said.

"This way, sir," a voice said from just beyond the doorway.

I turned to see Dad walking in, accompanied by a doctor in a white coat.

"Stay as long as you like," she said, leaving him alone.

Dad approached the table, placed his palm against my cheek, and said, "You're still warm." He then kissed my forehead and held my hand. "Sam, Sam, what have you done?"

His eyes were tearless as he paced the floor, giving the impression that he was trying to figure out a solution how to bring me back. Then, after a few minutes, he climbed onto the table, lay beside me, and said, "I'm so sorry, son, but I couldn't save you."

Father wrapped an arm across my chest, cradled his head on my shoulder, and wept.

CHAPTER TWO
OBSERVATIONS

A voice caught my attention, and when I turned to its source, I was standing in the backyard of my home. It was nighttime, the interior lights were on, and through the kitchen window, I saw my wife. Her cheeks glistened with streams of tears. Her face was pale and drawn, her long brown hair disheveled. Her family had gathered around her, trying their best to console her. Longing to do the same, I pointed toward the door and said, "Can I go in and—"

"No, I'm sorry, but that's impossible," Poppy said, interrupting me. "But we'll remain here for a while."

Another light turned on. This time in the next window, I saw Dad taking a seat before my work computer, which I used exclusively for our business. "Pops doesn't know the password," I said while Poppy and I took a few steps closer.

"Pops? Is that what you called him?" Poppy asked.

"I do; I mean, I did," I said with a pained smile.

"Why don't you help Pops figure out the password?" Poppy suggested.

"Help him, how?" I asked as Dad failed at several login attempts.

"You have to wait until he asks, then you can provide the answer," Poppy said.

"It's *Yankees*, all lowercase," I said, wondering how he would hear me.

Urging patience, Poppy held up a finger and said, "Let's watch."

I stared at Dad's face, focused on the task at hand. Until whatever had happened to me, it had been my responsibility to manage running the books for the window-covering business Dad had founded several years before my birth. I began working for him after my first job out of college with a luxury hotel in Manhattan. It was a good, well-paid position that I enjoyed. But six months in, I was dismissed after sending an essential package by regular mail instead of using the desired express service—a surprising reaction to what I considered a minor infraction. Dad suggested I could temporarily work for him while looking for a new position. That was eleven years ago, and until yesterday, I never returned to the hospitality industry and instead became his partner in his successful business and, ultimately, heir to its control once he retired.

Dad continued to make wrong entries, trying to unlock the computer where vital access to the business account resided. I knew the hard drive would lock up with several unsuccessful attempts. Then his only recourse would be the undesirable course of reaching out to Apple tech support for assistance.

Realizing his predicament, Dad closed his eyes and said, "Sam, what's the password?"

I quickly looked over to Poppy, who smiled and nodded. "Go ahead, tell him."

"Tell him how?" I asked.

"Just say it aloud. Dad will hear you."

I stroked my unshaven cheek and said, "Yankees, all lowercase."

Dad opened his eyes, typed the letters onto the keyboard, and as if he flicked on a light switch, both monitors lit up, illuminating Dad's face with its bluish glow.

"Oh my god!" Dad shouted, clapping his hands together.

"I did it," I cried, wrapping my arms around Poppy, who hugged me back.

"Thank you, Sam," Dad said.

Just then, Meghan entered the room, and with joyous animation, Dad explained what had just happened. They hugged, and I saw tears flowing down both their faces. I, too, wanted to cry but, as before, was unable.

Then Dad glanced out the window and pointed. "Is someone standing outside?" he asked Meghan while they gazed into the darkened backyard.

"Can he see me?" I asked, staring back.

Poppy nodded. "He sees a shadow of what remains of your body on the Earth, which happens occasionally. This is good, and your father will use this as a sign of your spirit trying to remain connected with him."

"That's possible?" I asked.

Poppy nodded. "But it depends upon the living, and it's up to them to try staying connected; otherwise, it will fade quickly."

"But what if I'm forgotten?" I asked.

Poppy closed his eyes and shook his head. "You won't be. Your father won't ever let go of you; your bond with him is everlasting."

I bit my lower lip and nodded. "I know that."

"Meghan, too, will keep you close. Though in time, she'll move on. She's young and will want a family," Poppy said while we watched her back in the kitchen, being attended to by her mother and sister.

"We spoke about having a baby this year."

"That would have been wonderful," Poppy said.

I closed my eyes and shook my head. "What have I done?"

"You have many things yet to consider and, in turn, to learn from. We will look back over the significant events in the thirty-two years of your life. This will be done in about a third of the years you were alive, about the same time you slept."

"That's over ten years," I said. "Why so long?"

Poppy wagged a finger. "In the soul world, time is not measured as on Earth, and you can be very productive here by being in several places simultaneously."

I closed my eyes and shook my head. "How's that possible?"

"You are no longer a physical entity. You now exist as part of the universal consciousness," Poppy said.

I stared at Poppy, trying to remember him before his death. But his presence seemed hazy, unlike those gathered in the house where I once dwelled. Meghan and her family appeared more substantial, as if their bodies had a purpose, while Poppy's was lighter, more like an illusion or a dream.

"Our minds," Poppy said, tapping a finger on his head, "are a microcosm of the greater universal consciousness. This endless expanse is where we exist after passing and before our calling to our eventual rebirth."

"I'll be born again?"

Nodding, Poppy said, "It's the nature of the universe. Except for those few who have lived a life that makes no demands on them to return, be it for good or bad."

"Good or bad?" I repeated.

"Yes, there are both *tzaddik* and *rasha* in the universe. *Tzaddik* are the hand of Hashem, of which there are only thirty-six on Earth at any one time. When their moment comes, they do not need to return, as they have given all they could and have earned the right to remain as higher beings among the cosmos."

"But what about the bad ones, the *rasha*? What happens to them?"

"*Rasha* are soulless," Poppy said, grasping my shoulder. "They are not permitted to return or amend for their misdeeds. Instead, they are destined to spend eternity within the lowest realms of Gehenna."

"Gehenna?" I repeated, rubbing the back of my neck. "What's that?"

"That's enough for now," Poppy said, waving a gentle hand across my eyes. "It's time we begin our work."

I swallowed hard. "But you said there was a *rasha* inside me, back at the ball field," I said, pointing in no particular direction.

"When alive, we have both within us—*tzaddik* and *rasha*. Each provides qualities to our essence or being. But your *rasha* seems strong, which may help explain things."

I bit my lower lip and asked, "Am I one of the soulless?"

"No, of course not. For most people, there's a balance between the dark and the light. Sometimes we can get out of balance, allowing the *rasha* within to lead us down pathways we should have avoided."

I nodded, thinking back on the cause of my death. "I always felt some sort of darkness consumed me."

"And that's why you sought the drugs."

I nodded.

"It seems the *rasha* is not done with you yet."

"What do I do?" I asked, knowing there were no more drugs to hide behind.

"I'll help you, Sam, but for now, there's much more to see," Poppy said, gesturing for me to walk into the darkness.

CHAPTER THREE
THE CEMETERY

"So many people showed up," I said, observing the crowd gathered among the cars in the cemetery's parking lot.

"Doesn't look like the cold kept anybody away," Poppy said.

The weather, according to the abundance of heavy parkas, hats, and scarves being worn, was well below freezing, though, once again, Poppy and I remained impervious to the frigid conditions.

"There's Dad," I said, watching him speaking with the rabbi, the same rabbi who presided over my Bar Mitzvah.

"And there's Max with your mother," Poppy said, pointing them out.

"Yes, I see them. But where's Meghan?" I asked, looking through the gaps of people huddled together under collective clouds of breath.

A black hearse made its way slowly into the parking lot and came to a stop. The door opened, and a tall, thin man wearing a black overcoat and a black-knitted hat emerged. Dad also spotted the funeral aide and joined him alongside the vehicle. They spoke for a moment, then the man nodded and walked to the rear end, where he opened the door, exposing a wooden casket.

"That's for me?" I asked, pointing to the polished mahogany.

With a few indiscernible maneuvers, the man reached in and flipped a latch, then lifted the lid, exposing my body.

I shared a look with Poppy, who was shaking his head and said, "This is not allowed."

Unaware of the Jewish custom of not permitting the viewing of a deceased body, several of my childhood friends, Hasan, Derek, Sky, and Jason, had formed a line, gazing into the open casket. From where Poppy and I stood, it looked like Hasan was saying something to my soulless body while Sky pulled out a fancy whiskey flask and placed it inside the casket.

"They're giving me gifts," I said.

When they dispersed, my brother Max approached, pulled out a necklace, and placed it inside. I took a step closer, wanting to take a look. But Poppy grasped me and said, "You mustn't see the body."

I nodded and turned my attention to Meghan, who appeared through the masked grievers consoling one another, ignoring the dangers of the contagious Coronavirus pandemic.

"There she is," I said, poking a finger.

"Come, let's get closer," Poppy said.

Meghan's family surrounded her. Her brother had his long arm wrapped around her tender frame. Frozen teardrops clung to her COVID mask. I cringed, feeling her pain, wanting to comfort her. "Meghan!" I cried out. But my words fell silent, caught in the winds swirling across the blacktop.

"They're heading on up," Poppy said, gesturing to the hearse inching toward the burial site.

We joined the solemn procession.

As we crested the hill, I saw several people gathering by the parked hearse, where the casket was pulled out along a series of rollers and then transferred onto a metal cart with sturdy-looking rubber wheels.

"Who will be the pallbearers?" the tall, thin man called out.

Dad, standing nearby, pointed to my friends, naming Hasan, Derek, Sky, and Jason for the honors.

Once the casket was secured onto the cart, the four men pushed it down the sidewalk to the gravesite, where another metal mechanism was perched over a rectangular hole dug out into the frozen ground. Each gripping a corner, my friends lifted the casket and, with audible grunts, carefully placed it onto the frame. Then they stepped aside, allowing two men with the cemetery staff to engage the device, slowly lowering the casket into the earth. Once it rested on the dirt six feet below, the men pulled the straps free and removed the frame.

People gathered around the fresh grave as the rabbi stepped forward and began the service, speaking through his mask.

"According to Jewish tradition, only certain people are obligated to be mourners. Yet, that doesn't preclude those paying their respects today of lending your support to the grieving," the rabbi said.

I shared a look with Poppy, who acknowledged me with a pained smile.

"It is tempting," the rabbi continued, "to try and offer perfect words to ease the suffering of the mourners. But frankly, no words can soothe such pain on this sad, sad day. All we can do is respond to the mourner's choices. If they choose to laugh, then we laugh with them. If they choose to cry, then we cry too. If all they need is a shoulder or just a presence, then that's what we're prepared to give. In the weeks and months ahead, we will be there for them and model what Sam would have wanted in his lifetime."

I took a moment to look at the array of masked faces, most of whom I recognized as friends from our community. It was a remarkable turnout, especially for such a frigid day.

"The Hebrew word *uriah* means 'tearing,'" the rabbi said. "This refers to tearing one's clothing and represents someone torn away from our lives, as Sam was. But instead of tearing one's clothes, we use a symbol."

I looked over to Dad, who wore a black ribbon pinned to his overcoat, as did Mom, Max, and Meghan.

The rabbi said, "I'm going to ask the Gordons to tear their ribbons."

After removing their gloves, each took a moment to rip the ceremonial ribbon.

"I will now recite the prayer. First in Hebrew, then in English," the rabbi said.

The rabbi closed his eyes, held his hands, and began, *"Baruch atah Adonai, Eloheinu each haOlam, Dayan helmet."* He paused momentarily, then continued, *"Blessed are you, Adonai, Ruler of the universe, the True Judge.* We pray and trust that Sam is among all those who have gone before him. The Lord has given, and the Lord has taken away. While we accompany the body to its resting place, Sam's soul has returned to Hashem and is bound within a band of protective light."

I took a moment to absorb the reactions of the congregation. Even with glazed-over, tear-filled eyes, all were riveted to the rabbi's sermon.

"The mysteries of life and death are beyond the limits of our earthly understanding," the rabbi said. "While overwhelmed and perplexed with grief, it is in such sorrow that we confront the reality of Sam being taken from our midst, and in turn, we feel our frailty."

Heads, donned with hoods, hats, or scarves, all nodded in unison.

"Now, a friend of Sam, Hasan, will share a few words," the rabbi said.

I had known Hasan since kindergarten, and we had been in the same class through seventh grade. We shared many beautiful memories, including playing on the same Little League team year after year.

Hasan stepped forward, unfolded a paper, glanced down at his notes, and said, "I spent much of my childhood down at Sam's. That house was the meeting point for all our friends and Mecca for our rule-breaking schemes. Like most young boys growing up, we all had our big dreams. Jason wanted to be in the NBA, Sky imagined becoming a fireman, Derek a baseball manager, and I . . . well, I wanted to be a cowboy. But thinking back on those childhood fantasies since Sam's passing, I can't remember his big dream.

"A few years later, well into our teens, we all went to get military-style dog tags inscribed with inspirational quotes for us to wear around our necks when going to the beach or gym. We chose among excerpts from our favorite films like *Gladiator*, one-liners from Muhammad Ali, or lyrics from our hero Eminem. When finished, we saw that Sam's dog tags were etched with three solitary words—family, friends, and love. We were, of course, pretty amused and ribbed on him endlessly.

"Now, all these years later, it's evident that Sky never became a firefighter, Derek gave up his dream of being a baseball manager, Jason never made it to the NBA, and sadly, I never became a cowboy. But Sam certainly fulfilled his dream of family, friends, and love.

"It's unfair to see my companion's story ending here today. Sammy, I will use you as a beacon of light, carrying you forward with me each day, leaning on our precious memories, using you as my inspiration for what kind of son I want to be and for the son I hope to one day have.

"And, of course, speaking for all of our childhood friends, I hope to be the friend to others that you always were to me. We are both thirty-two years old, and it breaks my heart that I get to continue with my journey and my story. On the other hand, I have to say goodbye to you here today," Hasan concluded, and stepped back into the assembly.

"Your friend is eloquent," Poppy observed.

I could only grimace at his words.

"We don't have to remain here if it's too hard for you," Poppy offered.

"Oh no," I said, holding up a hand. "I don't want to leave."

"Sam's brother, Max, will speak next," the rabbi said.

Max, wearing boots made from some animal he skinned, a fur hat, and a heavy canvas overcoat, stepped forward just as a strong gust of wind swept a dusting of snow into a whirlwind that hovered over the grave. My brother gestured toward this display and said, "According to Native traditions, the northerly winds are said to be sent from the Grandfathers. Proof that Sam's ancestors are among us today."

I looked at Poppy, who offered a smug smile at these words.

Max then looked at the surrounding people and said, "Sam would have been happy that so many people are here."

He stood for a moment in silence as tears filled his eyes. Picking up on his distress, Dad wrapped an arm around his shoulder, comforting his remaining son as Max continued, "Sam was so loved. He was a warrior who died in battle, and that is how I will always remember him in my heart."

Briefly choking away tears, Max said, "I pray for my father. I pray for my mother. I pray for Meghan to have peace. As for me, I hope to remain connected with Sam. It's an honor to have been his brother."

With that, Max and Dad embraced as the rabbi stepped forward. "Now Sam's father has words to share."

Dad removed his mask, made eye contact with those nearby, and said, "I want to thank you all for coming. It means a lot to my family and, of course, to my dear son. The rabbi mentioned how there are no words

20

to ease one's grief and pain we're all enduring. I, too, had similar thoughts, prompting me to compose these words."

With that, Dad pulled a folded paper from his coat pocket and read:

"There are no words to express the sorrow consuming me.

There are no words exposing the gash carved deep into my heart.

There are no words to share that speak to this excruciating pain.

There are no words to unwind the knots of confusion twisting within my mind.

There are no words for the anger of having my darling boy ripped from my arms.

There are no words, yet there are many, many tears.

There are no words to describe the abundance of love for my precious son.

There are no words to say that thirty-two years and forty-six days of life are insufficient.

There are no words, just prayers that he is greeted and cared for wherever he is now.

There are no words that can erase this moment, forever etched into my eternal soul.

There are no words—There are no words. . ."

CHAPTER FOUR
THE GLADIATOR

"Why are we here?" I asked as Poppy and I stood alone in Ben's disheveled apartment.

"Is this where you bought the drugs?"

I grimaced with a nod. "Yes. They were counterfeit Percocets."

"And the last one was spiked with a lethal amount of fentanyl," Poppy added.

I remained silent, hanging my head.

Poppy went on, "What I don't understand is why you would trust a drug dealer in the first place—especially when you almost died the last time he sold you tainted pills."

I sighed and said, "I guess I thought it would never happen again."

"Luckily, your father was there to save you the first time."

I stroked my chin and said, "Yeah, I know."

"But you risked your life to alleviate your discomfort."

I groaned with memories of the excruciating back pain I had suffered. "I had taken a tumble down the steps at home and landed hard on my back. I thought the drugs would help with the pain," I said.

"Did you also do drugs to escape from the drudgery of life?" Poppy asked.

"You don't have to answer that," came a voice from the adjacent room.

"Who's there?" I cried out.

"Don't speak, Sam," Poppy warned. "We must leave."

"Where are you going?" the voice said, followed by the approaching sound of heavy footfalls.

Poppy held out a protective arm in front of me.

A dark shadow filled the doorway a moment before a towering figure emerged. He needed to duck to pass through, and no wonder, as his head was crowned with an enormous bronze helmet featuring a significant, battle-earned dent on one side. His bare barrel chest was chiseled with layers of muscle and old scars. Clamped metal armor was along his right arm, from shoulder to wrist. In his hands, he gripped a long sword and, in the other, a round metal shield embossed with the image of a dragon. Strapped onto his legs were thick leather guards and metal plates covered his boots.

My mouth went dry as I tried to push out the words, "Who are you?"

"My name is Crixus," he said, pulling back his shoulders. "You don't need to go with this old man, Samuel. Come with me instead; I can make your time here more enjoyable. You can fight in the arena with the other gladiators, and I can guarantee you'll never lose."

"We must go," Poppy insisted. "Do not listen."

"Pfft," Crixus said, holding out his sword and shield. "I can offer you the glory of Rome. Isn't that what you've always wanted?"

I nodded as thoughts of fame, honor, and adulation filled my mind.

"This is nonsense," Poppy insisted.

"Why don't we let Sam decide," Crixus demanded.

Poppy gripped my shoulder and spun me around. "Look at me, Sam. Do you remember what you saw in the visitor's dugout?"

I nodded and said, "The *rasha*."

"That's right," Poppy said, pointing to the gladiator. "It knows you because it is you. All of your fears. Your darkest thoughts and hidden secrets. It's true; going with Crixus will be easier for now. But you must resist if you are to succeed with your work here. Be strong and follow me, not the *rasha*."

"But why not?" I said, looking at the magnificent warrior. "It's what I've dreamed of."

Poppy pinched the bridge of his nose and said, "Choices made in the soul world have consequences far beyond those decided upon in the earthly realm. If you go with the *rasha* now, you may never get a chance to do the work required."

"Work?" I asked, rubbing the back of my neck. "What kind of work?"

"I'll tell you," Poppy said, taking my hand. "But not here—let's go to a place that made you happy."

I thought momentarily, took one last look at the gladiator, and said, "Lake Mohonk."

Before I could blink, we were sitting on a wooden porch, perched on a cliffside, overlooking the serene mountain lake and legendary historic hotel. "It's Mohonk," I said with a smile.

"We had good memories here," Poppy said, referring to the several family reunions we had spent in this place.

"Where's the Lemon Squeeze?" I asked, looking over the railing for the challenging rock scramble below.

"Listen, Sam," Poppy said, gathering my attention. "You asked about the work you must do in the soul world."

I nodded.

"First, let me explain a few things. After you passed, you separated from your physical body, leaving you with your life body, soul body, and ego."

I understood that I had left my physical body buried in the cemetery, but the other concepts were lost on me.

"Do you remember when your dad thought he saw you through the window?" Poppy asked.

I nodded.

"That was your life body. Shortly after death, your *life body* begins to detach itself from the physical body."

"What's a life body?" I asked with a furrowed brow.

"The life body contains a record of your experiences during your lifetime. During its separation, you receive a panoramic review of your life, allowing you to reflect on your past experiences and relationships.

Once you've completed this assessment, your life body dissolves and disperses into the cosmic world."

"Is that what's going to happen to me?"

"That's right," Poppy said, nodding. "There will be a review of your life from a new perspective. You'll relive it by seeing events and significant moments of your history more objectively and detachedly. This will allow you to understand better the consequences you've endured and how you can learn from them."

"Is this the work you spoke about?"

"Yes," Poppy said, leaning forward. "Once we've reviewed your life, you'll become absorbed into the soul world. But you should know this look back is a gradual process, depending upon your ability to understand and take on the required work."

"Gradual?" I asked.

"Maybe 'gradual' is not the best word. In this realm, our experiences transcend the earthly limits of linear time, unfolding in a timeless dance where past, present, and future intertwine."

I scratched my head and asked, "Then what happens?"

"You'll meet others like me," Poppy said with his hand on his chest. "Your ancestors, angels, archangels, and other interesting beings will support you and help you navigate the soul world. You should know that this, too, takes quite an effort. As the gladiator has shown, you'll have many challenges along the way."

"Along the way to where?"

Poppy held out his hands and smiled. "Toward your rebirth."

CHAPTER FIVE
THE WEDDING

"Do you recognize this place?" Poppy asked as we walked along a sandy beach.

Observing the lack of palm trees, I realized this wasn't Florida, where Poppy and Nanny had made their home. But as we walked a bit farther, I saw a gathering of young men in swim trunks, engaged in a game of touch football, with a gaggle of young women lounging on chairs and beach blankets, cheering them on.

"Wait, I remember this," I said, jabbing a finger. "That's me with my friends at my wedding weekend."

"Yes, and your brother and father are playing, too," Poppy added.

"There's Meghan and her bridesmaids. That was so much fun," I said, quickening my pace. "Can we watch?"

"We can, but first, I want to finish explaining a few things," Poppy said, grasping my arm.

"You mean how I'm nothing more than my life body?"

"Oh, you're much more than that," Poppy laughed. "Your life body will remain with you for a while, but it's only one of the four bodies that create us. Along with the physical body and the life body, there's the soul body and the ego."

"Okay…" I said, absorbing these new words. "So what's the soul body?"

"The soul body is the vehicle that drives our emotions, desires, and passions. It's the part of us that experiences feelings and is most closely connected with our thoughts. It's not only part of us in our lifetime but travels with us into the spiritual realms," Poppy said, gesturing to the landscape. "It's what allows us to perceive and interact with the other spiritual beings."

"You mean like we're doing now?" I asked.

"That's right," Poppy said with a nod and a smile. "It also plays a vital role in our journey toward birth."

I nodded, trying to absorb this new and strange information. "I think I understand," I said, tilting my head to look past Poppy at the game.

"Good," Poppy said. "One more thing before I'll let you go."

"Okay," I said, recentering my attention to my grandfather.

"This is important," Poppy said and paused momentarily to gaze into my eyes. "The fourth body is that of the ego, which also carries on into the soul world. The ego is the core of our being, the source of our consciousness, willpower, and creativity."

"I understand," I said, trying to keep up.

"This body," Poppy said, holding out an arm, "is made of pure thoughts, feelings, and free will. We work within these elements, ultimately leading us to have a new physical body on Earth."

I scratched my head, trying to understand. "It sounds complex."

"Indeed it is," Poppy said, lifting his brow.

"But why are you still here?" I asked, cocking my chin toward my grandfather. "Shouldn't you have been reborn?"

"I passed away three years ago. There's still more work for me to do as well."

"Including helping me?" I asked with a smile.

"That's right. Who else would you expect?"

I sighed and shook my head. "I'm glad it's you, Poppy. You know how much I love you."

Poppy gripped my shoulders, pulled me tight, and whispered, "I love you too, Sam."

We released, paused momentarily, and then I pointed to the beach and said, "Can we go?"

"Yes," Poppy said with a wide smile. "Come, let's watch."

I closed my eyes and smiled, feeling the warmth of my grandfather's presence. When I opened them, we were no longer on the sun-drenched beach but stood on a music-filled, frenetic dance floor.

"It's my wedding!" I cried out, recognizing the song "Love Shack" by the B-52s.

"A happy memory," Poppy said loud enough to be heard over the thumping sound.

"It is," I agreed, turning my head from side to side, absorbing the whirlwind of delighted dancers swirling around us.

Poppy raised his arms and said, "Life is made of such moments."

"Everyone is so happy," I said.

"This is how the world of the living connects to the spirit world. You can think of this as *group soul*. It's why humans have craved such celebrations for thousands of years. It's an essential element for the evolution of humanity—friends, family, and love. Those same three words you had engraved on that dog tag."

"I want to stay here forever," I said.

"Me too," Poppy said. "But we must move on; there's much more to see."

"How did you learn about all of this *soul world* stuff?"

"I, too, traveled the spheres upon my passing."

"Spheres?" I asked.

"Come, let's find a quiet place. I have much more to explain," Poppy said, taking my hand.

CHAPTER SIX
SKIING

Heavy snowflakes fell from silver clouds. The ski lift dropped off round after round of skiers and snowboarders making their way either down the steep incline or into the luxurious ski lodge, clinging to the side of the mountain. Poppy and I observed the activity from the expansive, wrap-around wooden deck, overlooking the tops of evergreens and the zigzagging trails below.

"You have some wonderful memories," Poppy said.

"I loved our ski trips," I said with a smile. "Skiing in the morning. Lunch at the lodge. A few more hours on the slopes, then off to drinks and dinner. There was nothing better."

"I never skied, but I know how much you loved it."

I sighed. "It was one of the few times I felt free and unencumbered by the demands of life."

"We'll get to that," Poppy said, pausing me with a finger. "For now, I'd like to explain the journey you're about to embark upon. While it may sound unusual, you should listen and not worry about hanging on every word."

"All right, Poppy," I said, taking a deep breath and letting it go slowly.

"Beyond these clouds," Poppy began, gesturing overhead to the heavy cloud cover, "are the planets. These heavenly bodies are not just stars to gaze upon, but are integral to the spiritual journey of your soul."

"The planets?" I repeated.

Poppy nodded. "The seven planetary spheres are associated with unique spiritual forces you'll pass through as you embark upon your journey. Unless, that is, you get taken off course by the *rasha*. But we'll do our best to ensure that doesn't happen."

"What are these planets?" I asked, looking upwards.

As if pointing to its location in the sky, Poppy said, "First is the moon sphere, which one encounters first upon passing. It's the one you're in now. The moon sphere is associated with the forces of memory and healing. It's where you'll come to terms with your past life as a way to prepare yourself for your next incarnation."

I looked around with wide eyes. "Are you saying we're on the moon?"

Poppy shook his head. "It's more like a spiritual state of consciousness than a physical location."

"Aren't we still on Earth?" I asked, looking around at the familiar sight of mountains, trees, skiers, and snowboarders.

Poppy smiled. "Yes, it feels that way. But we're in an ethereal realm, where what you perceive is not real. In this moon sphere, you'll come to terms with the darkness that haunted your past life."

"You mean my inner *rasha*?" I asked.

"That's right," Poppy said, patting my arm. "By examining your life, coming to terms with the negative or the harmful, you can move on to the remaining six spheres to guide you toward birth."

I pinched the bridge of my nose and said with a sigh, "This doesn't appear to be easy."

"It's not easy at all," Poppy said, shaking his head. "Perhaps you're beginning to realize the magnitude of pushing open the gate to the soul world rather than remaining where you were and dealing with your earthly challenges."

I bit my lower lip and nodded.

"But don't despair," he said, cupping his warm hand on my cheek. "In this realm, you'll have the opportunity to improve things for your next incarnation."

"All right," I said, returning my gaze to the dozens of skiers carving around a mogul-laden black diamond run.

"After completing the moon phase, you'll enter the sphere of Mercury. Here you'll work toward gaining a deeper understanding of the Divine will and its healing forces. From an earthly perspective, the Mercury sphere offers insight into the nature of the universe."

I squinted and asked, "Who will teach me this?"

"The spiritual beings."

"Spiritual beings?" I asked.

Poppy nodded. "Yes, among the hierarchical beings are the angels and archangels. They will guide you."

I grimaced and scratched the back of my head. "Okay, Poppy, then what's next?" I asked with a dose of sarcasm.

Picking up on my frustration, Poppy pulled my arm, forcing me to look at him. "Sam, you mustn't resist. The more you close yourself off to the process, the more you open the door for the *rasha*. And trust me; you don't ever want the darkness getting hold of you. Especially not here, in these realms."

"Why? What would happen?"

Poppy wagged a finger. "There are places where darkness dwells and where souls like us dare not tread."

I offered a pained smile. "I'll try not to resist, Poppy."

"Good," he said. "Next, you'll encounter the Venus sphere. This is where the forces of attraction and love are engaged, though not as you experienced them on Earth. The spiritual energies of love offer a more profound sense of compassion and empathy. It's here, within the sphere of Venus, where you'll improve upon your moral and physical uprightness. Though I know these attributes were quite strong in your life."

A wash of warmth filled me at these words, giving me a more substantial presence. I placed my palm on my chest and said, "What's happening?"

"You're feeling something?" Poppy asked.

I nodded. "It's good," I said with a chuckle. "As if I just became more aware."

Poppy wagged a finger. "That's right. When we learn, we understand; it's a step forward. Remember this feeling and try to build upon it."

"I will," I said with a smile. "What's next?"

"After the Venus sphere, comes the sun. Within this sphere, you'll encounter the Sun Being, who presides over the principles concerning the cosmic order. The Sun Being will give you a deeper understanding of the cosmos and your place within it."

I closed my eyes and shook my head. "How is this possible?" I asked. "If we are given such knowledge, how come we stumble so often in our lifetimes?"

"That's a great question, Sam," Poppy said, patting a finger to his lips. "All I can say is, with each incarnation, we do our best to improve on the previous one."

"All right, Poppy, what comes after the sun?"

"Then it's the Mars sphere. Mars is associated with forces of courage. Here we learn how to channel our inner strength and determination to understand better our willpower and how it exists in the spiritual realm."

"There's so much to know," I said, rubbing the back of my neck.

"You don't need to memorize any of this," Poppy said, wagging a finger. "The knowledge will flow into you if you don't put up any barriers."

"That's a relief," I said with a chuckle.

"Good, then let's continue," Poppy said, now picking up his pace. "After passing through Mars, we move on to Jupiter. This planetary sphere is associated with the forces of wisdom, where we create a more profound sense of insight and the understanding of others."

I nodded, trying to be polite. But I couldn't help but think all of this sounded like make-believe. Though I knew if I voiced this opinion, Poppy would warn me about how I was opening a portal for the *rasha* or something like that.

"Finally, we arrive at Saturn," Poppy said, regaining my attention. "Saturn is where the forces of karma and destiny are evident, and it's where you'll confront the consequences of your past actions and be allowed to come to terms with them before you complete your journey toward birth."

I looked over to Poppy and held out my hands. "Is that all of them?"

"That's all seven, and as I said, you don't have—"

"How long does this all take?" I interrupted.

"As I told you before, in the soul world, we don't experience time the same way you once knew it to be. You may even experience several aspects of the planets at once or with large gaps in between. What's important is understanding your needs and how you can achieve the necessary insights and lessons from each stage of your journey."

"Okay, Poppy, I understand. But while this is happening, is it possible to stay connected with the living? Can I visit people like we did before?"

"I'm glad you asked," Poppy said with a wide-eyed grin. "I'm going to show you something thrilling."

CHAPTER SEVEN
STAYING CONNECTED

I looked around at the red-brick-lined thoroughfare, chock full of pedestrians. "Are we on Pearl Street?" I asked, recognizing the popular tourist destination in Boulder, Colorado.

Poppy smiled, gestured to the shops and restaurants, and said, "Do you remember this trip?"

"Yes. We had a good time here," I said.

"Come, let's walk. I want to explain how we can stay connected to those we left behind."

As we strolled along, it felt as real as if I were alive again, and I wondered if this was the connection Poppy was referring to.

"This is not real," Poppy said, tuning into my thoughts. "We cannot return to the earthly realm until it's our time. We're here because it's one of your pleasant memories."

I scratched at my stubble, trying to understand.

We continued for a moment before Poppy added, "It's not in our control to reach out to the living, and it's up to them to engage with those who've passed on. Only then can we respond."

"You told me this at the house," I said, "but what I still don't know is how the living engage with us."

"Let's sit," Poppy said, pointing to a bench, "and I'll explain."

Just as I leaned back, a man with long silver hair, dressed in an immaculate white gown, emerged from the crowd. I wagged a finger at him and said, "Hey, isn't that the guy Max met?"

Just as the words passed my lips, Max appeared and introduced himself to the stranger. The two spoke for a while, then, just as I remembered, Max exploded into a body-wrenching gush of tears and the man embraced him.

Poppy touched my shoulder and said, "Why is this an important memory for you?"

I shook my head. "I'm not sure. Maybe because it meant so much to Max."

"These recollections are not random. You're here for a reason, Sam. Why was this event meaningful, not just for your brother, but for you as well?"

I continued watching Max speaking with the holy looking man. "I remember thinking how easy it was for my brother to cry and how hard it was for me to express my emotions."

"That's a good observation," Poppy said, wrapping his frail arm around me. "Crying in front of others is difficult, especially for a man. I faced the same challenges during my lifetime."

I nodded, taking in my grandfather's wisdom, then asked, "Who would have been my guide if you hadn't died before me?"

Poppy shook his head. "That's hard to say. Your other grandparents, perhaps. But there's no need to speculate. Once you are in this realm, you'll soon realize there are no random events. I'm here with you because I was destined to be."

I swallowed hard, trying to absorb the significance of my grandfather's words.

"Now," Poppy said suddenly with a clap of his hands, "let me explain how the living can connect with the dead."

"Why is that?" I asked with a furrowed brow. "Why can't we reach out to them? Like I did when Dad needed the password."

"Uh-uh," Poppy said, wagging a finger. "Remember, it wasn't until your dad asked for your help that you were able to provide it. Only when the living continues to make an effort can our soul body respond."

I squinted and asked, "How do we respond?"

"In various ways," Poppy said, lifting his brow. "We can reach out to them in their dreams, for example."

"Dreams?" I asked. "But I thought dreams were no more than random images or some sort of replay of our experiences."

"They could be that. But sometimes dreams are messages from the soul world. But making the connection happen takes much work, and I've only done it a few times."

"You've entered Nanny's dreams?" I asked.

Poppy nodded. "I have, and it was wonderful."

"I want to do that with Meghan," I said, wide-eyed.

"Okay, once you're ready, we'll try."

"How else can we connect?" I asked, sitting up straight.

"There are intermediaries, like the angels and other spiritual beings, who can assist."

"You mentioned angels before. Do they really exist?"

Poppy nodded. "Not only do they exist, they are actually the beings most closely connected to the living."

"Pfft," I scoffed. "Next, are you going to tell me that fairies are also real?"

"Yes!" Poppy shouted. "And gnomes too. These creatures encourage the living to maintain a connection to the natural world."

I put my hand on my chest, took a deep breath, and slowly exhaled, trying to entertain these absurd notions. Then I asked, "But what about God? Isn't there a single being above them all?"

"That's what religion has taught us to believe. But actually, there is not a single unified entity, but rather a multifaceted, spiritual presence, evident in all things."

I rubbed my forehead, finding all of this hard to comprehend. "Can we go back to the idea of entering someone's dreams? I want to try to do that."

Poppy waved a hand. "We shouldn't rush. If you're unprepared, you may be vulnerable to the *rasha*."

I shook my head. "Why is that?"

"Do you remember what I told you about the soul body?"

I nodded and said, "It's part of our feelings, our emotions, and how it's connected to our thoughts."

"That's right," Poppy said, bright-eyed. "It also allows us to engage with other spiritual beings, including the *rasha*. At the moment when you seek out the living through their dreams, you're putting yourself in a vulnerable state."

"But you can protect me, can't you?"

Poppy shook his head. "I don't have that ability, and that's why I want you to become more aware of your soul body and its limits before venturing into the astral dream world."

"Okay, Poppy," I said and looked out onto Pearl Street, taking a moment to consider. "But what about channelers who can speak with the dead? Meghan was fascinated by them; is there any truth to their abilities?"

"Some legitimate individuals among the living possess a powerful soul body, enabling them with a form of communication that can contact the soul world."

"I hope Meghan reaches out to me through a channeler," I said, placing a hand over my heart.

"It's wonderful when the connection happens."

"Has it happened to you?" I asked.

"Oh yes!" Poppy said with a huge smile. "June has done it several times."

I slowly nodded, thinking about my Aunt June, my cousins Sophie and Ruben, and Uncle Craig and Cousin Rachel, and wondered how they reacted to my sudden death.

Poppy stood up from the bench and held out his hand. "Come with me; something is happening; you must see."

CHAPTER EIGHT
THE UNVEILING

"What's this?" I asked, finding myself standing among dozens of people at the cemetery. But unlike that snowy, bleak, midwinter day of my burial, this midsummer morning was warm, crowned with a canopy of a bright blue sky and a few puffy clouds drifting by.

"This is the unveiling of your headstone," Poppy said, pointing to the granite slab draped with a lightweight gauze.

"I want to thank everyone for coming," my dad said, stepping over to my grave.

It took me a brief moment to find Meghan. I walked over to her and stood no more than an arm's length away. Her eyes were glassy with tears, and she appeared thin and frail. Her brother kept a hand on her shoulder for comfort.

I looked at Poppy and asked, "Can I contact her?"

Poppy shook his head. "Not here and not now. Maybe in her dreams."

I sighed and turned my attention to my family and friends milling about.

Poppy tapped my shoulder and said, "Your dad's about to speak."

"We're gathering today to unveil my son Sam's headstone," Dad said, getting everyone's attention. "This Jewish tradition symbolizes the final act of laying a loved one to rest by providing a permanent memorial and a place to visit and remember the life of Samuel."

Heads bowed while birdsong accompanied the silence.

"If I may," Dad said, "I'd like to begin." He pulled a paper from his jacket pocket, unfolded it, and read aloud.

"Sam, it's been five months and eight days since you took off on your spiritual journey, and I would like to imagine that upon your premature arrival in the spirit world, you've connected with those already on this path, all of whom, I'm sure, have greeted you with adoring love, offering you their guidance and wisdom during this challenging transition.

"For me, over this same time, there's not been a day where my heart has not ached, my tears have not been shed, and my love for you has not been all-consuming.

"As any parent would, I remember that precise moment of your birth—your first breath of life and the joy it gave me holding you in my arms, my sweet, precious baby boy. And sadly, I can never erase the anguish watching you, as a beautiful young man, exhaling your last.

"Yet through all this pain, you have given me hope. Hope within the belief that there's much more to our existence than our first and last breaths. You've done this by piercing through the veil, separating the barrier between our two worlds.

"During these months since we laid you to rest, you have proven, while no longer of body, that you can still connect with me in tangible, verifiable ways. I have acknowledged your presence in my daily waking life, proving our love is vital and our bond unbreakable.

"I'm grateful for all your unexpected gifts, especially the dearest and most cherished, the birth of my spiritual wisdom. Though I should be offering you this knowledge, not the other way around. Yet, for some reason, God has chosen you, my thirty-two-year-old son, to lay this path before me to follow. How could a father be more proud?

"So, as we gather, with family and friends, forming this circle of tribute, I want to express my gratitude to you for being my beloved son and an excellent companion. Though that is not to say our connection has ended. It has begun anew in this form, with me here and you there, driving me forward while all the while I feel you by my side. All of this provides joyful fuel for the remainder of my days.

"When my time does come and our reunion is imminent, you will greet me and share all the wondrous things you have learned and experienced. But in the meantime, I will do my best not to allow your loss to consume me and will attempt to live my life unencumbered by the burdens of guilt, anger, and sorrow, knowing you have opened my heart and enhanced my soul in ways I could have never imagined.

"So while this chapter of your life has been put to rest, there is still much more to tell of your adventures among the upper realms, and I will remain here, awaiting with great eagerness these tales of your fantastic journey, knowing one day we will be reunited as father and son."

I looked over to Poppy, whose bright face mirrored my emotion. "How could he know so much?" I asked.

"It's the gifts you've provided him that have allowed your father to open this portal to you."

"But why does he celebrate my death?"

"He's obviously not celebrating it. It's how he's dealing with his grief—by trying to latch onto something positive."

After psalms, poems, and stories were shared by family and friends, Dad asked if anyone else would like to speak.

A close family friend said, "I would like to recite a verse from Rudolf Steiner's Calendar of the Soul, written for this week."

She then unfolded a paper and read:

"WITHIN MY BEING'S DEPTHS

THERE SPEAKS,

INTENT ON REVELATION,

THE COSMIC WORD MYSTERIOUSLY:

IMBUE YOUR LABOR'S AIMS

WITH MY BRIGHT SPIRIT LIGHT

TO SACRIFICE YOURSELF THROUGH ME."

I looked at Poppy and asked, "What does that mean?"

"The poem suggests that work is not solely about completing tasks to earn a living and can also serve as a vehicle for personal and spiritual growth."

I shook my head at Poppy's unexpected wisdom. "How do you know that?"

"I've learned many things while in this realm. You'll see once you get beyond the moon sphere," he said, shifting his brow.

"Let me explain a few details from the carving on the headstone," Dad said, regaining my attention as he removed the gauze cloth. "This top line, written in Hebrew, means—Here lies Schmuel, son of Nachum."

I stepped around and looked at the headstone and read the engraving.

TIME IS FLEETING

OUR REUNION CERTAIN

A LOVING WIFE AND

FAMILY AWAIT

"It's a wonderful message," Poppy said.

I nodded in agreement. "It's good."

"Before we conclude," Dad continued, "Sam's brother would like to share a few words."

Max, dressed in a tee shirt, shorts, and work boots, his typical summer attire, took his place alongside the headstone and spoke to the gathering about his childhood memories of growing up with me. After a few minutes, describing a few of the good-hearted antics between us, Max said, "There's one last thing I'd like to share."

Max took a breath, patted the headstone, and said, "Our cat Manu, has been missing for the past nineteen days. We sadly thought he was gone forever. But this morning at around four, we heard his distinctive cry from outside our bedroom window."

"Oh my," Dad cried, putting his hand over his mouth.

"Oh, Manu!" I said, thinking of our family's beautiful Bengal cat.

With eyes filling his tears, Max gathered himself and said, "My brother loved Manu. For many years they lived together, and it's special that he returned home on this special day."

I looked over to Poppy and held out my hands. "How is this possible?" I asked.

"Your life body leaves remnants behind of your thoughts and emotions. Animals like cats, dogs, and birds are susceptible to these spiritual senses. So are certain humans with clairvoyant abilities."

I scratched the back of my head and asked, "Can cats sense human souls?"

Poppy nodded. "Animals possess a level of perception and sensitivity that allows them to perceive spiritual qualities in their surroundings, including humans."

I sighed and thought about the connection I once had with Manu and was grateful some of it remained.

CHAPTER NINE
SOULMATES

Slowly, everyone departed the cemetery. I stepped toward Meghan, wanting to follow, but Poppy grasped my shoulder, holding me back. I groaned from the agony of missing my beautiful wife, yearning to be by her side, soothing her grief.

"I know how much you love her, Sam."

"Will I ever be with her again?"

"Do you mean in the soul world?"

I nodded. "Will I greet Meghan when her time comes?"

"It's possible," Poppy said, lifting his brow.

Thinking of my grandfather's wonderful sixty years of marriage with Nanny, I asked, "Are there such things as soulmates?"

"Of course," Poppy said with a warm smile and pointed to the tree line of tall pines along the sloping hillside overlooking the cemetery. "Come, let's sit under the shade."

Once seated, I wrapped my arms around my bent knees and waited for my grandfather to begin his lesson.

"There are deep and lasting connections that transcend our lifetime on Earth. It's what's called a karmic relationship, and it takes on many forms, depending on the nature of the connection. They can certainly span multiple lifetimes in romantic relationships, such as mine with Nanny."

"Karmic relationship?" I asked with a squint. "What's that?"

"A karmic relationship is based upon a deep connection, an understanding of a shared destiny. It's how partners play a role in the spiritual development of each other."

I looked at Poppy as he gazed at the array of headstones below. "So what you're saying is that Meghan and I could have known each other in a previous life?"

Poppy nodded. "It's possible. Some meaningful relationships are begun anew in a present lifetime, while others carry forward."

"How do I know when ours began?"

"It can be challenging to know for sure, but there are ways to identify a connection," Poppy said.

"What ways?" I asked.

"One way of knowing is when you first met, did you experience strong feelings of familiarity that created an instant rapport, defying explanation?"

"Oh," I said, jabbing a finger. "Yes, that's precisely what happened with Meghan and me. That first day we met, we connected instantly, as if we had known each other forever. That first night, we spoke for hours. It was like we had found the missing piece of ourselves in each other."

"That's wonderful," Poppy said.

I smiled, thinking about that special time.

"There are also karmic patterns," Poppy said.

"Karmic patterns?" I repeated.

Poppy nodded and said, "Repeating patterns in a relationship may indicate unresolved past life experiences. Often they are rooted in unresolved issues; they need to be addressed."

"Like what?" I asked, curious if any applied to my relationship with Meghan.

"Well," Poppy began with a grimace. "Issues like being attracted to an emotionally unavailable partner due to a past life experience of unrequited love, which I doubt was a problem with you and Meghan."

"No, it wasn't," I said, shaking my head.

"Then there are relationships with one partner becoming overly reliant on the other, possibly stemming from a past life experience of abandonment or neglect."

"Oh, you mean like codependency?" I said.

"Yes, that's right."

I shook my head. "No, we never had that problem."

"Well, there are many other possible issues like jealousy and possessiveness, fear of commitment, repeating cycles of abuse, the rescuer-savior complex, and infidelity," Poppy said, holding out his hands. "From what I remember, your relationship had none of these issues."

"We didn't," I said, shaking my head. "But we did have issues with painkillers."

Poppy raised a brow. "So this was a problem you both had?"

I grimaced. "It started in college."

"This must be worked out between you and Meghan if you're to move forward as a couple."

I took a deep breath, slowly rocked back and forth, and said, "I suppose I have sins to account for."

"The idea of repentance in the religious sense is not the work done here," Poppy said, rubbing his smooth cheek. "The process of our spiritual development involves understanding our negative tendencies. With such self-awareness, we can achieve positive growth and transformation. It's not about atoning for our mistakes, a concept many religions insist upon."

"And I do that by reviewing my life?"

Poppy nodded. "That's how you start."

I thought for a moment about my need to numb my pain.

"Why did you use drugs and painkillers?" Poppy asked, once again hearing my thoughts.

I shrugged and said, "I liked how they made me feel."

Poppy took a deep breath, exhaled, and said, "I think it's time we go there."

In an instant, we were no longer in the cemetery but instead standing in the bathroom of my home, watching my former self leaning over the marble countertop, using a pestle to crush a pill into powder.

"Is that Percocet?" Poppy asked.

"Yes, snorting is quicker and stronger than taking it orally."

I watched as I took a straw, cut to about three inches long, stuck one end into my nostril while pinching off the other, and then snorted up the neatly formed line of powder.

With a burst of energy, I jerked upright, shook my head, and cried out, "Ahh!"

"What are you feeling right now?" Poppy asked.

I looked at myself, remembering the effect. "Intense pleasure and well-being," I whispered with a moan. "It was as if every worry and burden had dissolved, leaving a profound emotional release from my pain as all my stresses melted away."

"Where you hurt?"

"No, not physically. It was just a way to…" I said, drifting off as my attention was drawn to a shadowy figure appearing beyond the bedroom window.

"Sam?" Poppy said, trying to get my attention.

"It's Crixus," I said, pointing.

"These were moments when he had his hold upon you," Poppy said, gesturing to my comatose self.

"He did this to me?" I said, putting my hand to my mouth.

Poppy nodded. "When you put yourself into this state, you allowed the *rasha* to grow."

Beyond the glare, I saw Crixus summoning me over with a crooked finger.

"We should go," Poppy said.

"But maybe I should…" I said, my voice drifting to a mumble.

Without warning, Poppy reared back and slapped me across my face. Stunned, I put a hand on my cheek and shut my eyes.

CHAPTER TEN
THE CHAMPIONSHIP

When I opened my eyes, Poppy and I stood on the same baseball field when I first arrived just moments after my passing, though now it seemed to be a beautiful, late spring day. The trees beyond the outfield fence were in full bloom; worn patches of green crabgrass and hard-packed dirt stretched from the rusty chain-linked fence to home plate. We were also joined by two teams of twelve-year-old boys dressed in colored numbered jerseys gathered by their opposing dugouts.

"What's this?" I asked.

"Don't you remember? It's your championship game," Poppy said, holding out his hands. "I thought you may need a good moment to visit."

"You're right; this was a wonderful memory," I said, smiling and walking over to where Dad had gathered our team along the first baseline.

"Dad was your coach," Poppy said.

"He was always my coach, ever since I was three," I said, recalling how he used to pitch to me in the house with a white wiffle ball, and I would smack it with a fat, red plastic bat.

"Let's get closer," Poppy said, cocking his head toward the boys.

Beside my thirty-two-year-old dad, was Hasan's father, a chiropractor, and our assistant coach. Gazing upward at the two coaches, like ducklings waiting for their worms, were my teammates.

And there I was, a pink-cheeked, chubby twelve-year-old, listening to Coach, who had guided us through an exciting season to the precipice of becoming champions. Dad never shied away from ensuring I was one of the team's featured players. I excelled and cherished our games.

"I want you to know," Coach said, addressing the team, "that even twelve-year-olds can achieve greatness, and that's what I expect to occur today on this field."

I looked at the innocent faces of my friends and teammates who hung on every word as Coach molded their overt nervousness into a sense of calm and confidence.

"Your dad," Poppy said, pulling back his shoulders, "learned the power of positive thinking from me."

I nodded, remembering Dad speaking of how his father preached this attitude to him.

With that, the umpire cried, "You ready, Coach?"

Coach nodded and gestured for the team to huddle, and as in every game before this final one of our Little League careers, we stretched out our hands into the center as one. On the count of three, we shouted in glee—"Go Reds!"

Poppy and I sat on the top row in the bleachers. Seated below us were my mom, my six-year-old brother, Max, and the other parents cheering on their children. Coach stood along the first base side as our team came to bat while Hasan's dad kept score in the spiral-bound official Little League scorebook.

Hasan led off. My childhood friend was an excellent player, and with the game's first pitch, he lined a base hit over the shortstop's head into left field. Cheers rose as Hasan reached first base, clapping his hands to encourage his teammates.

But that was it, as the pitcher for the Cardinals was a fireballer boy named Mike, who threw so fast that the pop in the catcher's mitt sounded like a gunshot. Inning after inning, we went down in order, unable to even foul a ball off. When Coach asked the boys, who sat with grim expressions side-by-side along the dugout bench, if they were afraid, they all nodded in fearful unison.

When our team took the field, Hasan pitched well, eventually shutting out the Cardinals through four innings. But in the fifth, with no score, the Cardinals finally put a few hits together. They combined two singles with a walk and a stolen base, resulting in two runs. Teary-eyed, Hasan looked over to his father.

Recognizing his son's distress, Hasan's dad headed out to the mound, and as everyone watched, he performed a chiropractic manipulation on Hasan's pitching hand. Seeming okay, Hasan gripped the ball and tossed a practice pitch.

We all watched, hoping Hasan would regain his control and confidence. But he shook his head and waved Coach over. He approached the mound, knowing we would need to bring in a new pitcher. With the infield players gathered around the mound, young Sam said, "Let me pitch."

Coach grimaced, as Sam's last performance had not been great. Plus, we only had one more inning to score, and our chances looked grim with how we were hitting. But Sam insisted, and Coach reluctantly agreed.

Sam took the mound with grit, and with the precision of the most dominating pitcher of the era, Atlanta Brave's ace Greg Maddux, Sam struck out the side on nine consecutive pitches. When he returned to the dugout, he was greeted with exuberance by his teammates and the dozens of fans in the bleachers.

But we were still down three to nil with our second to last chance to score runs. Still on the mound was Mike, pitching a gem. But when Zach got to bat, he lined the first pitch off the centerfield fence for a double. Next up was Erin, whose passion for the game was unmatched. He took the count to three balls and two strikes before hitting a slow roller to the mound. The catcher jumped up from his squat, pounced on the ball, and fired to first, but Erin beat the throw, allowing Zach to move to third.

Mike was able to regain his composure, striking out the next two batters. With two outs and runners on the corners, Sam came to bat.

He set himself in the left-handed side of the batter's box. Young Sam batted lefty, though threw righty. A quirk he acquired as a child when he would mirror his father swinging a bat.

Cheers of encouragement were shouted from both teams. Mike stared at the catcher, and as soon as he reared back and released the pitch, Erin took off for second base. Sam took the strike while the catcher ignored the baserunner and tossed the ball back to the pitcher. Sam worked the count to two balls and two strikes, then stepped out of the batter's box and turned to look at Coach.

Coach offered a nod and a warm smile, which he returned.

Young Sam stepped back into the box, and on the next pitch, he launched a moon shot over the rightfield fence. Bedlam ensued. Our boys rushed from the dugout and gathered around home, waiting for Sam as he rounded the bases and was greeted with backslaps and hugs the moment he touched home.

But the game was not over. Mike struck out the last batter with the score now three to two in our favor. The Cardinals would bat once more in the top of the sixth inning. Which meant we needed three more outs to win the game.

Sam took the mound. The first batter was able to foul off several pitches before being walked. If he scored, this runner would be the tying run, sending us into extra innings—a prospect no one wanted to consider.

But Sam settled down and struck out the next two batters. We were now only one out away. But the next batter was their star player—Mike. Not only their best pitcher but also their best hitter.

Once again, Sam looked over to Coach, who mouthed the words—*are you okay*? He nodded. Then, with all the intensity Sam could muster, he gripped the baseball and fired a pitch right down the middle.

With a lightning-fast swing, Mike connected, sending a lined shot over second base. As the lead runner rounded the bases, the Cardinal's third base coach waved the boy in. Erin, our centerfielder, caught the ball on a bounce and, using his body, coiled up and threw a beeline to our catcher—Hasan. There would be a defining play at the plate.

Hasan tossed off his mask and positioned himself in front of homeplate, steadying himself for the moment. The boy slid as the ball landed in his mitt, trying to sneak by him. But Hasan would have nothing to do with that and tagged him. Dramatically, the umpire shouted, "You're out!"

We all jumped joyously, tossing our gloves into the air and rushing home, where we piled on Hasan. The celebration was glorious.

Later on, after the congratulations, we met up as a team at DaVinci's. Our favorite local pizzeria, where we would gather after games.

The coach passed a baseball and a pen, asking the players to sign their names. Once done, he gathered everyone's attention and said, "Today, as predicted, was a great day. I want to congratulate all of you for today's victory and the entire season. A season of challenges and triumphs. I hope you'll all remember what you've accomplished."

Heads bobbed up and down, acknowledging Coach's words.

"Now," Coach said, picking up the signed ball, "while this is a team sport, we've had the tradition after each win to present a ball to the game's outstanding player, which every one of you has had the honor."

It was true; Coach had ensured we all received at least one game ball that season.

"Unlike before, I'd like the players to vote on who deserves today's honor," Coach said.

No more than a few seconds passed before several voices cried out in near unison, "Sam. Give it to Sam."

Coach flicked his fingers, summoning Sam to approach. With the air of ceremony, he handed the baseball to the team's champion and said, "Congratulations."

The children clapped and chanted, "Sam! Sam! Sam!"

"That was quite an honor," Poppy said as we watched the team's celebration.

"Thank you for letting me see it once more," I said as warmth flooded me.

CHAPTER ELEVEN
THE BAR MITZVAH

Outside the pizza place, Poppy asked, "Would you mind if we visited another happy time in your life; one we shared?"

"Sure," I said with a bright smile. "When would that be?"

"I think you know. Come, I'll take you," he said, and as we stepped toward the pizzeria's parking lot, we magically reappeared outside a large white stucco-faced building.

"Where are we?" I asked, finding myself among dozens of people dressed as if they were attending a wedding.

"This was your Bar Mitzvah," Poppy said, dramatically lifting his arms.

"Really?" I said, trying to find familiar faces.

"You were already sixteen when you began your studies."

I nodded and said, "Yes, and you were the reason why I got Bar Mitzvahed."

Poppy rubbed a hand on my back and said, "It was a great honor you bestowed upon me."

I looked down at my feet, kicked a small stone off the sidewalk, and said, "I didn't do it at thirteen because of my parent's divorce."

"That was a difficult time in your life," Poppy said. "And we'll look at that, but not yet."

Once inside, Poppy and I stood several feet off to the left of the Bimah, where the Torah was being unfurled. Leaning over the sizeable wooden podium clutching onto a *yad* was the rabbi, the same rabbi who, sixteen years later, presided over my burial ceremony. A yad, Hebrew for hand, is a long, narrowed, silver pointer that marks one's place when reading from the parchment. Its purpose is to avoid someone's hand touching and soiling the sacred text.

The ceremony began with family members being called up for traditional honors. Mom and Dad took turns reciting a blessing called the *Aliyah*, which acknowledges God's role in giving the Torah to the Jewish people and requesting the Almighty for guidance and wisdom.

All four of my grandparents recited a prayer called the *Shehecheyanu*, which expresses gratitude for reaching a significant moment in one's life.

When my turn came, I read from the Torah. According to the rabbi, based on the Hebrew calendar's time, my portion was about Joseph's adventures and his coat of many colors.

Upon my completion, the cantor led the congregation in the traditional Hebrew song *Adon Olam*. Then the rabbi turned to me, placed his hands on my shoulders, smiled, and said, "Mazel Tov."

To which the congregation responded in unison, "Mazel Tov."

"Now, Samuel would like to say a few words," the rabbi said.

I watched as my sixteen-year-old self reached into his pocket and removed a folded sheet of paper. He opened it, looked up at the audience, and smiled. He then refolded it, returning it to his pocket. Then he leaned closer to the microphone and said, "There's no need for notes."

Sam took a moment to survey the congregation, then began anew. "I'm sure many of you wonder why I waited so long before becoming a Bar Mitzvah. There are many questions and reasons but only one answer."

Sam paused momentarily, allowing the congregation to share their knowledge based on the presumed gossip in whispers.

"I did this for two reasons. The first one is that I did it to prove I could. During my life, there haven't been many accomplishments I can take claim to. You can say winning the Little League Championship was an achievement, and it was. But that was a team effort. This I did on my own," he said, pausing momentarily.

"The second reason," Sam said, looking at his grandfather sitting in the first row. "Was I did it for you, Poppy."

With his eyes glistening with tears, Poppy placed a hand over his heart and smiled.

"I want you to be proud of me, and I hope you are."

Tears rolled down Poppy's cheek, and barely able to choke out the words, he said, "I couldn't be prouder."

A chorus of "Ahh" cascaded throughout the sanctuary.

"But let me make sure to also thank my parents for supporting me and helping me reach this important milestone," Sam said, making eye contact with his parents, who sat on opposing sides of the center aisle.

"Days like today, celebrations, are moments in our lives intended to etch memories into our souls, never to be forgotten."

With many nods, the attendees acknowledged the significance of Sam's words.

"Getting Bar Mitzvahed at sixteen made sense to me. I'm much closer to being a man now than I was three years ago. At thirteen, I was a lost boy with no way to appreciate or understand the significance of this rite of passage. But above all, what's most important is that I did this of my own free will."

Sam stopped, took a moment to make eye contact with several of the attendees, and said, "I'm grateful for the love and support from my family and friends, and thank you all for coming."

Sam stepped aside while a round of applause echoed throughout the sanctuary.

"Thank you, Sam," the rabbi said. "What you say about being a Bar Mitzvah at sixteen makes sense; perhaps we should make it a regular option."

The congregants laughed.

"Now, if you don't mind, Sam, I would like to share with your loved ones a few words."

Sam nodded and stepped backward, giving his place before the podium to the esteemed rabbi.

"Today, Samuel, you read from the Torah the story of Joseph and his coat of many colors. And like Joseph, you have been blessed with many attributes that you'll find helpful as you embark upon your journey of growth and discovery. But it's important to remember that, like Joseph, your talents come with great responsibility. It would be best if you used your abilities to make a difference in the world, to be a positive influence, and to bring about a greater good. Just as Joseph's leadership helped save his family from famine, your leadership can provide for those around you in their time of need," the rabbi said and paused to look at the congregation.

"Joseph's coat symbolized his father's love for him and amplified his jealous brothers' dark side. You must be aware of the feelings of those around you," the rabbi said, waving a finger. "Be compassionate toward them, not shun them, and lead by example.

"So, Samuel, as you embark upon this next chapter of your life, I urge you to use your remarkable qualities to make a difference, be a leader among your peers, and persevere in adversity. And always remember, you, too, are blessed with a coat of many colors, a unique, special coat of potential meant for good. Mazel Tov on this special day, and may you continue to grow and thrive."

"Mazel Tov," the congregation responded.

After the ceremony, the rabbi directed everyone into an adjacent ballroom, where a celebration would commence. While the people filed out, Poppy said, "It seems you had no problem memorizing your Torah portion."

I shook my head. "No, I just kept listening to the recording repeatedly."

"I have a question for you," Poppy said, gently touching my chin and gazing directly into my eyes. "Three years earlier, when you were in seventh grade, your teacher asked each student to memorize a poem. Do you remember that?"

"Yes," I said with a sigh with a chuckle, "and I refused."

"But why?"

"I thought it was too hard."

"But you did it here," Poppy said, gesturing to the Bimah.

I shrugged with a sigh and said, "That's because I wanted to."

Poppy smiled and leaned in to kiss my cheek. "Come on, let's go watch the celebration."

*

The disc jockey had cued up a well-known Jewish traditional circle dance song—*The Hora.* Unable to resist the catchy melody and upbeat rhythm, the guests all held hands and formed a large circle. I watched my parents, grandparents, aunts, uncles, cousins, and many friends circling to the right and then to the left. With a unified cheer, they raised their clutched hands and rushed toward the center, then just as quickly backed away. Young and old joined in with huge smiles and bright eyes.

Suddenly, my dad left the dance floor to grab a chair. When he returned, he placed it in the middle of the circle and directed the Bar Mitzvah boy to take his place of honor. Once seated, Dad flicked his hand for three other robust men to help hoist his son. Dad's brother Uncle Craig, Uncle Tony—husband to Nanny's sister—and Poppy each took a leg of the chair, and with Sam gripping the edge of his seat, they lifted him high up into the air. Cheers exploded, and the circle charged in and out while Sam, his face filled with joy, was spun round and round.

After several more dances, the music stopped, allowing Poppy to step up to the microphone. "As I stand here before you today," Poppy said, "I'm filled with an abundance of pride and joy witnessing my grandson blossoming into a man. It seems like yesterday that I held you in my arms as a newborn, with you grasping one of my fingers with your tiny hand. And now you are, standing tall and beautiful, taking your rightful place as a Bar Mitzvah.

"Grandson, you're carrying on a tradition that dates back thousands of years, a ceremony passed down from generation to generation," Poppy said, stretching his arm outward. "As you read from your Torah portion today, sharing your insights, you are fulfilling a religious obligation and carrying on our ancestors' legacy. All of those who have traveled down this road before you have known what an important milestone this is. By nurturing your personal growth and fostering your inner freedom, I hope you can walk away from this day with an enhanced awareness of your inner self."

Poppy paused and lifted his glass of wine. "So let us raise a glass to my grandson on his Bar Mitzvah day. May you continue to grow and flourish, learn and explore, always be true to yourself, and know your values. L'chaim!"

"L'chaim," everyone cried out.

CHAPTER TWELVE
THE DIVORCE

"It's beautiful here," Poppy said, gazing out onto the still pond.

We stood on the wooden bridge stretching the overspill, where the water emptied into a meandering brook and to our left, and up the embankment, perched the house where I lived with my mom, dad, and brother. That was until the divorce when Dad moved out.

"I loved this house," I said, watching two geese emerging from the pond and waddling their way across the grass. "Dad hated those geese," I added with a chuckle. "They pooped everywhere."

Poppy laughed too. "He told me how he used to shoot them with a pellet rifle."

"He became obsessed," I said, wide-eyed. "When he heard their honking right before they landed, he would hurry into the house for his rifle, and while charging out the back door, he would load, then shoot them as they made landfall. One day, a new neighbor moved into a home toward the other side of the pond. Unaware of the incessant geese problem in our small enclave, she called the police, saying there was a man in the woods with a rifle."

"Did they come?" Poppy asked.

I nodded. "Just as Dad was pulling out the dead goose with a rake, two policemen approached, demanding that he drop the rake and turn around."

"Did he have the rifle with him too?"

"No, he left it at home when he retrieved the rake."

"Did he get in trouble?"

I laughed and shook my head. "No, they just gave him a warning."

Poppy rubbed his chin, directed his gaze onto the midsummer foliage, and said, "Do you know why we're here?"

I swallowed, expecting something unpleasant.

"We must look at your parents' separation and eventual divorce."

"That was a tough time," I said, shaking my head.

"You were only twelve years old. What do you remember?"

"Like my life was being torn apart. Dad leaving the house was hard for me to deal with."

"From your birth, you two were very close."

I furrowed my brow, ran my fingers through my hair, and said, "We were inseparable."

Poppy patted my back and said, "Let's go inside and see if we can understand more."

I puckered my lips and nodded as Poppy led the way.

Moments later, we were inside. Dad had taken great pride in the design and building of the A-frame-styled home. The living room featured an eighteen-foot-high vaulted ceiling with a fireplace sandwiched between large windows with a grand vista of the pond and surrounding trees. The house was within walking distance of the school and became a gathering place for my friends.

"I don't want to live here anymore," a voice cried out from the bedroom down the hall.

"Then go and live with your dad if that's what you want," replied the familiar voice of my mom.

Poppy cocked his head toward the shouting, and we headed to the disturbance.

Upon reaching the master bedroom, we saw pre-teen Sam, red-faced with hands on his hips, standing at the foot of the king-sized bed while his mother was fixing a red velvet pillow sham into place.

"Call your father and tell him," she said dismissively.

"I will," Sam said, storming out while at the same time reaching into his pocket and pulling out his flip phone. He scurried down the steps toward his basement bedroom, dialing the number.

"Dad, it's me," he said, slamming the door behind him and sitting on the edge of his unmade bed. "I can't do this, and I can't live here anymore."

He listened to his dad's response while pinching the skin on his forehead.

"She's making me crazy. I want to live with you. Can I please?"

I shared a look with Poppy, who offered a closed-eyed nod and a sigh.

"I don't care if I sleep on the couch. I want to be there with you."

Poppy tapped my shoulder and said, "Your father agreed, and you stayed with him for nearly a year before moving back home."

I nodded.

"There was also the issue of leaving school, which you attended since you were three. You were then sent to a public school, which was challenging. No wonder you had troubles."

"Yes, it was hard, especially after being in a small school where I had known everyone since kindergarten."

"Come, I want to show you something else," Poppy said, grasping my arm, and in the next instant, we were standing inside a small office.

I recognized Brian, my guidance counselor and a good friend of my dad's, who agreed to take me under his care upon my transfer to the middle school.

Twelve-year-old Sam sat slouched and teary-eyed.

"I know you're struggling with this," Brian said, leaning forward with his elbows on his desk. "But you must know your feelings are normal under the circumstances. You should also know that what's happening with your parents is not your fault and will never diminish their love for you."

"I know," Sam said, gazing down at the floor.

"You can always come and talk with me whenever you need to," Brian offered.

Sam looked up at Brian, wiped away the tears from his cheeks, and said in a barely audible mumble, "I want to kill myself."

Brian asked, unsure what he heard, "What did you say?"

Sam unfurled from his slouch, stared at Brian momentarily, then repeated, "I want to kill myself."

Brian pushed back his chair and said, "Stay right here. I'll be right back."

"Where are you going?" Sam asked.

"Just one second," Brian said and left the office.

While Sam sat alone, I said, "I wasn't serious about committing suicide."

"Then why did you say it?" Poppy asked.

I shrugged and said, "I don't know. Maybe to get back at my parents for putting me through this. Or maybe because it seemed like a way to stop the pain."

Poppy nodded. "And this behavior became a pattern, eventually leading you to explore other ways of dulling your emotions."

"Through drugs and alcohol," I said, shaking my head. "But I was never so abusive to myself that I couldn't function. I finished high school, earned a degree in hospitality, and worked effectively with my dad."

"But those types of wounds never heal on their own."

I rubbed the back of my neck and said, "No, I suppose they never do."

CHAPTER THIRTEEN
PLATTSBURGH

"So this is Plattsburgh," Poppy said as we walked among the students hurrying around campus.

"Yes, after graduating high school, I spent two years at community college before transferring here. Plattsburgh offered a bachelor's degree in hospitality, which I decided would become my major."

"Was this your first time away from home?" Poppy asked.

"It was, and I had a great time. I moved into an apartment off campus where I met my roommates and eventually Meghan."

"Before we get to Meghan, let's check out where you lived," Poppy said.

Then, in the blink of an eye, we stood inside a three-bedroom apartment I shared with two college roommates. The living room featured beige-painted cinderblock walls, a large flat screen tv, a battered, wooden coffee table littered with empty beer and vodka bottles, an overflowing ashtray of cigarette butts, and a half-eaten ham sandwich lying on top of a crumbled Subway wrapper.

"Gross," I said with a grimace.

"College life," Poppy said with a chuckle.

"I don't know how we lived like this."

"I suppose it wasn't unusual."

I scoffed at Poppy's assumption. "This was nothing. Some of my friend's places," I said, waving my hand, "were much worse than this. It's amazing how anyone of us ever got schoolwork done when there was so much partying."

"Was this where you first did the painkillers?"

I took a deep breath and slowly exhaled. "We snorted right there on that table. It's the best way to reach such a euphoric high, and that's because of the rapid release and absorption of oxycodone into the bloodstream. It's an amazing feeling."

"Until it wasn't," Poppy said with a grimace.

"Until it wasn't," I agreed, dropping my gaze.

"Where was your room?"

"Down here," I said, pointing to the hallway beyond the kitchen.

My room consisted of a single twin-size bed, with its long side pushed up against the wall. A wobbly table lamp stood on top of an oak-stained nightstand. I kept my clothes in a six-drawer wooden dresser with a cheap plastic framed mirror hanging off a nail on the wall above it.

"Nothing fancy," I said as we entered the small bedroom.

"I suppose you spent time with Meghan here?" Poppy said, gesturing to the bed.

"Yeah, I can't believe we slept together in that tiny bed."

"That's not surprising. When Nanny and I first met, we squeezed into one just as narrow. It's what you do when you're in love."

"We were in love," I admitted, remembering those moments we shared during our two years together at school.

"Then, after graduation, you returned to your mother's home with Meghan."

"That's right, and we lived in my bedroom."

"How was that? Bringing your girlfriend into the house with your mother and brother?"

"Challenging, to say the least. Of course, I was used to my mother. But it wasn't easy for Meghan."

"In what way?"

"You remember my mother. She had a big personality and tried to take control of our lives. Meghan often complained about her and wanted us to get our own place, which we eventually did."

"That's right," Poppy said, wagging a finger. "You got that apartment by the high school."

"Yes, I loved that place. We finally felt like a normal couple. With my degree in hospitality, I landed a job at a fancy hotel in New York City. While Meghan pursued her field of working with autistic children."

"Good jobs for a new couple."

"They were good jobs," I agreed.

"But what about your substance abuse?"

"We kept it under control, except on the weekends, when we locked ourselves in our apartment and binged on weed and oxy."

"And this became an ongoing habit?"

"For years," I said. "Even when we got the house with Dad."

"Do you think your addiction had anything to do with why you were fired from your job at the hotel?"

I thought a while, wanting to give an honest answer. "I'm sure it had an effect. The supposed reason for my dismissal was that I sent an important package in regular mail when I should have sent it by FedEx, and to be truthful, I was probably instructed to do so but zoned out and made the fatal mistake."

"Seems excessive," Poppy said, lifting his brow.

"Maybe it was just the last straw," I said, admitting to other more probable reasons for my performance.

"It doesn't matter," Poppy said, waving a hand. "The point is, you can understand the consequences of your abuse."

I sighed and nodded.

"After being fired, you went to work for your dad."

"I did," I said with a broad smile. "It was what I wanted more than anything. To be with him once again."

"Great, let's get into that," Poppy said, and with that, we vanished from my college bedroom and reappeared in Dad's office.

CHAPTER FOURTEEN
WORKING WITH DAD

Dad began his career in the window-covering business in 1985, three years before my birth. It was only a short time before his company thrived, supplying custom draperies, shades, blinds, and upholstery for the well-off throughout Southeast Florida.

A few months before my second birthday, Dad asked Mom if they could relocate to New York, where he had grown up. She agreed without a fuss. So he dissolved his Florida business, sold the townhouse I was born in, and moved us back to his childhood home.

Dad struck out on his own after working for a year with Poppy in his housewares store. Our family's history was chock full of successful, independent merchants, going back multiple generations, in various retail ventures. So when I was fired, I was eager to join Dad, continuing with the family's tradition of owning one's business.

"My son created a wonderful operation that would have been yours to take over once he retired," Poppy said as we sat in the empty office with two desks, computer monitors, piles of customer folders, and a wall of shelves filled with books of fabric samples.

"That was my intention," I said with a nod. "But I don't know if I could have succeeded."

Poppy squinted and said, "Why do you say that?"

I looked around the office where so many of Dad's creations were put into action and said, "I was afraid that once he retired, I would not have been able to carry on."

Poppy jerked his head back. "You thought you would fail?"

I bit my lower lip and nodded. "The business required Dad's constant involvement. Even when he was away on vacation, I needed him, and there was no way I could have gone on for long without his daily support."

Poppy wagged a finger and said, "It would have been hard, but I'm sure you would have figured it out."

I shrugged and said, "But what would have happened if I didn't?"

Poppy furrowed his brow and said, "You may have made some mistakes but would have succeeded."

I rubbed my fingers against my forehead and said, "I'm not so sure."

"This is another example of allowing your fears to control you," Poppy said, pointing the finger at me.

I swallowed hard, stepped toward the window, looked out, and said, "You mean my allowing my inner *rasha* to control me?"

"That's right," Poppy agreed.

As Poppy spoke, I noticed a figure moving about in the shadows. "Is someone out there?"

"Step away from the window, Sam," Poppy demanded. "By mentioning the *rasha*, you must have summoned him."

I stood frozen, unable to budge. Then, as if the words were meant for me alone, the *rasha*'s voice said, "Why do you allow yourself to witness these disturbing events of your life? You can leave that all behind you; it's ancient history, Samuel. Come with me, and I'll show you an eternity of peacefulness without this pointless effort."

With nothing more than a subtle nod, I was whisked away and found myself standing alone in an empty, unfinished office space on some upper floor in a tall building overlooking New York City. It was nighttime; the only light came from a full moon over the Hudson River.

"Where am I?" I asked, looking at my reflection in the floor-to-ceiling window wall of glass.

"This is where you belong," said my mirrored image.

A cold sweat ran down the back of my neck as I gawked at what appeared to be myself speaking back to me. "A-Are you the *rasha*?" I asked, my voice trembling.

"I don't like labels," he said, shaking his head with pursed lips. "After all, I'm a part of you. Your better half, perhaps."

I scoffed and said, "Hardly."

"Samuel, why don't you come with me," the *rasha* said, summoning me with a flick of his wrist. "Step through the glass and complete this useless trip down memory lane."

"But what about my journey through the planetary spheres and preparing for my birth?"

"That's all nonsense," the *rasha* scoffed. "I'll show you an easier way than—"

Suddenly my wrist was grabbed, and I was jerked away, and I found myself back in Dad's office.

"You need to be careful, Sam," Poppy said, holding out clenched fists. "This time, I was able to find you and bring you back. But the *rasha* is cunning, and I may not be able to do so again."

"He looked exactly like me," I said, pointing to the window in the office.

Poppy nodded, raising his brow. "That's because, as I told you before, he's part of you."

"Just before you pulled me back, the *rasha* said there was an easier way. What did he mean?"

"It's nothing but a lie. You don't want to go anywhere he wants to take you," Poppy warned.

"Where's that?" I asked.

Poppy shook his head. "It's best we don't speak of it. You see what happened when you mentioned his name."

I looked into my grandfather's gentle brown eyes and sighed. "Is my journey supposed to be this hard?"

"I'm afraid so," Poppy nodded with a raised brow. "That's because it's a process of self-discovery, introspection, and transformation. It's a way to help you learn from your past life and prepare you for your next incarnation. You can't avoid confronting your choices without dealing with the consequences."

"Am I being punished?"

"Oh no, it's not punishment," Poppy said, shaking his head. "You're not being singled out. This is how you progress and evolve toward a higher state of knowledge, and it's something all souls confront."

"Even you, Poppy?"

Poppy jerked his head back. "Of course. Even me."

"But you've had such a perfect life," I said, sweeping a hand outward.

"Hardly," Poppy chuckled. "It's true I never did any drugs or drank much. But I was no saint."

"Really?" I asked, wide-eyed. "What did you do?"

Poppy shrugged and sighed. "Ah, you know, there were times when running my business that I may have taken advantage of people, either financially or psychologically."

"What do you mean?"

Poppy shrugged and said, "There were several instances over the years. One, in particular, I am ashamed of was when I closed my store in New York and decided not to pay certain vendors, knowing they couldn't come after me."

"And when you died, did you have to deal with that?"

"I did," Poppy said, nodding. "It was a profound part of my purification process. We all go through it upon our passing."

"Does that mean we are also all reborn?"

"Not all of us," Poppy said. "A few have achieved an elevated level of spiritual development and no longer need to undergo another physical incarnation for their evolution."

I scratched at my stubble and said, "Have you met one?"

Poppy nodded. "I have, and so will you. But first, you have more work to do."

"*Pfft,*" I sputtered. "I don't know if I can."

Poppy stepped closer, reached out with both arms, pulled me in close, and whispered, "All of this is about to get much harder, so you mustn't give up. If you stay true to the path, I promise you'll find the peace you seek."

I took a deep breath and sighed. "Okay, Poppy, where to next?"

"Brace yourself. You're not going to like what you're about to see."

CHAPTER FIFTEEN
MOM'S OUTRAGE

"They're here," Dad said, gazing through the lower floor window.

He hurried outside and waited as Max pulled up the driveway, with Mom visible in the front seat.

"When was this?" I asked Poppy as we stood alongside, watching the event unfold.

"A day after your passing. Your brother picked your mother up at the airport upon her arrival from Florida."

We watched as Dad offered a pained smile and a wave. The moment the car came to a stop, the passenger side door swung open, and Mom jumped out. With the saunter of a prizefighter entering a ring, she confronted Dad, reared back, and punched him in the face.

Dad held his hands and cried, "What the hell?"

"You killed him!" she snarled, her bloodshot eyes swirling with hatred.

"What's wrong with you?" Dad barked back.

Then she let loose another fist, this time hitting Dad's chest. "You knew about this and didn't tell me."

Dad simply said, "Sam didn't want you to know."

Mom huffed, turned around, and headed into the house.

"How dare you accuse me of something like that?" Dad called after her.

Mom spun around, pointed a finger, and spewed, "It's your fault."

"You're a bitch," Dad yelled, taking an aggressive step toward her.

"Stop!" Max demanded, wrapping his arms around Dad, and keeping them apart.

"You're disgusting, a piece of crap," Dad shouted past Max.

Mom snarled and headed into the house, leaving Dad and Max in the garage.

"You told her what happened?" Dad asked.

Max nodded.

"And she thinks she could have done something to stop Sam?"

"She's upset you didn't tell her," Max explained.

"But Sam asked me not to, you know that."

"I know," Max said with a sigh.

Poppy grasped my arm, getting my attention, and said, "What were you keeping from your mother?"

"A few months earlier, I had a previous episode with tainted Percocet."

"Yes, I know?" Poppy said. "Tell me more about that incident."

"I crushed the pill into a powder and snorted it in my bathroom, and when I came downstairs to do some work with Dad, it consumed me. The only thing I remember before losing consciousness was Dad grabbing me and shouting, 'What did you take, Sam?'"

"Then what happened?"

I puckered my mouth and shook my head. "When I opened my eyes, I was lying on the carpet, with paramedics hovering over me. Surprised, I jerked myself up to sit. But I was gently pushed back down and told to lie still."

"Where was Meghan?" Poppy asked.

"She was standing off to the side with my dad and two police officers."

"All right," Poppy said, waving his hand for me to continue.

"The paramedics wanted to take me to the hospital for observation, and Dad asked if that was necessary, but the police told him it was mandatory after such an incident. So while I was lifted onto a gurney and carted out of the house and into an ambulance, Dad and Meghan said they would follow and meet me at the hospital."

"But something else happened?" Poppy asked.

"I didn't learn of this until later, but according to what Meghan told me, she went upstairs to get ready when the drug overtook her, and she lost consciousness."

Poppy, wide-eyed, shook his head. "She snorted it too?"

"We did it together," I said, shaking my head. "Good thing Dad went upstairs to check on her because she took too long. That's when he found her lying on the floor in our bedroom. He called 911 once again, and luckily the paramedics were nearby and gave her a shot of Narcan, the same medication that saved me and brought her back."

"Did they take her to the hospital?"

I nodded. "We were in separate rooms, down the hall from each other."

"Thank god your dad was there, or you both would have died."

I sighed and said, "I know."

"But why in the world, after that close call, did you do it again?"

"I don't know," I said, shaking my head. "I guess I thought it was a fluke, and I bought the Percocet from that guy many times before and never had a problem. When I hurt my back, I knew it was the best way to get immediate relief."

"But why didn't you want to tell your mother what happened?"

"Because she's no one to talk to. She grew up in South Florida during the seventies, where drug use was prevalent. She struggled with addiction her entire life, and I witnessed some of it firsthand. So I didn't believe she was in any position of authority to tell me what I did was wrong."

"Was that all?" Poppy asked with a squint.

"No," I said, shaking my head. "I also didn't want her calling the police on Ben."

Poppy scoffed. "Why would you want to protect him after he nearly killed you?"

"Because he was a good resource for my pot as well."

Poppy rocked back and forth as he thought. "I hope you can see how drugs weakened your will, dulled your consciousness, and caused a loss of your spiritual insight."

"Sure," I said, holding out my hands. "It's obvious now."

"I also hope you can see how you left a wake of destruction in the lives of those who loved you."

"I do," I said, lowering my head.

"It's a shame your parents have become such enemies."

I wagged a finger and said, "Mom had no reason to blame Dad for what I did. He couldn't have done anything to stop me. It was solely my fault."

"I know, Sam," Poppy said.

CHAPTER SIXTEEN
TECHNOLOGY

"We need to examine what led up to those moments that eventually took your life," Poppy said, as we now found ourselves sitting in my home office.

"All right," I said, swiveling in my chair to look at my grandfather seated on the brown plaid sofa.

"I remember that you were good with computers," Poppy said, pointing to the two large monitors on my desk.

"Yes, I was."

"It's a useful skill in this modern world and was a great asset to the business. I'm sure your dad relied on you to handle many technological tasks."

I nodded. "I did the QuickBooks, scheduled installations, wrote, formatted, and sent out our newsletters, updated the blogs and websites, handled the smartphones and other things like that."

"I wish I had you around when I ran my business," Poppy said with a grin.

"I was good at it," I admitted.

"But this attraction to the digital world became one-sided, even in your private life. You became obsessed, disconnecting yourself from the natural world."

I sighed and said, "This is true."

"Tell me more."

I held out my hands. "Well, when weekends came, even if it were a perfect mid-seventy-degree day, Meghan and I would lock ourselves in our bedroom and amuse ourselves with our favorite shows," I said and added, "We wouldn't even go out for food and we ordered in every meal."

"Was that because of the pandemic?"

"That's how it started," I said with a grimace. "We were apprehensive about mingling in public places, so we developed a habit of getting everything delivered. There was no need to leave the house with Amazon, Door Dash, and Instacart."

"This could be the root cause of your downfall. We must maintain a deep spiritual connection with the natural world as earthly beings. By losing touch, it becomes harder accessing your higher self or having the ability to experience spiritual insights."

"It's true. I lost my balance," I confessed.

Poppy jabbed a finger, agreeing with my remark. "It's critical to maintain a balanced approach to life by incorporating the physical, mental, emotional, and spiritual aspects of our being."

"Well," I said, taking a deep breath, "I certainly worked on my physical well-being. I went to the gym nearly every day."

"That's wonderful, and you were quite fit," Poppy said, waving his hand toward my body. "But your disconnection from nature, coupled with an overreliance on technology, weakened your personal development."

"I understand."

"It's not hard to see how the digital world seeped into your consciousness, becoming part of you."

I squinted. "What do you mean?"

"What did you like to watch on TV?"

I shrugged and said, "Um, I liked *The Last Kingdom*, *The Witcher*, *The Mandalorian*, any of the Marvel or DC movies, and um—"

"*Spartacus?*" Poppy reminded me.

"Yes, and *Spartacus*," I said, recalling Crixus's visit earlier in my journey.

"And what do you think attracted you to those shows?"

I puckered my lips and shrugged. "I guess I related to the warrior."

"That's interesting because the warrior represents strength, courage, discipline, and an ability to confront challenges and adversity. Attributes you struggled with in your lifetime, though your impressive physique states otherwise."

"Strong body, weak mind?" I offered.

Poppy grimaced. "There was nothing weak about your mind. Do you remember how I explained how we are made of four bodies?"

I nodded, held out my hand, and counted them off. "The physical body, the living body, the soul body, and the ego."

"Good," Poppy said. "And which body relates to our ability to think, reason, and make decisions?"

I thought a moment, then said, "The soul body?"

"Correct," Poppy said, pointing a finger at me. "It's the soul body that relates to a strong mind. As you review and assimilate experiences from your past life, you'll learn from them, allowing your soul body to purify and strengthen."

"And this makes my mind stronger?"

Poppy nodded. "This is the essence of the work you'll need to do to prepare for your rebirth."

"So by reviewing significant moments in my past life, I'll cleanse my soul body?"

Poppy squinted and said, "Not quite."

"What else must I do?"

"You're only in the journey's first stage—the moon sphere. This is where you'll encounter your shortcomings, reflect upon them, and be forced to realize the consequences of your actions. Then there's the purification process."

I swallowed hard and said, "What's that?"

Poppy reached over and patted my knee. "You'll see. In the meantime, let me show you something to make you feel better."

CHAPTER SEVENTEEN
DREAMS

"Where are we?" I asked, scanning a large lake cradled within rolling green hills.

"Beautiful, isn't it?" Poppy asked as we climbed a large boulder along the water's edge.

"Peaceful," I said, crouching to sit.

Poppy joined me and said, "Not everything in the soul world is difficult to maneuver."

"That's good," I said.

"You like the view?" Poppy asked, sweeping an arm outward.

"I do," I said with a light-hearted chuckle.

"You may want to call this place paradise," Poppy suggested.

I shrugged and said, "It reminds me of the state park near home."

"How often did you go there?"

Sam shook his head. "I don't know, a few times."

"Perhaps you'll want to immerse yourself more in nature in your next incarnation."

"I want to," I said.

We sat silently, absorbing the natural beauty, before Poppy said, "You remember how you helped your dad with the password?"

"With the computer? Sure," I said, nodding.

"That occurred because your soul body allows you to send such messages."

I squinted. "Are you saying I can do that again?"

"Yes, you can," Poppy said, nodding.

I slid off the boulder and onto the rocky shore, where I picked up a flat stone and tossed it sidearm across the lake's surface, watching it skip several times before it sunk into the water.

"Can you teach me how?" I asked, keeping my eyes on the ripples pushing outward from where the stone settled.

"Sure," Poppy said. "There are several ways, and one is by influencing the thoughts and feelings of those you left behind."

With a furrowed brow, I turned around and asked, "How do you do that?"

"I found the most effective way was through dreams."

"Dreams?" I repeated. "You mentioned dreams before."

"Yes, you can communicate to the living through the dream world," Poppy said, shimmying down the slick side of the bolder. He, too, reached down for a stone, reared back, and tossed it. The smooth stone skipped off the glass-like surface a few times more than mine before the water swallowed it up.

"Good throw, Poppy!" I called out, surprised at the power of his slender arm.

"Thanks," Poppy said, stepping to the water's edge lapping onto the shore. "When the living sleep, their soul body separates from their physical body, allowing their consciousness to access the soul world. In a way, it's as if dying into the spirit world without crossing the threshold of death. That's the time when we can connect."

I furrowed my brow and nodded, trying to absorb Poppy's words.

"The soul bodies of both entities create this communication bridge, allowing the soul to share insights, guidance, and messages with the living."

"That's great," I said, wide-eyed. "Say I want to enter Meghan's dream; how do I do it?"

"First of all," Poppy began, "you must understand the ability to enter a dream happens infrequently. Maybe twice a lifetime, or it may not happen at all."

"I still want to try," I said.

"All right," Poppy said, nodding. "It's important for the living to be receptive to a visit from someone who's passed. I gather Meghan was a believer."

"Without a doubt," I said. "She loved watching all those shows; her favorite was *Long Island Medium*."

"Good," Poppy said, bending over to pick up another stone. "Then you should be able to enter Meghan's dream."

I rubbed my hands together and said, "Can I try now?"

"Go and lie down on this rock," Poppy said, stretching out an arm and pointing.

"Okay," I said, climbing back up the steep side. Once on top, I lay on my back and closed my eyes.

"Once your life body has completely dissolved, there will be no need to act this out, and you'll just call upon your soul body to enter someone's dream. But in the meantime, it works better if you mimic sleep as if you were in your physical body."

"Do I need to think of Meghan?"

"Yes, of course. Imagine being with her, saying something sweet to comfort her. If your soul body connects with hers, she'll receive your spiritual guidance."

"Okay," I said and thought of us embracing, and with my arms wrapped around her, I leaned in and whispered, "Everything will be all right."

I opened my eyes, lifted my head, and asked, "How do I know if it worked?"

Poppy looked up at me and shrugged. "You don't know. But you can keep trying. Making the connection can only happen when our soul bodies are in sync. Meghan must also be dreaming while you're trying to reach her, and that's why it happens infrequently."

"All right," I said, getting to my feet. "I'll keep trying."

"You can also try with your family," Poppy suggested. "Anyone you were close to."

We lingered in silence, then I said, "What about channelers? Those who reach out to the soul world? Do I need to ready myself if one tries to contact me?"

Poppy sighed, bent down, picked up a stone, held it in his hand, and said, "Oh, you'll know when a legitimate channeler reaches out to you."

"Legitimate?" I said, climbing down the boulder.

Poppy nodded. "Well, they're the only ones who can contact."

"What does that mean?"

"Those who can open a channel to the soul world have developed virtues of selflessness, humility, and compassion. These qualities help purify their soul, preparing them for perceiving our world. They have learned, through exercises, how to quiet the mind, which helps develop their clairvoyant faculties."

"Exercises?" I repeated. "What kind of exercises?"

"Oh, you know, like visualization, certain mantras, or meditation. These sharpen the channeler's spiritual senses, enabling them to perceive and interact with the soul world."

"What about the four bodies you spoke about?"

A huge smile spread across Poppy's face. "Excellent question, Sam. You've been paying attention. Yes, it's important for a channeler to access the soul world, to have all four bodies—the physical, the life, the soul, and the ego in balance."

I considered this for a while, wondering if Meghan or Dad would engage me with a channeler. I then asked, "You mean like you did with June?"

"Oh yes," Poppy said. "June has used a very accomplished channeler several times. Maybe she'll try to reach out to you, too."

"I'd like that," I said, and then a thought occurred to me. "I'm curious, Poppy; why haven't we looked at events of my life when I was very young?"

"Great question," Poppy said, tossing another stone. "I have an idea of something wonderful you would love to see."

CHAPTER EIGHTEEN
MAX'S BIRTH

"Who's that?" I asked, pointing to a newborn baby with oxygen tubes inserted into its nostrils and other medical devices taped to its tiny arms.

"That's your brother, Max," Poppy said, staring at him with an engaging smile.

"Really?" I said. "He's so little."

"And over there are you and your dad," Poppy said, pointing to the observation window.

I looked through the glass and saw my six-year-old self standing alongside Dad, who must have been about thirty-eight by then.

"Why was Max here? Was something wrong with him?" I said, having no memory of that day.

"He swallowed fluids during your mom's c-section. He's fine; they're just making sure. You know, the same thing happened to you."

"It did?" I said with a grimace.

We stood there a while, watching Max wiggling his arms and smiling as if he knew we were present.

"I see his physical body," I said, pointing to my baby brother. "But what about his other bodies? Are they part of him now too?"

Poppy, wide-eyed, held out his arms and said, "Great question. You're right. His physical body is fully formed, but the others, his life, soul, or ego bodies, will grow as he does. It takes some time. His life forces will take seven years to rebuild every cell from its heredity body to make his body uniquely individual. The last sign of this physical transformation is when the first adult teeth replace the baby teeth. Max's soul body, which relates to his emotions and desires, will integrate with his life body at around fourteen. At the same time when he experiences more complex emotions and starts to develop a greater sense of himself."

"What about his ego?" I asked.

"When he turns twenty-one, just as his self-consciousness is being realized. You know, when you think, feel, and act independently."

I thought about the ages and said, "There seems to be something happening every seven years."

"Another wonderful observation," Poppy said, clapping my back.

"Thank you," I said, pulling back my shoulders.

"The development of our beings, starting at birth, is based upon seven-year cycles. From birth to age seven, it's the time of physical and life body development. Then the child's emotional or soul body forms between the ages of seven and fourteen," Poppy said, holding up a finger.

"Okay," I said, nodding. "What about from fourteen through twenty-one?"

"That's the time of the intellect, the time of the ego."

I scratched my cheek and said, "I imagine the next seven years have to do with seeking career paths and relationships. Would that also be the ego?"

"That's right," Poppy said with a deliberate nod. "Now, from twenty-eight through thirty-five, your last age group, what would you expect these years to enhance?"

I shrugged and said, "More responsibilities?"

"Excellent," Poppy said.

I sighed. "That's what I was burdened with," I said, thinking of the stresses of my life just before my passing.

"Let's stop and listen in on what the two of you were talking about," Poppy said, flicking his hand toward Sam and Dad.

I shook my head as I listened to the heartwarming conversation between my six-year-old self and my dad. It seemed I was more interested in the knobs and lights on the walls than the birth of my brother.

"You know, Poppy," I said, tilting my head to speak to him, "I just had a thought. This moment of Max's birth was not his beginning, was it?"

Poppy squinted and asked, "What do you mean?"

"It's like me and my journey toward birth. Didn't Max also have time before being born? What was that like?"

"Oh, Sam! You're figuring it out," Poppy said, rubbing his hands together.

"I imagine that Max came into the world with something more…" I said, searching for the words.

"Go on," Poppy said, rolling a hand.

"From what I've learned, we bring our history into our next life."

"That's right. It's called your karmic history. But we have a long way to go and much more work to do before we're ready to examine yours."

I sighed, looking at Max and wondering about his experiences with his *in-between* time. *Did he come to terms with his shortcomings? Did he feel ready to take on the challenges of his new life?*

"Life is wondrous," Poppy said, picking up on my musings.

~ ACT TWO ~

CHAPTER NINETEEN
THE *TZADDIK*

"What's this place?" I asked, looking out onto a desolate landscape between two soaring ranges of black rocky mountains poised under a silver, cloudy sky.

"This is known as the Valley of the Shadow of Death," Poppy said as we stood upon a gravel-laden roadway that meandered onward, vanishing into a thick fog.

"That's a frightening name," I said with a furrowed brow.

Poppy nodded. "This is the first level of Gehenna."

"Gehenna?" My jaw dropped. "What are we doing here?"

"You've been summoned to meet someone," Poppy said, pointing off into the distance.

I followed his hand and saw a figure coming from the shadows. But it was so far off that I couldn't make out the face. "Who's that?" I asked with a squint.

"You'll see," Poppy said, crossing his arms over his chest.

We waited and observed what looked like a man approaching. Once close enough, I could make out that he was elderly, with two bushy growths of gray hair on either side of his round head, connected with a short combover. His soft blue eyes spoke of his kindness. He stretched his arms and said, "Schmuel, it's good to see you."

I took a step backward at his use of my Hebrew name. "Do I know you?" I asked.

"You may not remember me. I died when you were maybe five or six."

I glanced over to Poppy, then back and said, "Are you Beebop?", referring to the endearing name bestowed upon him by his eldest granddaughter.

He smiled. "I haven't heard that name spoken in a long time," he said, stepping close and embracing me. "But you can call me Moshe."

"You're my great-grandfather," I said, wide-eyed.

"I am indeed," he said, releasing me.

"It's good to see you," I said.

Moshe reached out, took my hand, cupped it between his soft hands, and said, "I'm very sorry for what happened to you."

"You know about it?" I asked, cocking my head.

"Sure," he said, patting my hands. "We all know."

"Okay," I said deliberately. "But why are we here in this Valley of the Shadow of Death?"

Moshe looked over to Poppy, then returned his focus to me and said, "We need you to do something crucial for our soul family."

"Soul family?"

"Yes," Moshe said, waving a hand between me and Poppy. "Souls that have traveled together through multiple incarnations are called soul family, and members play different roles in each other's lives and support each other's spiritual growth and evolution."

"All right," I said, scratching my chin. "What do you need me to do that's so important?"

Moshe sighed, stepped closer, and said, "I need you to find my father, Pincus."

"Pincus?" I said with a furrowed brow. "And where did you lose him?"

Moshe jerked his thumb behind him.

I tilted my head to look past him into the shadows. "I don't understand."

"Come," Moshe said, "let's sit, and I'll explain."

Once the three of us perched ourselves on an outcropping of stones, my great-grandfather shared his story.

"During my past life, I grew up in a small shtetl in what's now considered southern Poland. I lived there with my parents, Pincus and Clara, my brother Hymie, and my sister Jennie. Father left us behind when he set off for America. I was only nine, and Mother was pregnant with Anna."

"He left you?" I asked. "Why would he do that?"

Moshe shrugged. "It was common for the heads of the household to go on ahead. Father was a cobbler and ventured to the New World to establish his business, find a place for us to live, and then planned to return and retrieve us within a year. But he stayed too long, and World War 1 broke out. Our little village was suddenly in the middle of a war zone. That was when I learned that I had a special gift."

I blinked and said, "What kind of gift?"

"The kind that comes from Hashem," Moshe said and paused. "You know this word?"

I nodded. "It means God."

"Do you also know the word *tzaddik*?"

"Yes, it's the counterpart to the *rasha*," I said, looking over to Poppy, who nodded.

"Good, Sam," Moshe said, tapping my knee. "During my time on Earth, I was a *tzaddik*."

"No way," I said, jerking my head back.

Moshe laughed. "I know; it sounds crazy, but it's true."

"How did you know you were *tzaddik*? Did you have some superpower?"

Moshe laughed. "You mean like Batman?"

"Or maybe Thor?" I suggested one of my favorites.

"Well, not exactly," he said with a grimace. "For one thing, I was able to foreshadow bad events."

I squinted and said slowly, "You knew when something bad was about to happen?"

Moshe nodded. "I would get sick. Like during the war when Russian soldiers murdered our Jewish men, I felt nauseated moments before they barged into the synagogue."

"That's it? That was your superpower?" I asked, disappointed.

"Well," Moshe said with a shrug and a tilt of his head, "there was something else."

"What was that?"

"Several times throughout my life, I comforted those at the moment of their passing."

I furrowed my brow and asked, "What does that mean?"

"There's much fear for those in pain and close to death, and I was able to give them peace just by touching them."

"How did you do that?"

"I would grasp their hand or gently touch their face, and their anguish drained when they looked into my eyes."

"Why?"

Moshe held out his hands and said, "Because they saw the Almighty."

I reached out and grasped his hand, hoping for a vision.

Moshe smiled, squeezed back, and said, "There's no need, Samuel. You're already connected."

I thought about this for a while and then asked, "But what's that got to do with your father?"

"I'll tell you," he said, holding a finger. "Years later, in America, I was working in my cobbler shop in the Bronx when I was summoned by a man who heard of me and knew of my gift. His name was Arnold Lieberman, and after much convincing, he recruited me to fight Solomon Blass, a corrupt gangster, and *rasha*."

I rattled my head and said, "A *rasha* on Earth?"

Moshe nodded. "Blass was a rasha who had the power to foresee future events through the dream world. To destroy him, I had to learn to become lucid in my dreams so we could meet up."

I waved my hand. "Slow down," I demanded. "You were recruited to fight some gangster in the dream world, who also happened to be a *rasha*?"

Moshe laughed. "I know it sounds convoluted, but it's true."

"And how did you destroy the *rasha*?"

"While flying in our lucid dreams, I grasped onto him and dragged him down to the fiery pits of Gehenna, or as it's known in these realms— the River of Fire."

"That's how you destroyed the *rasha*?"

"I thought I did, but it was a mistake."

"A mistake? Why?"

"Because I believed that the River of Fire was where souls were destroyed. But instead, all that's done in that realm is cleansing their sins by passing them through churning rivers of black lava and flames."

"That's all?" I said with a grimace.

"Sure, all souls survive the River of Fire. I should have brought Solomon to the Frozen Wasteland, where there's no salvation."

I waved my hand back and forth and said, "You're telling me that this is a true story?"

Moshe put his hand over his heart and said, "A *tzaddik* never lies."

I took a deep breath and let it go slowly. "Sounds outrageous, but can I ask a question?"

Moshe held out his hands and said, "Sure."

I looked at Poppy and said, "How come I never heard this story?"

Poppy smiled and said, "Because Moshe decided it would be best if it remained a secret, and he didn't want future generations to know of his gift."

"But why?" I asked, turning to Moshe.

"Until I turned sixty, I kept it private my entire life. After encountering the *rasha*, I insisted that no one speaks of it. For I was worried that it would put my family at risk, and not a word was spoken for the last twenty-three years of my life."

I stared at my great-grandfather, wishing he had lived longer. It would have been amazing knowing him as an adult. "So, what does this have to do with your lost father?" I said, pointing off into the distance.

"Solomon is out for revenge."

"Are you saying the *rasha* has kidnapped your father, Pincus?"

"That's right," Moshe said.

"But you're *tzaddik*. Why don't you go and rescue him?"

Moshe lowered his eyes and said, "I'm too old, and you're a young, strong soul."

"Am I?" I said, pointing to myself.

Moshe nodded. "By passing at thirty-two, you've carried forward a healthy portion of the spiritual energies you would have used if you'd lived on. As a result, these extra life forces enable you to have an impact within the spirit world. In essence, Sam, you have what you may like to call a superpower."

I scoffed and said, "You're joking."

"I do joke," Moshe said with a dimpled smile, "but not about this."

CHAPTER TWENTY
FAREWELL

"Where do I go?" I asked.

Moshe swung an arm outward and said, "Into the valley."

"Is there a map or signs to follow?" I asked.

"I'm afraid not," Moshe said, shaking his head. "The landscapes of Gehanna are fluid, always changing. A map would be useless."

"But what about this place? What's the Valley of the Shadow of Death like?"

"This is where souls are sent with minor transgressions or who have not fully embraced the idea of the Divine presence. Here souls undergo purification before being allowed to move on in preparation for their rebirth."

I looked over to Poppy with a grimace and asked, "You mean like me?"

Moshe waved a hand and said, "Do you accept that the Divine is present and active within the created world?"

"After what I've seen," I said, nodding, "I most certainly do."

"You're being sent into this realm, or if necessary into the other realms, for no reason than to find Pincus."

"But what's it like?" I asked, pointing in the dark, shadowy gloom ahead.

"It's a place of utter silence and stillness. Where repenting souls dwell within solitude, facing their fears, to test one's faith and resilience."

"So I just wander about, looking for Pincus?"

"Use your life body forces to guide you," Moshe advised. "It will provide you with an edge over the others."

"But what if I don't find him? What do I do then?"

"Then you go onto the next realm, and then the next, until you do."

I scratched the top of my head and said, "Maybe it's a good idea to tell me about these realms."

Moshe leaned forward, resting his elbows on his knees, and said, "After the Valley of the Shadow of Death comes the Pit."

"The Pit?" I repeated, swallowing hard.

Moshe nodded. "Within the Pit, you'll witness intense suffering where souls endure excruciating physical and emotional torment."

"But I thought our physical bodies don't exist anymore."

Moshe looked over to Poppy and smiled. "You taught him well."

"Sam's a good student," Poppy said.

"It's true that physical torment seems contradictory, since souls lack a physical body. Those subjected to the Pit undergo an intense and transformative experience. This involves working through their remorse, guilt, and regret of their past actions and understanding the consequences of what they bestowed upon others."

"Suppose I can't find your father in the Pit; what's next?"

"Then there's the River of Fire." Moshe sighed. "The place I banished Solomon to. Hopefully, you won't need to go that far."

I swallowed hard and said, "You told me about that."

Moshe nodded. "Next comes the Clay of Yaven, where souls experience shame and regret for their past life by undergoing intense emotional pain and humiliation."

I sat quietly, awaiting Moshe to describe the last level.

"Lastly, Samuel, there's the Frozen Wasteland. This level is associated with the complete spiritual annihilation of the soul. As its name portends, it's a frozen wasteland where souls are entirely cut off from Hashem. Do not step onto this final level, for the sake of your everlasting soul."

I took a breath and slowly exhaled, then asked, "How do souls end up there?"

"The Frozen Wasteland is for those who are forbidden to be reborn because of depraved acts committed during their lives."

"But what's to stop Solomon from going there?" I asked.

Moshe reached out, poked a finger into my chest, and said, "He may go there. That's why you must hurry before it's too late."

The three of us rose to our feet. I looked back and forth between my grandfather and great-grandfather, bit my lower lip, and said, "Am I doing this alone?"

"You are never alone," Moshe said, dropping a heavy hand on my shoulder. "Higher beings are looking after you."

"Higher beings?" I repeated.

"The *Malakhim*, the angels," Moshe said. "These beings are messengers and agents of Hashem, performing various tasks, such as guiding and protecting souls on their journey like yours."

"There's such a thing as angels?" I asked.

Moshe smiled. "There are angels and higher-ranking angels, called archangels, holding greater responsibilities and powers."

"So why can't you call upon these angels or archangels to rescue Pincus?"

"It's not so easy. You see, Pincus did some things in his past life that required significant purification and cleansing."

"What did Pincus do?" I asked.

"That's not important now. Solomon captured my father before he could complete his journey through at least one of the levels of Gehanna. The hierarchal beings cannot interfere with souls until they have done so."

"But *I* can interfere?"

"Most definitely. You're soul family."

Poppy and Moshe offered their heartfelt farewells, accompanied by hugs and kisses on my cheek. Standing before them, I brought my hand to my chest, bowed to my elders, and said, "I will do my best; I can at least promise you that."

"Should you succeed with this quest you're about to embark upon, it will do much to elevate you among those within the soul world,"

Moshe explained. "As well as save your great-great-grandfather's soul from extinction."

I swallowed hard and asked, "What if I fail?"

Poppy touched my shoulder and said, "Think positive, and you won't."

CHAPTER TWENTY-ONE
THE BRONX

I turned for one last look, but Poppy and Moshe had already gone, leaving me alone between two soaring ranges of mountains built of solid black rock and shadows. There was neither a breath of wind nor a bit of scent to stimulate my senses. All was still; all was silent.

As I walked the pathway into the darkness before me, the only audible sound was gravel crunching beneath my feet. I was alone for the first time since arriving in the soul world.

I continued upon the pathway, absorbed into the thick, silvery fog, and wondered how to find Solomon when I couldn't even see my hands without holding them inches from my face.

After walking for some distance, I felt my blindness and disorientation leading to those feelings Moshe warned me about—isolation and disconnection from the Divine presence. Not that I considered my relationship with the Divine before. But now, I understood what floundering within such a void meant. While considering my circumstance, I felt a longing for the familiar embrace of an earthly existence wash over me. I yearned for physical sensations and the warmth of loving relationships—a gentle holding of hands or a kiss. Tender memories, once cherished, were haunting me, causing me to wonder if I was ready to move on.

I had already gone through the spiritual assessment of my earthly life and understood the consequences of my choices. But to be truthful, I had many unresolved emotions, resulting in an abundance of remorse, guilt, and regrets, especially concerning the harm my actions may have caused others.

"Hello!" I cried out. But my voice was mute, no sound escaping my lips.

For the first time, as Poppy suggested it would happen, I was indeed a being of *thought*, nothing more. But that's not to say I lacked feelings. Because I was frightened, worried I would remain in this void forever, just wandering.

My thoughts consumed me. *I have no one to blame but myself. I chose this path of passing through the gate of death, thinking it would be easier, peaceful. There was so much I didn't know. How I wish I could return to my life.*

"Samuel, you need to keep moving," said Moshe's voice entering my consciousness.

"Moshe?" I said, curious about his presence.

"Yes, I'm with you."

"I don't understand. You said angels would help me. Are you an angel?"

"No, I'm not an angel, but because I am *tzaddik*, I am considered the equivalent of an angel within the hierarchy."

"Did you also do this?" I asked, gesturing at the barren land before me.

"I did, but that was before. I no longer need to travel the planetary spheres as my karmic footprint has been cleansed. I'm released from the cycle and will not be reborn."

"Is that what's happening to me? Am I being purified?" I asked, unable to move.

"That's what happens to souls within the Valley of the Shadow of Death."

"But if I'm only here to find your father, why am I subjected to its forces?"

"No one is immune to its forces."

"Pfft," I said. "Hardly seems fair."

"Did you think this quest would be easy?"

"I suppose not," I sighed.

"I will do what I can to help you, Sam, but your struggles are your own."

"All right," I said. "But could I at least see where I'm going?"

"That, too, is up to you. Try thinking as if you're in a lucid dream. Imagine you can see, and it will be so."

"But I do want to see," I insisted, and just as I thought these words, the fog lifted, and I stood on the sidewalk of a city chock full of pedestrians, cars, and trucks whizzing by on a wide boulevard. On either side stood two endless rows of stores of all types. As I tried to make sense of my surroundings, I realized that the parked cars, and those rambling along, came from a time I saw in old movies, with the people dressed in similar dated fashions.

"Where am I?" I said; this time my voice was audible as I returned to my physical body.

"The sixties," Moshe said. "Nineteen-Sixty to be exact."

"I don't understand," I muttered.

"You're looking for Solomon, the man who kidnapped Pincus. This was the time when we met."

"But I thought I was in the first level of Gehenna."

"You remain there," Moshe said. "But the collective consciousness of the universe has created this landscape, similar to how our subconsciousness creates scenes in our dreams. This will help you find Solomon and, hopefully, Pincus."

"So what do I do now?" I asked as I stepped aside from the rush of people pushing along the concrete sidewalk.

"Try to find Solomon. He lived and worked in this neighborhood and had an office on Southern Boulevard, which is not far from here."

I held out my hands and said, "But where am I?"

"Ah," Moshe's voice exclaimed. "This is the Grand Concourse in the Bronx. During the sixties, it was the premier shopping street. My cobbler shop is just ahead, and the famed Lowe's Paradise Theater is across the street."

I looked beyond the four lanes of traffic and saw the large marquee announcing the movie *Spartacus*. Then I twisted my head to this side of the street, searching for Moshe's cobbler shop. But it wasn't until I walked a dozen steps that I found a large plate-glass window with piles of disheveled old shoes filling the sill and a faded sign hanging overhead that said COBBLER.

"This all feels so real," I said, marveling at the details of a world I had never even been a part of. "What did you mean when you said the universe created this landscape?"

"The collective consciousness assembles our fellow souls' memories, narratives, and intelligence. We can tap into this phenomenon while we dwell in the soul world."

"So, can I interact with these people? Ask them questions about Solomon and your father?"

"You certainly can," Moshe said.

"All right," I said, pushing my hands deep into my jeans pockets. "So, where do I begin?"

"Try the Paradise Theater. My friend Arnold Lieberman was the owner and had an office on the third floor. Go and talk to him."

"Arnold Lieberman," I said, stepping to the crosswalk. While waiting for the light to change, allowing the pedestrians to cross, I shook my head, wondering what lay ahead in this search for an ancient man kidnapped in this imaginary world.

CHAPTER TWENTY-TWO
MEETING GRAY

Cupped hands shading my eyes, I pressed my forehead against the brass-framed glass doors, trying to peek inside the theater. The lobby looked dark and abandoned. *"Mmm,"* I murmured, grabbing the handle and tugging it. Surprisingly, the door was unlocked, and as I pulled it open. I took one last look up and down the street before stepping inside.

What appeared to have once been a magnificent lobby was now in desperate disrepair. The reeded wooden columns that supported decorative carved cornices were soiled with black streaks of creeping mold. The ceiling, painted in geometric patterns of faded colors, was in tatters, with large chunks broken away and crashed to the cracked marble floor below.

Once passing through the lobby, I came upon deeply tufted, upholstered doors leading into the theater. The fabric was torn open, exposing its horsehair stuffing bursting forth in patches. I entered the auditorium and saw it was flooded with beams of natural light. This was caused by a large opened gash in the elaborately decorated ceiling, painted to look like a galaxy with abundant stars and planets.

"Hello!" I called out. "I'm looking for Arnold Lieberman."

The only response came from a flock of pigeons, agitated by my intrusion, rapidly escaping through the hole in the roof.

I stood momentarily, then remembered Moshe saying that Arnold's office was on the third floor. I charged up the aisle, pushed the double doors open, and searched for the stairs without pause. After a few strides into the lobby, I found the carpeted, sweeping staircase leading to the upper floors. I soared up each level two steps at a time until I reached the third floor.

There, as before, the interior was in tatters. The once-patterned red and gold carpet was pulled back from the water-damaged walls. But what struck me for the first time since crossing the frozen baseball field was the return of my sense of smell and taste. I inhaled the musty odor and paused to feel it seeping down the back of my throat. *How remarkable.*

It took me only a short time to find the door marked OFFICE. Without hesitating, I turned the knob and entered, and not unexpectedly; this space was an abandoned mess. Papers and files were tossed around as someone had scrounged through the desk drawers and cabinets, tossing their contents about.

"Arnold?" I called out meekly, not expecting a reply.

"Who's there?" came from a room behind a closed door.

"Arnold?" I inquired and hurried to the door, opening it.

A man dressed in a gray business suit stood by a large window.

"Are you Arnold?" I asked.

"Me?" the man said, pointing a finger to his chest. "No, my name is Gray."

I looked around the office and then back to Gray and asked, "Can you tell me where Arnold is?"

Gray flicked a wrist and said, "Mr. Lieberman has long since moved on."

"Moved on? Moved on to where?"

"To his new life, wherever that may be. We were sad to see him go."

"Do you mean Arnold Lieberman was reborn?"

"That's right," Gray said. "And you must be Samuel, Moshe's great-grandson."

"I am. But how do you know that?" I asked and took a moment to study this soul more closely. Gray's skin tone appeared to be a pale shade of gray, eerily matching his suit color. Even his eyes looked gray.

"You can say I'm a friend of the family. Someone who helped Moshe while battling the *rasha*—Solomon Blass."

I stared at Gray, not knowing whether to trust this man.

"You can trust me. Just ask Moshe," he said, hearing my thoughts.

I put my hand to my cheek and tilted my head.

"I'll be joining you on your quest," Gray said, moving the conversation along.

"Do you know where to find Solomon?" I asked.

Gray shook his head. "No, I can't say that I do."

"Moshe said his office was nearby," I said, pointing to the window.

Gray wagged a finger and said, "None of what you see here is real. Come, I'll show you."

I followed Gray down the staircase and out the front doors. The moment the doors shut behind us, the Bronx scene of the Grand Concourse vanished, and we stood once again in the Valley in the Shadow of Death. What were once tall buildings were now black rock mountains, and the boulevard stretching in between had returned to the gravel-laden pathway I first walked upon.

I held out my hands and said, "What's happening?"

"We created that little scene for you," Gray said with a prideful shrug.

"We?" I asked. "Who's 'we'?"

Gray nodded. "Your soul family."

"But for what purpose?"

"Our time in this realm is not only about our personal soul development," Gray explained. "We also need to collaborate with other souls and the higher spiritual beings for the betterment of humanity."

"So far, you're the third soul I've met. Where are the others?"

Gray stretched his arms outward and said, "Did you not just see hundreds of them when you walked among them on the concourse?"

"Those were souls, like you and me?"

Gray nodded.

I looked at Gray once more, this time with more interest. From head to toe, the man was indeed gray, from his gray leather shoes down to his gray slacks poking out under his gray overcoat. He wore a gray dress shirt and tie and sported a nice full head of gray hair.

"Can you tell me how you and Moshe are connected?"

"I knew your great-grandfather in his past life when he was a cobbler," Gray said.

"And that's it? Nothing to do with this business about the *rasha*?"

Gray showed me his gray palm and said, "Oh, plenty to do with Solomon."

"Oh!" I nodded with a squint.

"I was the one who taught Moshe how to move about in his dreams."

"To fight the *rasha*?"

Gray pointed at me and said, "Correct."

"How did you know about doing this in the dream world?"

"I learned when I was a child," he said and held out his gray hands. "Would you like to hear my story?"

I nodded. "Sure."

"I was born in 1915 in Amsterdam. My father was Frederick van Eeden, the famous Dutch writer and psychiatrist. He loved poetry, and his artist friends described him as bohemian, which I gathered to mean he lived an unconventional lifestyle."

I nodded, encouraging Gray to continue.

"Anyway, it was Father who coined the term *lucid dreaming*. He was strongly influenced by Hindu practices and their beliefs of being awake in the dream world. In his lab, Father used me as his test rat. I was eight years old when we started. He would observe me in my sleep, and after a while, he could tell when I was dreaming. When he thought there was a break in my dreams, he would wake me up and have me describe them. That was the first step. Next, he figured out a way of sending me a signal to let me know that I was in a dream without needing to wake me."

"How did he do that?" I asked.

Gray cocked his chin to me. "Open your palm."

I did, and Gray ran a gentle finger across it.

"That was it, and it worked. The light brushing of his finger was just enough for my conscious self to become aware when I was dreaming. Soon, I became lucid without the stimulation, and I've been that way ever since."

"What happened to your father?"

Gray smiled strained and said, "He passed away when I turned twenty. But he gave me a gift few people have."

"That's great," I said. "But what's this connection with Moshe?"

"When living in the dream world, you sometimes see disturbances. I observed Solomon for years. His manipulations created an imbalance, and I tried to find a way to stop him but never could. That was until I met your great-grandfather."

"What do you mean, he created an imbalance?"

"Within the dream world exists laws of proper conduct. When someone crosses the line at the expense of others, people like me, experts in lucid dreaming, take notice and try to instill order. We're like a lucid dreaming police force," he said with a broad smile, showing off his shiny gray teeth.

"And I suppose it was you who guided Moshe into his lucid dreams, where he captured and vanquished the *rasha*'s soul into the fiery pit of Gehenna."

"That was me," he said with a nod. "But it was a mistake."

I nodded and said, "Yes, Moshe told me about this and how the *rasha*'s soul survived."

Gray nodded. "I'm afraid so," he said, picking up his pace.

I hurried alongside him and asked, "And now he's worried that something will happen to Pincus?"

Gray stopped and turned around, nearly causing me to bump into him. "Yes, he's worried. As we all are, and that's why I'm going with you."

"We're both going?"

"That's right."

I grimaced and said, "But why do you need me? What do I know about fighting a *rasha*?"

"I understand if you want to turn back, Samuel. Please don't let me stop you," Gray said, spinning around and marching ahead.

I took a breath and let it go slowly. If I chose not to go on, what would become of me? Certainly, Poppy and Moshe would be disappointed. But, even more important, how would this decision affect the evolution of my soul? Could I be cleansed in the Pit or the River of Fire? So with all the courage I could muster, I called out, "Hold on, Gray, I'm coming with you."

CHAPTER TWENTY-THREE
RIVER OF SOULS

"There it is," Gray said, lifting a finger to the cliffside.

"What are you pointing at?" I asked, squinting.

"The entrance to the *sheol*," Gray said as he ascended the incline.

I hurried along to follow. "The *sheol*? I thought we were in the Valley of the Shadow of Death."

"We are, but up there is the *sheol*. It is the purification cave within the valley."

"Purification cave?" I said, stopping short. "But why would we go there?"

Gray halted his climb, turned, and said, "To look for Pincus and Solomon."

"But what if they're not there?"

"Then we'll ask if anyone has seen them," Gray said, shaking his head to emphasize his frustration with me.

I peeked beyond Gray and saw shadowy figures moving further up the hill. "All right," I said and cocked my chin forward, encouraging Gray to continue.

As the entrance came into view, Gray asked, "Are you ready?"

I took a deep breath, exhaled, and nodded.

Gray took the first step, and I followed closely behind him. Once inside, the darkness subsided, and I saw dozens of souls mingling. They looked strangely like ordinary people wandering around a shopping mall.

"Is this the *sheol*?" I asked, observing them.

Gray gestured with a broad sweep of his arm and said, "Yes, these souls have just arrived. They're being prepared for the purification process."

"And how exactly are souls purified?"

"For most of those here, by detaching themselves from what they loved dearly—money, power, and possessions, though I'm not sure in what order. Not that it matters."

"No one seems worried," I said, observing the men, women, and children casually chatting.

"That's because they have no idea what lies ahead," Gray explained. "Most of them think they're passing through a check-in process, like when immigrants arrived at Ellis Island."

I furrowed my brow. *Do I even really want to know about their true fate or mine?* I wondered.

"Come on," Gray said, flicking his hand and walking deeper into the cave. "We need to find Hadriel."

"Hadriel? Who's that?"

"Hadriel guards the gates of the *sheol*. It's his responsibility to ensure that all the souls undergo the appropriate purification process."

I jerked my thumb behind me and said, "But no one stopped us. We just walked in."

"Oh, anyone can enter," Gray said with a chuckle. "It's getting out of the *sheol; that's* a different story."

"Getting out?" I said with a grimace.

"The way to exit the *sheol* is by cleansing yourself of your misdeeds. Only then are souls permitted to continue with their journey toward birth. For those who don't figure things out," Gray said with a shrug and a squint, "they remain here until they do."

"But we're just here searching for Pincus and Solomon," I said. "Will Hadriel expect us to get purified too?"

Gray looked at me, puckered his lips, and said, "You know what, Sam? I don't know."

*

As Gray and I maneuvered our way among the sea of souls, I noticed most of the elderly were somewhat transparent, while the younger ones appeared more defined. I presumed this had to do with the age of their passing. I looked over at Gray, who seemed more solid. "How old were you when you died?" I asked.

"I was thirty-five when I was shot dead."

"You were murdered?"

Gray nodded and said, "I was walking back to the Paradise Theater with Arnold when Henryk Appel, Solomon's rabbi, called out my name.

When I spun around, he pointed a gun at me. Before I could move, he fired, striking me in my heart."

"That's terrible," I said, shaking my head. "But why would a rabbi want to kill you?"

"He wasn't a real rabbi," Gray said with a twist of his mouth. "He was thrown out of rabbinical college for his beliefs in Kabbalah's dark side. He learned I was teaching your great-grandfather to become lucid in the dream world and wanted to stop me."

"Stop you from destroying Solomon?"

"That's right."

"You were a good man, Gray," I said. "I'm sorry about what happened to you."

"Thank you. But it seems my story has more to tell, as does yours."

This remark caused me to dwell upon the idea that my life story didn't end with my death but has since carried on, and for the first time, I had the thought that, as a soul, I could be eternal. This newfound awareness inspired a deep sense of liberation, no longer confining me to the temporal limitations experienced in the earthly realm.

I smiled at this epiphany as we marched with hundreds of other souls, all moving like a river through the massive canyon of caves toward some mysterious destination.

The deeper and deeper we traveled, the walls and ceiling encompassing us narrowed until the tube of stone was only wide enough for Gray and me to advance side-by-side. I tried looking ahead but couldn't see beyond a few souls. Just as I was about to ask about our fate, we each took a turn squeezing ourselves through a slender crevice in the cavern wall, and, like a baby being birthed, we stepped into a tremendous, magnificent chamber as large as a baseball stadium. We stood among thousands of other souls of all ages, genders, and body types. We were crammed together while the feeding tube from which Gray and I had just emerged continued spilling more souls.

"Get closer," a booming voice called out. "There's plenty of room."

"Plenty of room?" I said with a groan as strangers squeezed in from all sides, pushing me further and further away from Gray.

"All right," the voice returned. "Welcome souls to the *sheol*. My name is Hadriel."

The souls around me, following the source of the voice, lifted their arms and pointed upwards. I followed the hands to the cavern ceiling, where a golden-haired man hovered above the crowded cavern floor.

"That's him," a voice said. "The angel Hadriel."

CHAPTER TWENTY-FOUR
HADRIEL

"Welcome, dear souls, to the *sheol*," Hadriel said.

A collective gasp escaped the mouths of the congregants.

"During your stay here," Hadriel continued. "You'll find this to be a place of reflection and purification—a home where you'll confront the consequences of your actions during your earthly life. Do not fear; I will guide and protect you on this journey. Embrace this moment and know that the light of Divine love and mercy will lead you to your redemption and renewal."

A buzz of conversations ensued upon Hadriel's words. It sounded to me like we were being welcomed to some wellness retreat.

"In the *sheol*," he continued, silencing the agitated souls, "the purification process is tailored to your unique needs. Each of you will undergo profound introspection, examining the choices you made during your life and their impact upon yourself and others. You may find this process challenging and uncomfortable as you confront your shortcomings and misdeeds."

As Hadriel spoke, I wondered how the angel would judge my shortcomings and misdeeds.

"The purpose of your time here is not to punish, but rather to help you gain a deeper understanding of your actions and their consequences, allowing you to let go of any lingering negativity, embracing the transformative power of Divine love and forgiveness."

Listening to his comforting words sent a pleasurable calmness sweeping through my being. This wonderful expression seemed to be absorbed by the multitude of other souls, evidenced by the space around me expanding and allowing me to spread my arms out wide, drinking in the moment.

"Trust in the wisdom of our work here, and with sincere efforts on your part, you will emerge from the *sheol* more enlightened, ready to continue your journey toward your birth," Hadriel concluded.

While the assemblage of souls reacted to the angel's rousing speech with conversations and comments, Gray shouted over the hubbub. "Hadriel, my friend Samuel and I are not here for remediation. We're searching for the *rasha* known as Solomon Blass. Can you tell me if he's been seen in the *sheol*?"

"A *rasha* in the *sheol*? Nonsense," Hadriel said as his ethereal presence drifted downward.

The crowd backed away, clearing a space for the white-gowned angel, who settled in the center of the cavern floor. I gawked at the rippling blond hair surrounding his slender face. His smooth-as-glass cheeks were tinted with the slightest tinge of pink. But what was most unusual were his two colored eyes—one blue and one brown. Hadriel looked young, perhaps no more than fourteen or fifteen years old.

"How would you know when there are so many souls?" I questioned.

Hadriel paused momentarily, assessing my presence, and said, "I'm pleased you've arrived, Samuel. There's much work to be done."

"Oh no," I said, waving a hand. "Not me. We're here looking for Solomon the *rasha*, and Pincus, my great-great-grandfather; nothing more."

Hadriel ran his long slender fingers across his cheeks and said, "Are you saying, Samuel, that you lived a life absent of any misdeeds?"

I looked upward at Hadriel, who stood at least a full head taller than me. Knowing I had lived a far-from-perfect life, I asked, "What sort of misdeeds?"

Hadriel rocked his head back and forth and seemed to consider my question. "Oh, let me see," Hadriel said. "There's dishonesty, theft, violence, abuse, greed, envy, and pride."

"Pride?" I repeated. "What's wrong with pride?"

"Ah," Hadriel said, lifting a finger. "Pride is the most interesting. Many believe pride is a positive emotion, providing self-esteem, motivation, and emotional resilience. This could be true, but there's also the flip side. Pride can also encourage a sense of arrogance, self-centeredness, and a refusal to acknowledge one's flaws and limitations."

A sudden dread overwhelmed me. What if Hadriel forced me to experience the purification process before I could be released from the *sheol*?

"There's no need to be afraid, Samuel. The work here is based on love. Gradually you will release those negative energies, emotions, and patterns that have caused you problems. Your soul body will transform and become lighter, allowing you to continue with your journey toward birth."

"But as I said, there's no time," Gray said, stepping forward. "We must find the *rasha* before it's too late."

Hadriel pointed at us and said, "No one leaves the *sheol* without being purified. Unless, of course, you need further remediation. Then I can recommend you to the Pit. Though, for the two of you, that seems unnecessary."

"No, no." Gray wagged a finger. "I've already been here in the *sheol*, though it was long ago."

"I know this," Hadriel said with a slight smile. "But you've returned."

"That's because we're—"

"I know why you've returned," Hadriel said, interrupting Gray's plea. "You will remain in the *sheol* until I deem you're ready. Then, if you want to move on to the other realms, you are free to do so."

With those words, Hadriel levitated off the floor. Quickly, the souls rushed toward the center, closing the open space around Gray and me, their arms outstretched upward toward the floating angel, their fingers spread wide apart.

"Now what?" I asked Gray while the adoration continued.

Gray tilted back his head, watching the gatekeeper of the *sheol* rise and vanish into the mist clinging to the cave's ceiling. Gray then returned his attention to me. He leaned in close and whispered, "There's no way we can wait for Hadriel's blessing. We must find our own way out of here."

CHAPTER TWENTY-FIVE
GRAY EXPLAINS

We sat upon two large stones among a field of boulders. Gray leaned forward, resting his elbows on his knees, and said, "We need to find our way out."

I pointed to the direction from where we entered and said, "Why not go back the way we came in?"

Gray shook his head. "These corridors are constantly shifting, and the one that brought us here probably doesn't exist anymore."

"So, how do we get out?" I whispered.

"I don't know, but we're wasting time sitting here," Gray said, stroking his chin.

"How is it Hadriel can float and disappear?"

"Angels are not like souls. Though we share similar qualities, their soul bodies are built upon emotions and desires, just like ours."

"They have feelings like we do?"

Gray nodded. "But it's their life body that sustains their existence, enabling them to float about and disappear into the mist."

"*Mmm,*" I said, pondering the existence of these hierarchal beings. "You said you already experienced the *sheol*—what was it like?"

"It was long ago when I first arrived, and just like you, I reviewed my life," Gray said. "But it wasn't until my time here that I understood the consequences of my choices."

"What were they?"

Considering my question, Gray rocked his head sideways, then said, "I was obsessed with lucid dreaming so much that my waking life suffered. I became aloof and uninterested in other people, and that caused my life to be out of balance."

"Out of balance," I repeated. "That's similar to my life, though for other reasons."

"Yes, I'm aware," Gray said.

"Can you tell me about your purification process?"

"There were several steps in the process," Gray began. "I had to acknowledge my misdeeds, but none were too severe like yours. After that came the cleansing."

"How were you cleansed?" I asked with a grimace.

"I was separated from the negative energies and impurities that accumulated inside me during my lifetime."

"Separated? How?"

Gray rubbed his hands together and said, "All I can tell you is that it wasn't pleasurable."

"Is that so?" I sighed and asked, "What happened next?"

"A time of deep solitude, allowing me to reflect upon the harm I may have caused others. Then, I could ask for forgiveness, which opened the door to making amends."

"Did anyone help you?"

"I was assigned a guide to help me through the purification process."

"Was it an angel?" I asked.

"Sort of," he said with a wiggle of his head. "She was more of a hierarchal soul, someone versed in furthering my education toward my spiritual growth."

"She?" I asked, wide-eyed. "Your guide was a woman?"

Gray laughed and patted the side of my leg. "All spiritual beings transcend gender and are pure emanations of Divine energy. Depending on their purpose, they take on certain physical qualities we recognize as male or female."

"So you've been cleansed and purified, ready to journey toward your rebirth?"

"I suppose so," Gray said.

"Then why haven't you been reborn?"

"Haven't you figured that out by now?" Gray said and smiled, his grayness taking on a more silvery presence. "It's because we must stop the *rasha* Solomon Blass and rescue your great-great-grandfather, Pincus. Until we accomplish that, I will remain in the soul world."

*

Gray and I remained by the scramble of boulders, watching the other souls huddling in conversations or wandering about. Everyone seemed to be waiting for something to change. Then, as if summoned by some silent voice, the thousands of souls formed lines, dozens of them, all facing the surrounding stone walls of the cavern.

"What's happening?" I asked Gray.

"The purification process has begun."

Just as the words passed his lips, a voice spoke. "Find your place, Samuel."

I jerked my head back. "Did you hear that?"

Gray shook his head. "I heard nothing."

I pointed to my ear and said, "You didn't hear?"

"No, like I've explained, I've already gone through this."

I swallowed hard, curled my hands into fists, and asked, "What do I do?"

Gray held his hands and said, "This is not a choice. You must go."

"But shouldn't we stay together?"

"If it's meant to be, then we'll reunite. In the meantime, best of luck, and don't be frightened. Everything will be fine."

Before I could acknowledge Gray's advice, an energetic force took hold of me, pulling me into one of the many long lines weaving through the massive canyon floor.

As I joined a particular queue, more souls filed in behind me. I tried looking ahead, wanting to see our destination. From what I could make out, those in front seemed to be vanishing into a thick fog. Our line started taking steps, and with each one, more and more souls were swallowed. I tried to turn my head for a last glimpse of Gray but could not.

With each forced stride, I approached the gathering mist clinging to the cavern wall. Unable to comprehend my fate, I shut my eyes, putting my faith in the hands of the Almighty, and stepped into the abyss.

CHAPTER TWENTY-SIX
PURIFICATION

When I opened my eyes, I stood alone in the center of an open-aired stadium. Multiple rows of long ivory marble benches rose steeply off the expanse of a sand-covered arena up to the pole supports, where an elaborate canvas awning system was engineered to cantilever out over the stands. Such details suggested this was not a modern-day structure; instead, it was from the ancient time of the celebrated gladiators.

"Hello!" I shouted, and within an instant, I heard my voice echoing back.

As I gazed into the desolate stadium, a sharp creaking sound caught my attention. I spun around just as a wooden gate leading onto the bloodstained arena of sand swung open; before me stood Crixus, dressed in breastplate, helmet, and sword. My breath caught in my throat as a wave of disbelief washed over me, and all I could do was stare in silence.

"Are you ready to prove yourself, Samuel, or will you cower and slither away like the coward you are?" Crixus said, taunting me, his helmet tucked under one arm.

Cautiously, I took a few steps backward and caught my heel against a bump of blood-hardened sand, causing me to trip and fall. Crixus belly laughed at my clumsiness. But in a heartbeat, he turned serious. He squeezed his large, scarred head into his battle-tested bronze helmet, reached for his gladius from his leather belt, and pulled it out in one swift motion. He swiped the sword back and forth with a grand gesture, creating a metallic hum that vibrated through the coliseum air.

"B-but I-I have no weapons," I stuttered, getting back up.

Crixus swung his gladius out to my left, where another gate opened. From out of the shadows ran two skinny slaves dressed in white gowns. One carried a breastplate, while the other held onto a trident, net, and a bronze helmet.

"That's for me?" I said in a near whisper.

Without answering, the slaves approached. The one carrying the breastplate slipped it over my shoulders and pulled tight on the straps, buckling me in. The other lifted the helmet and shoved it down upon my head. Once in place, I opened my eyes and looked out through the tiny slitted cut-outs.

Lastly, one of the slaves grabbed my right forearm and placed the trident into my hand and the net in my other.

"Are you ready, Samuel?" shouted Crixus.

"But I can't see," I cried out.

I didn't expect a response, nor did I expect Crixus to charge me without warning. Sweat poured down my forehead and into my eyes. All I could do was hold up my weapon, hoping to block the gladiator's assault.

With my eyes squeezed tight, I waited for the death blow. I knew my demise was not possible, but I didn't know if I would experience any pain or perhaps lose my head.

But the strike never came, and when I dared to open my eyes, I stood before an enormous waterfall crashing upon magnificent boulders, sending clouds of mist toward its source. I was no longer facing the fierce Crixus but instead admiring the image of some man emerging from the mists above. With the roaring falls as a backdrop, a piercing blue-eyed figure lowered himself until he stood before me.

"Who are you?" I asked, wondering if this was an angel like Hadriel, who also could levitate.

The man looked at me with a gentle smile and golden curls cascading down his neck. His skin looked like milk, not just in color but in texture. "I am Michael," he said without moving his lips, though his eyes seemed to smile.

"Are you an angel?"

"I am the archangel Michael."

"Archangel?" I frowned. "What's the difference between you and an angel?"

Again without seeming to speak aloud, Michael said, "Angels have specific duties and functions, like delivering messages, providing protection, and executing Divine judgments."

"Like Hadriel?" I asked, as he was the only angel I had ever met.

"Yes, like the protector of the *sheol*."

"All right," I said. "But what about you? What do you do?"

"You can say that my tasks are to oversee the angels."

"You mean like a manager?"

Michael laughed. "My position is more about assuming a prominent role in executing the will of the Divine."

Unsure of what that meant, I furrowed my brow and nodded.

"There are certain souls whose journey requires me to guide them through the purification process. Especially those who have died young."

"Like me?" I asked, placing my hand over my heart.

Michael nodded. "Your arrival into the soul world has been celebrated."

"Celebrated?" I repeated with a grimace. "Why would anyone celebrate my death at thirty-two?"

"Because with your early death, you still possess a significant amount of your life forces."

I nodded. "Yes, I've been told this, and how a portion of my life force has carried over, offering me abilities older souls may lack. That's why I was chosen to find my great-great-grandfather Pincus, who was taken by the *rasha* Solomon."

Michael seemed to nod. "Yes, that is your quest. But it's not only to benefit your ancestor; these new life forces help the angels and archangels with their tasks and contribute to the overall evolution of the spiritual realm."

"That sounds wonderful," I said, focusing on the mysterious figure hovering before me. "But how do I move past the *sheol*? Can you help me find my way back to Gray?"

The archangel raised his smooth palm and said, "These episodes between you and the gladiator Crixus are evidence of how the *rasha* has infected your essence. It's also apparent that this taking of Pincus was instigated to lure you into the lower realms of Gehenna. Your life body has the power to assist not only the upper realms but the lower ones as well. It would appear that you are a most wanted soul."

"So what do I do?"

"Continue until you find Pincus and return him to his rightful place."

"But what about Gray? I left him back in the caves."

"This is your quest, Samuel, not Gray's."

"But I don't know where to go or what to do."

Michael waved his open palm and said, "Samuel, I recognize your forgiveness and bestow upon you the purification and redemption required to move beyond the *sheol*. Those who receive such a blessing can continue their journey among the planetary spheres and eventually toward birth. But unlike those souls, you've been chosen for a purpose, and should you succeed, your karma will reflect your outstanding efforts and be rewarded in your next lifetime in ways you can't even imagine."

CHAPTER TWENTY-SEVEN
THE PIT

A big whooshing sound and a burst of stale air rose from a large pit beneath me, just as a frail, bony arm smacked me across my chest when I tried leaning over to see its source.

"Be careful," the stranger warned. "You don't want to fall in."

Without moving, I did my best to gaze outwards over the ledge and saw a massive hole no farther away than the tips of my shoes. Trying to understand my whereabouts, I raised my awareness to the circular perimeter, where what seemed like thousands of souls were teetering along this narrowed stone ledge.

I twisted my neck and asked, "What's this place?"

A very old man, thin with a drawn, droopy face and a few remaining strands of silver hair clinging to his otherwise bald head, said, "This is the Pit."

"Ah, right. That's what Michael told me."

"Souls here have much to atone for," the old man lamented.

"There are so many," I said.

"What's your name, son?"

"My name's Sam. What's yours?"

"I'm Hal," he said. "I'd shake your hand, but I'm afraid to lose my balance. I shouldn't have risked saving you before; I acted impulsively."

"Oh, I'm grateful, Hal. And you're right; I might have fallen in."

"If you don't mind me asking, you seem very young. How old were you when you died?"

"I was thirty-two," I said. "What about you, Hal?"

"Oh, I lived to a ripe old age of ninety-two."

"That's a good age," I agreed with a nod.

"It was, but I'm sorry, I wasn't a good person. That's why I'm here."

"Why? What did you do in your life?"

"I was a lawyer for the dishonest."

"Do you mean like gangsters?"

"You can say that, sort of. I represented those in powerful political positions, doing dirty deeds worldwide to fill their pockets with riches," Hal said, pausing to catch his breath. "I've had trouble breathing ever since I got here."

I tested the air by taking a few deep breaths and granted, there was a distasteful staleness to it, but nothing debilitating to affect me as it did Hal.

"Granted, I was a rich man, but if I'd known this would be where I'd end up, I certainly would have lived differently. But enough about me; what about you, Sam? You're so young; what misdeeds could you have committed at such an age that sent you to the Pit?"

"Um," I said. The last thing I wanted to do was to share the true purpose of my quest. "I'd rather not say if that's okay with you?"

"Sure, I don't need to know."

"Thanks, I appreciate it," I said.

Hal grunted a low, guttural noise in response.

"Do you know what's down there?" I asked, jerking my chin forward.

"The Pit is bottomless, with rings of stone shelves like this one, going on and on, both above us and below."

I saw the same silo-like hole rising and vanishing into the darkness. Then I heard wailing cries and howls echoing in all directions. Flickering light from an unknown source cast lively shadows, which had a disorienting effect on my balance. Feeling dizzy, I clutched a handful of stone on the wall behind me to steady myself.

Once the feeling passed, I asked Hal, "How do you know what's above and below?"

"I speak with these fellow souls on the ledge. It's what the others have told me."

"That's helpful," I said.

"Not that I believe any of these scum. Like me, we're all liars and thieves. The souls that—"

A scream interrupted Hal, followed by what appeared to be a body falling from above and disappearing into the void below.

"What was that?" I shouted just as flames shot upward, nearly reaching us.

"Oh, that poor soul," Hal lamented. "If you fall in, that's what happens."

"Your soul burns up?" I said, though the answer was obvious.

"It does, but from what I've heard, you recover. It's all part of the plan of repenting for our sins."

"Seems harsh," I said with a grimace.

Hal sighed. "Well, if you think about why souls are here, it seems pretty reasonable considering the offenses they've committed."

"Like what?" I asked.

"Well," Hal said, scratching his silver stubble, "there's physically and emotionally harming others. Betrayal in a marriage. Engaging in corrupt or dishonest business practices for personal gain."

"Like you," I offered.

"That's right," Hal said. "Oh, and their malicious acts of deception. There's this guy over there," Hal said, pointing over to his right, "who's tricked people into giving out their credit card numbers."

"You mean like a phishing scam?" I said.

Hal wagged a finger. "Yes, that's what he called it. A clever name, by the way."

"How long have you been here?"

"*Pfft*. I don't even know. It feels like forever if such a thing exists. Nothing ever changes, except now and then a few souls topple in, or some new ones appear." He gestured to me.

Remembering my purpose, I asked, "Have you seen or heard of someone named Pincus?"

Hal twisted his wrinkled face. "Pincus, *mmm*," he murmured.

Without waiting for a reply, I asked, "What about an old man named Solomon?"

"Solomon?" Hal squinted. "Sorry, I don't think so."

I sighed and wondered why the archangel would send me here. But even more worrisome was getting out of this new predicament. As far as I could see to my left and right, these tortured souls encircling the Pit shared my same concerns.

"Hal," I said, pointing into the Pit. "Besides falling into the abyss, how else do souls leave?"

"When you're ready, you jump off and float out," he said, pointing upwards.

I shook my head. "What do you mean, you jump? Wouldn't you burn up in the flames below?"

"Oh, those poor souls, they just weren't ready. But we can't leave until we understand the cause of why we're sent here and have gone through the process of repentance and rectification."

"Well, have you repented and fixed whatever was wrong with you?"

"Oh, I'm sure I did that long ago."

I peeked over the ledge at the darkness below. "Why haven't I seen any souls floating upwards?"

"I'm not sure, but from what the others are saying, it's because we become invisible to the observing souls upon our redemption."

"It's a big risk jumping off," I said, wondering how a soul would know it was time.

"That's why I'm still here. I'm afraid," Hal confessed.

"Mmm," I murmured.

"I've almost jumped. Many times. But at the last second, I always chicken out."

I took a deep breath and slowly exhaled. "I can see why."

"I get it, I do. I hurt people. Lots of people. If I'm lucky to get another shot, I'll be a better person. But I can't find the courage to jump."

"You can't stay here forever," I reasoned.

"I know," Hal said in a pitiful tone.

I rubbed my forehead, searching for an answer, and said, "How about this, Hal? What if we jumped together?"

"Together?"

"Sure. We can even hold hands if you want."

"But why would you do that? You just got here, and there's no way you're ready."

"I disagree," I said, shaking my head. "I think I'm ready. What do you say? Let's do it before I change my mind."

Hal tugged on the loose skin hanging from his neck. "You're right," he said, offering me his bony hand.

I grasped it and said, "On the count of three."

CHAPTER TWENTY-EIGHT
FIRST CONTACT

The moment I stepped off the ledge, Hal released my hand. I jerked around to see him remaining plastered against the stone wall. His face was frozen in a silent scream. All became quiet, and as Hal suggested to be a possibility, I floated upwards. Moving swiftly, I passed ring after ring of souls poised on the narrow ledges.

Then, just as suddenly, my trajectory stopped, putting me directly in front of a group of trapped souls. While hovering like an archangel, I caught the glare of an old man staring back. As I looked into his glassy brown eyes, I wondered how he could see me if I was supposed to be transparent. Not only could this strange man observe me, but he appeared to have a hold upon me, halting my upward motion.

"Hello, Samuel," the old man said.

I gritted, not knowing if I should respond.

"I understand you've been looking for me," he said.

"Are you Solomon?" I asked, then looked over to the man standing alongside him.

"Yes," he said, noticing my observation of the thin, frail man. "And this is your great-great-grandfather, Pincus."

"Pincus," I said softly. Pincus stared back behind wire-framed spectacles but remained silent.

"Well, here I am, Samuel. Come and get me," he said in a taunt and with a smirk.

Hovering over the bottomless Pit, I held out my hands and shrugged.

"Pfft," Solomon said before shutting his eyes, and instantly, I soared upwards into the darkness.

Without an understanding of how, when I opened my eyes, I was no longer swallowed by the Pit. Instead, I found myself in the passageway between the Valley of the Shadow of Death's black mountains, and Gray stood before me.

"Gray!" I called out, happy to see him once again.

"Hello, Sam," Gray said, patting my back. "I'm happy we've reunited."

I pointed behind me, though I had no idea what direction I came from, and said, "I saw them in the Pit. Solomon and Pincus, and they were there."

"What did you do?"

"What do you mean?" I asked, holding out my hands with a shrug. "I couldn't do anything; I was floating like a hummingbird. Solomon took control of me, mocked me, and laughed before releasing his hold."

"What about Pincus? Did you see him?"

"I think so. The man beside him was small, thin, and wore wire-rimmed eyeglasses."

Gray nodded. "That's him."

"What were they doing there?" I asked.

"They're making their way through the levels of Gehenna," Gray said.

"What do you mean?"

"They must pass through each level. There's no other route."

I rubbed my eyes and said, "Does that mean they're heading for the River of Fire?"

Gray nodded and said, "Then the Clay of Yaven and, if they make it that far, the Frozen Wasteland."

I pinched my forehead, giving thought to venturing where my soul, my very existence, could face complete annihilation.

"I hope that we can catch Solomon at the River of Fire," Gray said, breaking my anxious spell.

"And then what?" I asked. "Solomon held me in the Pit, just by his will."

Gray sighed. "The *rasha* is formidable."

"Formidable?" I said. "He's more than that, and it's not a fair fight. I am no *tzaddik*."

"You may not have your great-grandfather's gift, but you are young."

I rolled my eyes. "I keep hearing this. But it hasn't given me any special powers."

"That's because you have yet to be challenged," Gray said.

"You can't be serious," I said, pointing to the cliffs. "After what I've been through?"

"That's nothing, Sam," Gray said, wagging a finger. "I promise you where you've been so far will look like a walk in the park compared to the River of Fire."

I looked at the silverly shadowed landscape and said, "All right, Gray, where is it?"

"It doesn't matter where it is, Sam," Gray said, folding his arms across his chest.

"You mean, I just need to imagine it."

Gray smiled, shifted his brow, and said, "That's right."

"Will you be coming with me?"

"I want to if Michael allows it."

"Michael?" I asked with a squint. "Do you mean the archangel?"

"Ah, you've met," Gray said.

"Yes, he appeared before me out of a waterfall."

"Ah, the Divine beings love the drama."

"That's interesting," I said, remembering the lessons about the Greek gods in fifth grade. "Do you ever get the idea that these angels and archangels use souls like us for their amusement?"

"Oh no," Gray said, wagging a finger. "They are Divine beings, serving as messengers, helpers, and protectors of humanity. Their only motivation is guided by love, compassion, and a desire to help us evolve and grow spiritually."

"All right," I said, not wanting to argue with Gray about something he knew far more about than I.

"Are you ready to move on?"

"I am," I said and closed my eyes.

CHAPTER TWENTY-NINE
RIVER OF FIRE

I stood on the embankment of a glowing, molten flow of fresh lava spewed from an unseen source up the mountainside. Red and orange flames sparked off its surface, creating a blinding light and ear-piercing hissing sounds that crackled and popped. The River of Fire crept along while its vapors emitted a noxious gas that exuded a sulfurous stench.

"Don't get too close," Gray warned.

I turned to the sound of his voice and saw him standing a few feet farther back. Naturally, I backed up to the higher ground, a safer distance from the churning inferno, and pinched my nose and mouth as the stink was too much to bear. "How's it possible for souls to survive this?"

Gray shook his head. "I don't know, Sam, but somehow we do."

With my free hand, I pointed and said, "You expect me to jump into that?"

"I'm afraid we must," Gray said, with hands on his hips.

"But won't we burn up?"

"You keep forgetting that these physical bodies are nothing but an illusion. We are beings of pure consciousness," Gray said with a grin, "and there's nothing of us to burn."

I scoffed. "But there must be pain, agonizing pain."

"I'd imagine so," Gray said. "How else would a soul eliminate its impurities and the negative traits accumulated in a lifetime of sins and misdeeds? All souls must be cleansed and purified before ascending to the higher spiritual realms and eventually preparing for one's birth."

"Listen, Gray," I said, shaking my head. "I've already been through the *sheol* and the Pit; any more cleansing, and they'll make me an angel."

Gray smiled. "It's good to see you still have your sense of humor."

I released an exasperated sigh.

"Come on, Sam. You didn't think this would be easy."

"Nothing has been," I said, focusing on the dancing flames.

Gray took a few steps down the embankment toward the river's edge, then turned his head to me and flicked his hand. "We'll go together."

I immediately thought of Hal and my offer to hold his hand while jumping off into the Pit. Which, upon reflection, seemed as easy as leaping into a swimming pool. As I stared into the boiling bile, I heard a voice barely audible over the crackling flames. "You can do this, Sam."

I reached out my hand to Gray, who grasped it firmly, and unlike Hal, he didn't let go as we leaped together into the River of Fire.

*

I remembered moments from my life when, just before I submerged myself in the delightful water of a swimming pool, I would shut my eyes, hold my breath, and not open them until I swam to its surface. But in this thick stew of magma, I couldn't move freely or float about; instead, it felt like a tub of lard. Stuck in this constricted space, I cautiously tested my vision by peeking out through one eye, and to my astonishment, I saw a melded world of reds, oranges, and yellows. With both eyes wide open, I experienced the entire expanse of what being submerged in an immense lava lamp looked like. Though I knew I did not need to breathe, I inhaled and filled my imaginary starved lungs.

While floating with no sense of what was up or down, I searched for Gray through the opaque mix of colors. After twisting about, I realized I could use my arms to move. I soon realized the breaststroke worked best at allowing me to push through the thickness.

I continued with no sense of direction but with distinct gratitude for having not vaporized myself in the River of Fire. Not much farther along, I noticed faint figures off in the distance. I kicked my legs to swim faster. Upon my approach, many souls came into my field of vision. Hundreds of them, floating around me in all directions.

When I got close enough to a few of them, I saw their contorted faces, expressing what appeared to be their excruciating pain. Soon I was mixed among them. Not only could I witness their agony, but I also heard their cries of distress. There were high-pitched shrieks and loud moans. Many shouted while others howled on endlessly, like wounded animals.

Soon several of these poor souls took notice, and for some reason, I became a curiosity as they pointed at me and swam closer. Soon I was surrounded, and by their troubled expressions, I felt threatened.

Closest to me was a middle-aged man, engaging with an angry scowl and clenched fists. He reared one arm back and leveled a punch through the soupy mix. But inches before striking me, his knuckles crashed into an invisible barrier. Frustrated, he tried again and had the same result.

When I pushed out my hands all around me, I realized I was encased in some sort of protective bubble.

Soon, others approached, curious about this transparent egg surrounding me. Some banged on its shell with fists, trying to crack it, while others ogled over it by gently rubbing its smooth surface. I remained unaffected, shielded from these tormented souls.

After being pushed around, I floated toward a group of congregated souls who seemed focused on a disturbance. Soon I realized that I no longer needed to use my arms or legs to move; with my thoughts alone, I could push myself in the desired direction.

As I walked through the crowd of souls, I saw Gray; his face pinched with fright.

"Gray," I called out.

Then I saw the cause of his anguish. The *rasha* had grasped Gray's neck, causing my friend to flail his arms in an attempt to break free. Then in Solomon's hand appeared a rope. With a swift, one-armed motion, he tied a noose knot, looped it over Gray's head, and pulled it around his neck. He then grabbed Pincus, who floated within arm's reach, and with the same length of rope, he added a second loop. Solomon had both men tied by the neck while he held onto the end of the human leash.

Solomon tugged, ready to move on, when he spotted me. With a snarl, he swam over, and once close enough, he reached out, and like all the others, his hand banged into the bubble.

"Ah," he cried, pulling his hand back while maintaining his hold on the prisoner's rope. "What have we here?"

"Let go of them, Solomon, and I'll spare you," I said, surprising myself with my bravado.

Solomon wagged his head, seemingly impressed. "It seems you found yourself some protection. Is this the work of Moshe?"

I put my palm against the inside of the bubble and said, "That's no concern of yours."

Solomon pointed a finger at me, his eyes squeezed to a squint, and said, "Don't you understand, Samuel? You don't belong to the *tzaddik*. The very essence of your soul screams *rasha*, and you know this. Come, join me, and I'll show you true power beyond this silly notion of having a special advantage just because you died young."

"You keep trying to lure me. But you should know I am not the same naive soul I was when I arrived. I've learned much already, and you should know this: I want nothing to do with you or your kind."

Solomon laughed. "You think you've changed; that's nonsense. We've known each other from previous lifetimes, and we're destined for more. You have no power to break this karmic cycle."

"*Pfft,*" I said. "That's a lie."

"Our accumulated karma shapes us. You don't remember, but you've tried before to overcome our connection and failed."

I stared at the old man, whose watery eyes tried to draw me in. I forced myself to look away and glanced over to Gray and Pincus.

"Don't listen," Gray implored.

Pincus offered nothing but a blank stare.

"If you insist on stubbornness, I must say farewell for now. We still have a long way to travel, and I suggest you don't follow because next time, I'll figure a way of breaking that shell and looping a third noose for you."

CHAPTER THIRTY
SAMAEL AND RAZIEL

I watched Solomon pulling Gray and Pincus away by their necks while their feet dragged along, fluttering in their wake. *Now what do I do?*

While pondering my next step, a man appeared before me. Unlike the souls committed to the River of Fire, this man didn't greet me with a knock, bang, or a gentle stroking of my protective egg. Instead, he stood before me, his face inches from mine, and said, "Greetings, Samuel. My name is Samael."

"Samael, that's almost the same as mine."

"That's right," he said, holding up a finger. "Just one letter different."

"What do you want, Samael?"

He shook his head. "There's nothing I want or need, and I've come for you."

"For me?" I asked, worried this was some messenger from Solomon.

Samael shook his finger. "I'm no messenger," he said, able to hear my thoughts.

"Are you an angel?" I presumed.

"I am the angel Samael."

"And what do you do?" I asked, learning that these angels have responsibilities.

"Some call me the Angel of Death."

My eyes widened. "Angel of Death?" I said. "But I'm already dead."

"This is apparent," Samael said. "When someone dies, I'm responsible for separating the life, soul, and ego bodies from the physical body."

"I didn't know there was an angel overseeing that process."

"I was there for you when your time came," Samael said.

"I see," I said, observing the blue-eyed angel. "So why are you here now?"

"I also guide souls through the purification process in the River of Fire."

"You're the busy one," I scoffed.

"Not only that," he said, holding up a finger, "I'm also a symbol of the transformative power of perseverance and spiritual endurance."

I shook my head and asked, "What does that mean?"

"I challenge souls on their journey, pushing them to develop resilience, strength, and determination. Souls develop spiritual depth and maturity through adversity and struggle."

"Ah," I said, wagging a finger, "my brother Max called that hormesis."

Samael beamed. "Excellent! Yes, hormesis is a process by which a small amount of a potentially harmful substance or an act can have a positive effect. In earthly life, it's been observed that these challenges can stimulate cellular repair when stresses are employed, such as intense exercise or fasting."

"Well, I've been getting a healthy dose of soul-driven hormesis."

"Indeed you have," Samael said, sounding enthusiastic.

"You're making all of this sound very upbeat," I said, gesturing to the nearby poor souls.

"They'll all be fine," Samael said. "I've seen this billions of times."

"I assume you know I'm not here for any more purification."

Samael, his long black curls dancing in the magma, smiled and said, "That may be so, but this bubble of yours is not permitted in the River of Fire."

"Hold on!" I said, showing the angel my palm. "Without this, I would have been taken away by the *rasha*."

"I'm sorry, but I must insist on its removal."

"But I'm only here because of the *rasha*, and I do not need to repent for any sins worthy at this level."

"Perfect," Samael said, holding out his slender arms. "Then you should have nothing to worry about."

"But you don't understand. I need to leave here. You know I was sent by your boss, the archangel Michael."

"Of course I know Michael has sent you. But we have rules to follow, and there are no exceptions. I hope you understand," he said.

"So, how do I follow your rules and leave?"

"You must go through the process of *tikkun*."

"Tikkun?"

Samael nodded. "It's where you confront and rectify your past mistakes."

"But I've done that already in the *sheol* and again in the Pit."

"This is different," Samael said, wagging a finger. "Through *tikkun*, you'll rectify your imperfections and elevate your soul to higher spiritual realms. It's essential for your continued evolution and growth."

"All right," I said with a sigh. "What choice do I have?"

And at that moment, my bubble, along with Samael, vanished, and I found myself sitting cross-legged in the middle of a ring of fire, its flames stretching up into a blackened sky. There I remained, looking across at another being.

"Hello," I said.

"Hello, Samuel. My name is Raziel."

"Raziel," I repeated, staring into her large brown eyes, which shimmered in the flames.

"Do you know who I am?" she asked.

I shrugged and said, "Another angel?"

Raziel chuckled. "I understand you've met quite a few."

"You can say that again."

"You should be honored. Most souls never meet even one."

"Why am I the lucky one?"

"You're on a great quest, which we seldom witness in the soul world."

"I wish someone had told Samael. He took my bubble away from me."

Raziel shook her head. "You no longer need that."

I looked around at the ring of fire and said, "I hope not."

Raziel folded her hands on her lap and said, "I was the angel who bestowed to Adam, the first man, the book revealing the secrets of the universe and the mysteries of the Divine."

"Wow," I said wide-eyed. "That must be some book."

Raziel laughed. "You have a sense of humor, Samuel. That's good because you'll need it where you're going."

I put my hand to my chin and said, "And where would that be?"

"I'll tell you in a moment, but first, you should know that I'm also the guardian of the Tree of Life, a symbol of the universe's Divine flow of energy and consciousness. That means I assist souls with the knowledge and wisdom to guide them on their righteous path."

"And how do you do that?" I asked.

"With the gift of foresight, Samuel," she said, holding her hand.

"You mean like the *rasha*?"

"Yes, the *rasha* has this ability. But his intentions are immoral."

"Tell me why this sinner is allowed to gallivant, unheeded in the soul world?"

Raziel wagged a finger. "Oh, he's not unheeded, and his presence is only permitted in Gehenna. That's why, to stop his torment, you must meet him among the five realms."

"Tell me more about your ability to see into the future," I said.

Raziel nodded. "Unlike Earth, where time is linear, here in the spiritual realms, time can be thought of as simultaneous, where past, present, and future events can coincide."

I thought momentarily, then said, "I must say, time has seemed pretty much the same as it was on Earth."

Raziel jabbed a finger at me and said, "That's how you perceive it. But, in many ways, your destiny has already concluded."

"And what happened?" I asked, holding out my hands.

"That I cannot say because I'm sitting here with you now, in this time."

I pinched the bridge of my nose and said, "So how do I see time this other way?"

"Only souls with a higher level of spiritual development can transcend the limits of linear time."

"All right," I said, figuring that wasn't me. "So what do I do in the meantime?"

"Stay upon your righteous path, Samuel. There's much to lose if you don't," Raziel said, waving an open palm, and at that moment, all went dark.

CHAPTER THIRTY-ONE
THE CLAY OF YAVEN

I opened my eyes inches away from some wet, gritty, rust-colored blob. When I tried to lift my hand, my entire arm refused to budge, nor would any other part of my body. That was because I was stuck neck-deep in thick, heavy mud. I twisted my head back and forth, trying to figure out my whereabouts. "Where am I?" I called out.

"This is the Clay of Yaven," a voice replied.

I twisted hard, trying to see behind me. "I don't understand," I shrieked.

"Try to remain calm," the voice advised.

"Who are you?" I asked.

"My name's Jared. I murdered my wife and then killed myself. It's called a murder-suicide."

"Yeah, okay, but what's this stuff I'm in?"

"As I said—it's the Clay of Yaven."

"The fourth realm," I said under my breath.

"The worst of the worst are sent here. However, I hear others have done even more unspeakable things. Those condemned souls go to the Frozen Wasteland. What about you?"

"What about me?" I asked while wiggling my shoulders, trying to free my arms.

"What did you do? You look young. Were you killed?"

"Oh no," I blurted. "I'm not here for the same reason as you."

"Why are you here?"

"I'm looking for someone. Have you seen them? Two old men. Solomon and Pincus."

"Nope, never heard of them. But it's not like I get to meet many souls. Though I had a friend once," he said with a sigh. "But he was taken."

"Taken? Taken where?"

"Down below. After that, I don't know what happens to us."

"You mean under this clay?"

"That's right. We were talking, and the next minute, he was yanked under."

"So, how long have you been like this?"

"I don't know. There's no sense of time. Things here never change, nor do I ever move."

Besides the mounds of clay at eye level, I could see slowly drifting rust-colored clouds above me. "I can't stay here. I must get out," I said, thrashing. But to no avail; I was held captive, buried neck-deep.

"What's your name?" the voice asked.

"My name's Sam, but I must get out of here." *And not talk to you*, I wanted to add.

"How are you doing, Sam? As I said, I'm Jared. My poor wife was Marlene. I'm sorry for what I've done, and I certainly deserve this," he said with an exasperated sigh. "If I ever get a second chance, I swear to the Almighty I'll be a better man."

"Oh, come on." *This is ridiculous. How am I supposed to find Solomon? I need help.* "Jared, is there an angel in charge here?"

"Well," Jared said with an audible swallow. "I wouldn't call him an angel, but there is Asmodeus."

"Asmodeus?"

"Yes, Asmodeus is more like a demon. Some have said a fallen angel."

"And when did you see him last?"

"Oh," Jared said, taking a moment to remember. "It was when I first arrived."

"When you first arrived?" I repeated.

"Oh no," Jared said, realizing the significance. "That means Asmodeus is coming for you. Let me give you some advice. Don't speak; listen and nod. This demon is tricky, cunning, and powerful."

"Understood," I said, biting my lower lip and wondering how to convince Asmodeus to release me.

"It's been said that Asmodeus tempts the living, encouraging them to do terrible things. That's where my bad thoughts came from. Because I was a good man, and I don't know..."

I ignored Jared's incessant yapping and instead wished to move beyond this need for my imagined body. According to what Poppy had said, I understood that my transition required the physical, earthly part of me to remain for a while, and I was okay with that until now. My physical body had become a nuisance or, even worse, an existential threat.

After a while, Jared tired of speaking and fell silent. This allowed me to reflect upon my journey through the realms of Gehenna and wonder again if these angels had an agenda that wasn't in my best interest.

"You're right not to trust the angels," a baritone voice said.

My eyes darted back and forth, looking for who was speaking. "Who's there?"

"You want to know why I was sent here?"

"Where are you?" I asked, twisting my head back and forth.

"It's because I spoke the truth and was condemned to look after these poor souls buried in the Clay of Yaven."

"Asmodeus?" I asked.

"Though I can see why the likes of Hadriel, Samael, and especially Michael, have taken an interest in you."

I shook my head and said, "I don't understand."

"A *rasha* in Gehenna is like a virus, poisoning its purpose. Once infected, it's impossible to rid itself of the disease. The angels need a young soul like you to disinfect and remove the *rasha*."

"But what about Pincus?"

"Ah," Asmodeus said. "How do you know who've you seen with Solomon was your great-great-grandfather and not an impostor?"

I grimaced, giving it some thought, then said, "I suppose I don't know."

"You have a choice, Samuel. You can forgo this pointless quest and move on to the cosmos, readying yourself for rebirth. Or you could remain here in the Clay of Yaven until I decide to release you, depending on my whim, which could be quite a while."

I twisted my lips, contemplating my decision. I wanted to avoid remaining neck-deep in this heavy clay for who knows how long. What if Asmodeus was right and this quest was a hoax? How could I, a simple soul, be expected to rid Gehenna of a notorious *rasha* while simultaneously rescuing an ancient forefather of mine who might be a pretender?

"All right," I said, giving in to the easier path. "I'll agree to move on."

"Excellent. I'll make the arrangements," Asmodeus said and fell silent.

While I waited, my neighbor's voice returned. "Still waiting for Asmodeus?"

"Oh, no. He was here. Didn't you hear him?"

"I heard nothing," my neighbor said. "Whoever spoke to you, I can assure you, was not Asmodeus."

"Then who was it?" I asked, and as those words passed my lips, I was yanked under the sticky and dense Clay of Yaven.

CHAPTER THIRTY-TWO
CAPTURED

Helpless, I was pulled through the depths. I felt wet clay abrading my skin before depositing me into some rocky shelter. When I got to my feet, I saw my clothes and skin were covered with dried clumps of red clay. I picked them off while looking around, shivering for the first time since my transition to the soul world.

While I wrapped my arms around myself, trying to generate some warmth, I wondered why I was here and not in the cosmos as Asmodeus promised.

I surveyed the cave, and all I could tell of this place was that it was freezing. Then a terrible thought occurred to me—*Have I been dragged into the Frozen Wasteland?*

As my teeth began to chatter, I heard voices, and they were coming from somewhere in the shadows. I hurried, and as I turned the corner around an outcropping, my eyes bulged out at the sight of Gray and Pincus.

"Ah, Samuel," Gray said, showing his hands, "I see the *rasha* has finally caught you."

My eyes bounced between the two men huddled close together on a stone shelf. From the looks, they had been here a while. Gray's skin looked even more ashen than usual.

As for Pincus, he had never appeared to be in good health. But now, his tone lacked color; he was nothing more than a pale shade of white.

"I-I thought I m-made a bargain with Asmodeus," I said, shivering out the words.

"Come close; we'll keep you warm," Gray said, summoning me over.

"I understand why I am still of body, but why are the two of you?"

"All souls traveling through Gehenna must maintain the illusion," Gray said. "It's only upon our freedom from these realms into the cosmos that we lose the need."

I climbed up and sat next to Pincus. Though he was my great-great-grandfather, it was apparent we shared only a tiny percentage of our genetic makeup. He was a tiny man, less than half my size. His thin nose featured a bony bump at its bridge, and the lenses in his wire-rimmed glasses magnified his beady black eyes. I had difficulty imagining how any part of this man's genes was within me. Blood was blood, but I wasn't sure. "Is this the real Pincus?" I asked Gray, squinting.

"Why don't you ask me?" Pincus said with a snarl. "I'm sitting right next to you."

"Oh, I'm sorry. I was just told that you weren't real."

"Who told you that?" Gray asked.

I explained what had happened during my last moments in the Clay of Yaven.

"And you thought you made a deal with Asmodeus?" asked Pincus.

I released an exasperated sigh and said, "Solomon tricked me."

"Don't feel so bad," Pincus said, patting my leg. "He tricked us all."

"I'm afraid to ask," I said, pointing into the shadows, "but is this the Frozen Wasteland?"

"Oh no," Gray said, wagging a finger. "This is some in-between place. But I believe the icy realm is close by."

"I hope you don't mind me asking," Gray said. "But why did you agree with Asmodeus to move on?"

"I felt hopeless," I said, shaking my head and lowering my eyes. "And now I feel ashamed."

"Nonsense," Pincus said firmly. "You did what it took to survive."

"I don't know," said Gray, wagging a finger. "With your karmic history, you might have consequences for making such a decision."

"You think so?" I asked.

Gray puckered his lips and nodded.

"You don't know that," Pincus said. "Maybe Sam made the right decision. Though at this moment, things don't look too promising."

"No, I suppose it doesn't," I said.

We sat a while in silence while I contemplated our situation. That was when I decided I would be proactive. "Where's Solomon now?" I asked.

Gray shrugged. "Who knows, and does it matter? We're caught and no longer a threat. I wouldn't be surprised if we never see the *rasha* again."

"So that's it?" I said, flipping out my hands. "This is where our stories end? In some frozen cave in Gehenna?"

Neither Gray nor Pincus answered.

"But what if we can find our way out?" I said, gesturing with a sweep of my arm.

"Out into the Frozen Wasteland?" Pincus replied, wide-eyed and startled.

"Well, we can't just sit here," I argued.

Gray leaned forward to look at me and said, "Do you know what's out there, Sam?"

I shrugged and said, "I've heard a few things about it."

Gray pointed at me and said, "The Frozen Wasteland is desolate and barren. The unfortunate souls wandering this level are surrounded by an icy mist that makes winters on Earth seem like a warm summer's day. Because of their unspeakable sins, the soul's purification process is painful and everlasting."

"Okay," I said, knowing I may have no choice but to venture into Gehenna's last and most dastardly realm to find my way out.

CHAPTER THIRTY-THREE
PINCUS'S STORY

I don't know how long we had sat huddled in bored silence when Pincus lifted his chin and said, "Would you like to hear how I rescued my family during the war?"

I turned to him and said, "Sure, I'd like that."

"It was 1917. I'd lived in New York's Lower East Side for over four years when, one day, I gave the newsboy a nickel for the *Forward*, a popular Jewish newspaper. I got my usual table at Katz's Deli and ordered my favorite—a corned beef sandwich with cabbage on rye, a half-sour pickle, and a cream soda."

"*Mmm*, that sounds good," I said, remembering the deliciously soft, warm meat.

"Oh," Pincus said, licking his lips, "mouthwatering. Anyway, I sat down, folded my paper for easy reading, took a bite into the pickle, and nearly choked. Across the top, in huge letters, I read 'War Declared. All of Europe in Turmoil.'"

"Was that World War I?" I asked.

Pincus nodded slowly and said, "The Allies against the Central Powers. Our small village of Krzywcza was now in a war zone, and bloody battles raged in our backyard between the Russians and the Austrians."

"From the story I was told, you planned on returning home within a year but waited too long, and war broke out."

Pincus sighed. "It was the biggest mistake of my life and one I had to face, especially dealing with the consequences here in Gehenna."

I rolled my hand and said, "Please continue."

"While in my cobbler shop in the Lower East Side, I shared the news with my good friend Jakob, a young man I met onboard the steamship SS *Amerika*. To my surprise, Jakob had just arranged with a gangster named Leo Gorpatsch to go to Germany."

"Another gangster?" I said, sharing a look with Gray.

Pincus nodded. "Jakob agreed to smuggle guns from America to Jewish fighters in Krakow, a city not far from Krzywcza, my home village. He proposed that I tag along to help him with the delivery, then, afterward, we would go and rescue my family."

"During the middle of the war?" I said, wide-eyed.

Pincus nodded. "I know it sounds crazy, but it's true."

I held out my hands and said, "Go on."

"Well, I closed the cobbler shop, and we bought two tickets onboard the same steamship and sailed for Hamburg. But this time, instead of traveling in steerage, Jakob and I had enough money for a first-class cabin."

"First-class," I said, sounding impressed. "It must have been great."

"Oh, Samuel, it was luxurious. But remember, it was also winter, and we were sailing across the Atlantic in a world at war. But most regretful were my troubled thoughts. I had fantasized about this trip being my triumphant return home."

"What did you imagine?" I asked.

"Oh, it was a grand vision," he said, straightening his spine and lifting his chin.

"Pincus Potasznik, the disrespected man who ventured to the New World with only a few coins in his pocket, had established a successful business, was the founder of the Krzywcza Landsman Society, and was now coming home to an adoring family. Ready to spit upon those uppity Torah scholars who once shunned him as a second-class citizen."

"And if the war hadn't broken out," Gray offered. "That might have happened."

"What was it like when you reached Germany?" I asked.

"Hold on," Pincus said, holding up a finger. "Before that, while onboard the steamship crossing the Atlantic, we met a real German prince and princess."

"Really?" I said, realizing my great-great-grandfather had a fascinating life.

"His Royal Highness Prince Adalbert, the son of Kaiser Wilhelm, and his wife, Princess Adelaide."

"The son of the Kaiser?" I asked.

"It was because of Jakob that we met them. He was very outgoing and had no qualms about approaching the royal couple, even with their entourage of bodyguards. Jakob shared the reason for our mission with the prince about transporting guns to the war effort. And to our surprise, the prince offered to help us with official papers of the court and a horse-drawn wagon to traverse unaccosted across the German countryside."

"That's amazing," I said, riveted by the story.

"But that's not all," Pincus said with a smile. "One early morning, during breakfast, I had a private conversation with Princess Adelaide. After I shared my plans of rescuing my family, she gave me the name of her cousin, who worked for the Norwegian America Line. This was important because that's how we eventually returned to America."

"But how did you get your family out?"

"Wait," Pincus said, holding up a finger. "I'm going to tell you."

I bowed my head and held out my palms, offering for him to continue.

"After two weeks at sea, we finally docked at the Port of Hamburg and thanked the prince and princess for securing us a wagon and two horses. With a wooden crate packed with rifles in tow, we left the shipyards and crossed the frozen countryside through Germany, heading to our destination in Krakow. We had a few close calls along the way, but eventually, we crossed the border and found the renegade militia of Jewish soldiers. But when the crate opened, we discovered the guns were gone."

"Gone?" I asked. "What happened to them?"

Pincus laughed. "The prince stole them from the crate while stored on the steamship. We traveled throughout Germany, a country at war with an empty crate."

"Were the soldiers angry?"

Pincus nodded. "They were upset at first, and who could blame them? But when we shared how the prince swindled us, they let us go on our way."

"How far was Krakow from your village?" I asked.

"About two hundred and forty kilometers. Which by wagon was about two days' ride."

"But what about the war?" I asked. "Did you stumble upon any soldiers or battles?"

"We ran into several roadblocks and saw many dead soldiers lying in fields and on the side of the road, from both sides—Russian and Austrian. But by the blessings of Hashem, we were able to push our way through to Krzywcza."

"What was it like when you got home?" I asked.

Pincus smiled. "It was a moment I'll never forget. Seeing my wife and children for the first time in four years was emotional, as you can imagine."

"Wasn't Clara pregnant when you left for America?" Gray asked.

"She was," Pincus said, nodding. "That was also the first time I met our baby girl Anna."

"How did you get them out of there?" I asked.

"In the same empty wooden crate that held the guns. That's where we hid Clara, Jennie, Moshe, Hymie, and Anna. After many weeks and dangerous conditions, we eventually returned to Hamburg and found our way to Norway, where I sought out the princess's cousin, who secured our passage home."

"That's an incredible story," I said. "You should've written a book."

"It's a worthy story of perseverance and courage," Pincus said, sounding prideful for the first time.

"What happened to your friend?" Gray asked.

"Shortly after returning home, Jakob was shot dead by Leo Gorpatsch," Pincus said, shaking his head. "Poor man was only thirty-two."

"Just like me," I said, touching my chest. "Did you ever see him again in the soul world?"

"I haven't," Pincus said. "He may have already moved on."

"That's quite a story, Pincus," Gray said. "I had no idea of your courage and fortitude. Maybe with your smarts, you can figure out how to get us out of here."

Pincus shrugged, dropped his gaze, and shook his head.

CHAPTER THIRTY-FOUR
THE BAIT

The three of us remained in the desolate, frigid cave, where nothing changed. Besides the ice cracking within the stone walls surrounding us, Pincus's incessant and annoying groans were the only sounds. Occasionally, one of us had something to say, and it was during one of these conversations I asked Gray to tell me more about Francesca Sarah of Safed.

"Of course, my father told me about her wisdom of the dream world," Gray began. "As part of his studies into lucid dreaming, he traveled to Safed in northern Israel, the birthplace of Kabbalah, to learn more. He discovered that back in the seventeenth century, Francesca Sarah taught her followers of Kabbalah that the dream world was a realm of consciousness where boundaries between the self and the external world were blurred. In this altered state, one could access deeper levels of understanding and insight into the nature of reality. She believed that by paying attention to our dreams and reflecting upon their meanings, we could gain valuable insights into our inner world and spiritual journey. She explained that through this process, we would uncover hidden aspects of ourselves, leading toward greater self-awareness and enlightenment."

"*Mmm,*" I said, absorbing Gray's words. "I wish we could still dream."

"You know, Sam, it's possible for souls to reach a similar dreamlike state."

"How do we do that if we don't sleep?"

"We need to move on beyond these realms of Gehenna and transition into pure consciousness."

I wrapped my arms across my chest as a shiver cascaded through me. "I don't understand a few things," I said. "If our bodies are necessary for our travels among the five realms, why can't we dream? I have regained all my senses—taste, smell, sight, touch, and sound."

"Okay, then let me ask you this. Since your arrival, have you fallen asleep?" Gray asked.

I shook my head. "No, I haven't even been tired."

"These experiential things, Sam, are nothing more than illusions. What's true is that souls retain their capacity for sensory perception, but in different forms. For example, we possess a unique set of spiritual senses. We can perceive light, hear sound, and feel warmth, but it's done collectively with other souls."

"But none of that's useful, being stuck down here," I complained.

Gray sighed and nodded. "This is true."

"I don't know about you, but I need to rid myself of this body," I said, patting my leg. "And this can't be done while in Gehenna."

"It seems we don't have much choice," Pincus said.

I thought a while, trying to figure a way out, when I realized there was only one solution. "What we need to do is to lure Solomon back here," I said, pointing a finger to the stone floor. "Then figure out a way of swapping places with him."

"It's good to be young," Pincus said and sighed. "I'm too old for such *mishegoss*."

I looked at Pincus with my hands held out, shaking my head.

"*Mishegoss*, it's Yiddish for 'craziness.'"

"Do you want to continue sitting here for an eternity on this cold stone with Gray and me?"

Pincus shrugged. "No, of course not. I want to be born already. There's much I need to do."

"Great," I said, patting his boney leg.

"So, Sam, what do you propose?" asked Gray.

I thought a while, then asked, "Who's the gatekeeper of this realm?"

"Oriphiel," Gray said with an eye roll. "This is one angel you don't want to meet. It's been said that Oriphiel guards the Frozen Wasteland with a flaming sword, which I gather is not used for releasing souls into the cosmos."

"That is a frightening prospect," I agreed. "But what if I could speak with Oriphiel and convince him to exchange the *rasha* for our freedom?"

"*Pfft,*" Pincus said. "How do you propose you do that?"

"I don't know," I said, exhaling a breath and watching the cloud of mist floating upwards. "Maybe I'll figure it out when the time comes."

Gray said, pointing into the darkened corridor, "The Frozen Wasteland is not like any of the other realms. Some have called it the

Other Side because of its association with the forces of impurity and its separation from holiness."

I listened to Gray's ominous description, then asked, "You're saying there's no chance for redemption once a soul enters the Frozen Wasteland?"

"Listen to me carefully, Sam. You can't just walk out there. This is the realm of darkness, confusion, and chaos, where souls are permanently cut off from the Divine."

"Gray's right, Sam," Pincus said. "It's too dangerous."

I furrowed my brow and said, "I'm not going just to sit here and wait for something to happen. Because nothing will."

"You don't know that," Gray said.

I got to my feet and jumped off the stone shelf. I stepped toward the way out, then turned back to face Gray and Pincus. "My great-grandfather sent me on this quest to rescue Pincus and destroy the *rasha*. I'm halfway there," I said, pointing to the mealy man. "All I need to do now is finish the job. I understand if you want no part of walking out there with me."

Gray smiled. "I admire you, Sam, and you've certainly come a long way. But I'm sorry, I cannot join you."

I looked over to Pincus, who offered me a troubled smile and said, "Perhaps if I had some of my life forces remaining. But I'm an old soul and would be more of a hindrance, and you'll have a better chance without me tagging along."

I took a deep breath and a moment to gaze into Gray's and Pincus's eyes. "I'll return for both of you, and we'll travel the cosmos together."

"That would be wonderful," Gray said, touching his heart.

CHAPTER THIRTY-FIVE
THE OTHER SIDE

I entered the darkened corridor, where a faint glow guided me. This illumination remained constant, drawing me toward some destination. I followed it through a meandering array of stone passageways while I tried imagining what a confrontation would be like with Oriphiel. I struggled with the idea of an evil angel and assumed these Divine creations lacked free will, making them incapable of rebelling. In other words—a being of obedience, destined to serve humankind. But what about Asmodeus, the fallen angel who had turned away from the Divine and become a corrupted, destructive force—though, based on what Gray had said, Oriphiel was considerably fiercer and more formidable than even the protector of the Clay of Yaven.

I don't know how far I followed the light, but eventually, I approached the tunnel's end and stood in awe at the vision before me. As far as I could see, vast blocks of jagged ice filled the landscape with no signs of souls or vegetation. Above me, the sky was dark, like the late hours of a moonless night.

Cautiously, I climbed down the slippery cliffside to the landscape below. Once there and sure of foot, I came to grips with the scale of these blocks of jagged glaciers, each the size of a house. Along with being surrounded by the immense structures, I came to the joyous resolution that I was no longer freezing. Pleased not to be shivering, I advanced along the pathways carved out between the gigantic obstructions, though to where I had no idea.

I pushed ahead, further and further away from the safety of where I offered my farewells to Gray and Pincus. There was no question I thought more than twice about my wisdom of leaving them. As I wound my way, I wondered if Oriphiel would appear or if I would wander aimlessly and alone in this frozen land forever.

Though I still experienced time in an earthly way, I could not determine its duration. There was this constant advance of my existence, where each moment built upon the previous one.

I hadn't realized that this realm was also void of sound until I heard the faint high-pitched whistling of a wind pushing its way through the channels of ice. Accompanying this change was a chill that caused my body to shiver uncontrollably. I stopped walking and braced myself by bending over and grasping onto my knees, hoping it would cease.

My body continued to experience tremors, and these vibrations spread to the frozen ground beneath my feet. Soon, the entire realm shook so hard that chunks of ice began cracking off and crashing all around me. I covered my head with my arms, trying to avoid being hit by the falling debris.

Then, as if someone had flipped a switch, the violence stopped, and all was still. A dark shadow enveloped me, and as I looked up and saw a being hovering over me, its fiery eyes locked onto mine. Suddenly, a warm wind pushed me backward as the creature flapped what appeared to be a pair of large black wings.

Could this be Oriphiel?

The birdlike being settled on the ground before me. I looked up at the towering bare-chested figure with long black hair falling over his shoulders, a belt with a geometric symbol on its buckle, and tight black pants tucked into knee-high boots. With an effortless motion, he folded his wings neatly behind him.

"Are you Oriphiel?" I asked, wide-eyed and slack-jawed.

"Ah, Samuel, Oriphiel is pleased to meet you," the winged angel said, holding out its arms. "Welcome to Tohu."

I squinted and scratched the back of my head. "Tohu? But isn't this the Frozen Wasteland?"

"That's an unfortunate name given by those jealous of Oriphiel's realm."

"Jealous?" I repeated.

"Yes, that's right. You would think angels could suppress the sin of envy. They all know that Tohu is the precursor to the world's creation."

"But how is that possible when nothing exists?"

"Ah," Oriphiel said, pointing at me. "Tohu produces the raw material from which the universe is formed. At first glance, this may seem like a spiritual wasteland where nothing grows or flourishes; however, it's in this state of emptiness and chaos where new possibilities emerge."

"I don't understand."

"Tohu is where souls play an active role in repairing the earth and bringing it closer to its ultimate purpose."

"But there's nobody here," I said. "Where do these repairs take place?"

"We don't have many visitors because most souls are purified before reaching Tohu."

I looked around at the giant-sized blocks of ice surrounding us and said, "Am I the only one here?"

"Well, your friends, Gray and Pincus, are here."

"You know of them?" I said, thinking of them waiting for me at the threshold.

"Oriphiel knows all. Now, Samuel, follow me," he said, sweeping his long arm to his left.

"Just one moment," I said, trying to slow down the giant black-winged angel. "May I ask, does Oriphiel know if the *rasha* Solomon has been here?"

"Ah, yes, Solomon. He is waiting for you. Please come," Oriphiel said and turned.

With a full view of his black wings, I stayed close. Could it be that Oriphiel was not the evil angel I'd expected? Maybe he could assist in freeing me, then Gray and Pincus. With much hanging in the balance, I fell in step behind him.

We walked a dozen paces, though I needed to take two or three times that due to his long strides. When we stopped, the angel turned and gestured for me to stay back as he spread his magnificent black wings. Then, the ice cracked open in the space before us, revealing a long staircase leading to a mysterious destination below.

Oriphiel retracted his feathers and descended. I stood there momentarily, still gathering my wits, when Oriphiel cried, "Are you coming, Samuel?"

"Yes, I'm coming," I said, stepping toward the edge.

By the time I got there, I had caught sight of the tips of Oriphiel's wings before the being was swallowed into the darkness. "Oriphiel!" I shouted.

There was no response. I stood there momentarily, hands on my hips, trying to gaze into the abyss. Once again, second thoughts plagued me, causing me to reconsider returning to the safety of the cave where Gray and Pincus were huddling.

I breathed, allowing myself to reminisce about those I left behind. If only they could only see me now, deep into the fifth realm of Gehenna, face to face with a black-winged angel, searching for Solomon, the wicked soul out for revenge against my great-grandfather, the righteous one. *Rasha* verse *tzaddik*: a heavyweight bout in the soul world.

The sports analogy gave me the courage to descend the stairwell of ice and into the unknown with a clear duty to protect my soul family.

After a few steps, any light reflecting off the ice quickly diminished, and I remained, once again, alone in the dark. Though luckily, this lasted only a few moments as my eyes adjusted. It took quite a while to reach the bottom as the stairs cut back and forth dozens of times. But eventually, I arrived, and to my astonishment, I saw stretched out upon an open plain, tens of thousands upon thousands of souls with tortured expressions, crying out, all squeezed closely together. They appeared locked into place, with their lower portions, from the hips down to their legs, buried into solid ice.

"What's this place?" I said, pausing on the last step.

"This is the Frozen Wasteland," said a familiar voice.

"Who's there?"

"Hello, Samuel," the voice said, emerging from the shadows.

The moment I saw his face, I recognized the *rasha*. "Solomon."

"Well, this was easier than I thought," the old man smirked.

"Why are you here? And who are all these souls?" I asked, gesturing to the endless field of writhing bodies, trying to twist themselves free.

"The ones who have committed the most egregious sins against humanity. The souls here cannot be purified. They will never be reborn."

"But I don't understand. I just spoke with Oriphiel," I said, pointing upwards. "He called this place Tohu, where work is done in repairing the earth, bringing it closer to its ultimate purpose, or something like that."

Solomon laughed. "Oriphiel has his aspirations. But, there's no such work here. These souls," he said, holding his arms outward, "are despicable."

I put my hand over my mouth, realizing I'd been tricked. "What's going to happen to me?"

Solomon rubbed his wrinkled hands together and said, "You'll join your friends here."

"But I left them back in the cave," I said, pointing up the steps.

Solomon wagged a finger. "No, no. They're right over there," he said, pointing to Gray and Pincus, who were encased waist-deep in the ice like the multitude of souls surrounding us.

"Oh no," I said, wondering if turning and charging back up the steps was still possible. But I knew making a run for it was futile.

"This is all working out better than I planned," Solomon said. "I intended to capture the *tzaddik*'s father, but who knew I would also snare his great-grandson."

"Come on now, there's no need for this," I pleaded.

With a squint, Solomon stepped closer and said, "Do you know what the *tzaddik* did to me?"

I nodded. "Yes, he brought you to the River of Fire. But you were fine, though the purification didn't seem to stick."

Solomon chuckled and pointed at me. "That's funny. No, it didn't stick."

"So you're fine; you still exist and seem to have found a place that accepts you," I said, sweeping an arm toward the field of souls.

"You're the clever one," Solomon said, nodding. "It's a shame doing this to you. You're very young, with so much potential."

I furrowed my brow and said, "Potential for what?"

"To join me," he said, touching his chest. "By my side, there's much we can accomplish."

"And betray my soul family?" I scoffed, shaking my head. "What makes you think I would do that?"

"Because it's your nature, Samuel. There's no need to resist."

I held up my hand and shook my head. "There's no way."

"Very well," Solomon said with a shrug. Then, with an upward swipe of his hand, **Oriphiel** appeared before me. The angel opened its black-feathered wings and wrapped them around me. In one sweeping motion, my body was lifted and deposited into the solid ice between Gray and Pincus in one move.

I struggled for a few moments, trying to wiggle free, but soon gave up, coming to grips with my predicament.

"So nice of you to join us," Gray said mockingly.

"You can't get away with this," I shouted after Solomon, who had already ascended the stairs.

CHAPTER THIRTY-SIX
THE FIRST *RASHA*

"Now what do we do?" I said as the switchback staircase, the *rasha*, and the great dark angel vanished, leaving the three of us perched like potted plants.

"Looks like we found our final resting place," Pincus said, though it was hard to hear him over the screams and cries of the tens of thousands of souls.

"Is this what will happen to us?" I said, twisting my head back and forth. "Will we go crazy like all of them?"

Gray took a breath and snorted it out. "Probably. I'm already starting to feel frantic."

"Me too," Pincus said.

"Let's try to remain calm," I said.

"This is all my fault," Gray said.

"What do you mean?" I asked.

"Bringing you on this so-called quest was my idea. Your grandfather Poppy thought it would be too dangerous. But I convinced him otherwise."

"How did you do that?" I asked.

Gray lowered his gaze and said, "I promised him that nothing bad would happen to you."

I closed my eyes and sighed. "I doubt my grandfather based his decision on your promise."

"Yeah, you're probably right. He doesn't seem to be the gullible type," Gray said.

"You did your best, and I don't blame you, Gray. Trust me; I would have objected if I didn't want this. Saying no was never a problem for me," I said, recalling the numerous times I refused to do things because I thought them too challenging.

"What do you mean?" Gray asked.

"For example, when I was in school, I didn't want to perform in our class play. Then, at work with Dad, I shied away from doing certain tasks, like giving presentations to architects."

"All right, Sam," Gray said. "However, you surprised me with how you made it through all five realms of Gehenna."

"I've only made it through four. But it looks like my luck has run out."

"So many regrets," Gray said, clasping his head with both hands. "Why did I seek out Moshe to take on Solomon? I can't believe I'm paying for something I did in 1960, now in my afterlife."

"Bizarre," I agreed.

"What are the odds of running into a *rasha* in one's lifetime?" Gray asked with a scoff.

"I've done it twice," Pincus said, holding two fingers.

"Twice?" I asked with flared nostrils.

"Yes, the first time was in '64, when Moshe was sixteen. A *rasha* kidnapped him."

"That's right," Gray said. "I completely forgot. Moshe told me how you and your wife rescued him. Tell Sam the story."

Because of the incessant buzz of the tortured souls, I leaned in closer, not wanting to miss a word.

"Sure," Pincus said. "After our daring escape from the war, we'd been back in the Lower East Side for nearly four years. Moshe had just taken over the reins from me at the cobbler shop, and the customers loved his friendly demeanor. Then one day, he went missing. Clara and I looked everywhere but couldn't find him."

"Where'd he go?" I asked.

"He was taken by a woman named Dora Meltzer, who happened to be the same person I met onboard the SS *Amerika*. My friend Jakob and I had learned of this famous palmist offering readings. So we decided to try her out. Jakob went before me while I waited nervously in her first-class cabin. On that initial voyage, we were both in steerage. So you can imagine how impressed we were."

"I'm sure you were," I said.

"When my turn came, I remember sitting across from her. She had the most beautiful eyes I'd ever seen, along with these blonde curls, and her breasts were—"

"Pincus," Gray interrupted. "Stick to the story."

"Oh, sorry," he said, batting away the memory. "The moment I sat across from her, she asked for my hands. She grasped them, turned them over, and looked at my palms. Keeping her gaze upon them, she traced the lines in my palm and said, '*You're on a journey of discovery, Pincus, where you will find great challenges and significant successes in your new life. I see that you are a craftsman . . . that you work with your hands,*' gently stroking my calluses. 'Yes, I'm a cobbler,' I told her. '*You will open a business in America, and it will surpass your expectations.*' Then she dug her nails into my palm and said, '*Pincus, you have a family you left behind.*' I told her this was true. Then she warned me, saying I should wait no more than a year before returning for them. She said she sensed danger if I stayed in America too long."

"But you didn't listen," I said.

Pincus shook his head and said, "She asked if I had a son. I told her I had two sons. She pointed to my palm and said, '*Your eldest son, he's the special one.*'"

"Was that Moshe?" I asked.

Pincus nodded. "Of course, I wondered why she thought Moshe was so special. He seemed like a normal nine-year-old boy, perhaps more sensitive than most. But years later, when I returned to my village during the war, our rabbi, Rabbi Shapira, spoke with me and Clara. Based on what he had witnessed, he said he was certain that Moshe was a *tzaddik*. He also warned of the dangers from those wishing to harm him."

"Wise man," I said.

"I shared with the rabbi how I met this palmist on the voyage to America four years earlier and what she told me about Moshe having a gift."

"And what did the rabbi say?" I asked.

"He told me that Dora Meltzer could be a *rasha* and warned me that Moshe should never meet her until he had fully matured and developed all his defenses."

"So what happened when he went missing from the cobbler shop?" I asked Pincus.

"When I searched for a clue to his whereabouts, I found a work ticket lying on the floor in the back workroom. In Moshe's handwriting, it read:

DORA MELTZER

97 ORCHARD STREET

BLUE SHOES - REPLACE SOLES—$2."

"It was the *rasha*," I said.

"It was," Pincus said, nodding. "We figured Dora was trying to take advantage of Moshe's gift. Eventually, we found a rabbi who introduced Clara and me to a seminary professor who was an expert in Kabbalah mysticism. He warned us about the *rasha* and how Moshe was in danger."

"What did you do?" I asked.

"Clara and I devised a ruse."

"A ruse?" I said, sharing a wide-eyed look with Gray.

"The professor was to contact Dora and seek to entice her with an idea of how to harness the power of the *tzaddik*. But to do this, she must bring Moshe to the Willet Street synagogue, as it was a special place to engage the spirits. Dora agreed and brought Moshe. That's where Clara and I waited and rescued our son from her clutches."

"That's quite a story," I said. "You were fearless."

Pincus laughed. "That's the craziest thing. All my life, I wasn't—I cowered from confrontation."

"But when it counted, you were there," I said, reaching over to pat Pincus's back.

"Thank you, Sam. But we'll need more than courage to get us out of this mess."

"You mentioned your wife, Clara," I said. "Has she moved on?"

Pincus shook his head. "Oh no, she's still in the soul world. Though I haven't seen her since Solomon took me away."

"By the way, how did that happen?" I asked.

"That, too, is an interesting story. It's been a while since Clara journeyed through the *sheol* as all good souls do, while I needed to pass through the Clay of Yaven for my purification. My misdeeds were more severe than my wife's, and she never did anything wrong." He chuckled. "Though something strange happened to her during the war, she refused to tell me what, no matter how many times I asked. That's how Solomon lured me into his web."

"How do you mean?"

"He told me he knew Clara's secret."

"Are you serious?"

Pincus nodded. "He offered to tell me, but only if I agreed to meet him in the Valley of the Shadow of the Dead."

"Why there?" I asked.

Pincus shrugged. "From what he said, he could not journey through the cosmos because of misunderstanding. I didn't know who he was; if I had known he was a *rasha*, I would have never gone."

"So you agreed?"

Pincus nodded with a shrug. "I wanted to know what she hid from me for many years."

"And did he tell you?" Gray asked.

Pincus thought a moment, twisting his mouth, considering. "Well, I really shouldn't say, but I don't think we're getting out of here, so what the heck."

Gray looked over at me with eyes filled with surprise. Equally curious, I leaned in.

"It occurred while I was still in New York. War had broken out, and in our province of Galicia, Russia was fighting fierce battles with the Austrian-Hungarian army and Jewish militia, who readily took up arms to kill Russians. During a battle near Krzywcza, many of our people were wounded and taken to our synagogue, which was converted into a makeshift hospital. They tried their best to offer aid, but with only one elderly doctor and minimal supplies, it was more to make them comfortable. Moshe offered the most, helping those ready to pass."

"Yes," I said, remembering what Moshe noted about how those close to death were put to ease just by his touch.

"That's when Rabbi Shapira realized he was a *tzaddik*," Pincus said.

I nodded.

"Anyway, during this time, this Russian Army captain named Berbecki and his soldiers entered the synagogue, ordering the wounded men outside where they lined them up against the wall and, by firing squad, shot them all dead."

"Oh my," I said, wondering if this Russian captain was among the throngs of souls exiled in this realm.

"When the deed was done, the captain wanted to take Rabbi Shapira into custody. But Moshe stepped forward and offered himself instead, to which Captain Berbecki readily agreed. When Clara learned that the Russian captain had taken our son, she hurried to the station, demanding his release. From what Solomon said, Captain Berbecki had his eye on my wife for some time. So when Clara insisted he hand over Moshe, the captain obliged, though under one condition," Pincus said, shifting his eyes up and down.

"No way!" I said, anticipating the worst.

Pincus nodded. "She allowed that pig to violate her for the sake of our son. It was hardly a sin."

"Certainly not," I said with a grimace. "But I can understand why she kept it a secret from you."

"Clara was a remarkable woman," Gray added.

Then, all three of us let out loud sighs, returning to our mutual states of gloom.

CHAPTER THIRTY-SEVEN
EZRA

"Hey, you," a soul called out. He was a few feet away, with his back facing me. So, to make eye contact, he needed to twist his upper body around almost a full one hundred and eighty degrees, demonstrating remarkable flexibility.

"What?" I replied, cocking my chin.

"Who are you?" the man asked.

He was a middle-aged man dressed in a business suit that looked fine, even here, stuck in the frozen mud. "My name's Sam," I said curtly, not wanting to converse with some scum of the souls.

"My name's Ezra," he said, taking a moment to adjust his blue tie. Though I'm not sure, it was blue, as the Frozen Wasteland seemed to suck the colors from everything.

"Hello, Ezra," I said.

"So what dastardly deeds are you paying for?"

"Pfft," I blurted. "I'm not."

"Oh, come on now. Are you too ashamed to say?" he said with a white-tooth smile that even the dread of this realm couldn't quash. "How about this? I'll go first."

"Suit yourself," I said with a sigh.

Without unwinding, Ezra began his story.

"My full name is Ezra Porkevitch. I was killed when Sadie Wollman stabbed garden shears into my neck," he said, and did a reverse twist, spinning around in the other direction to show me a nasty open wound on the left side of his neck.

I gawked, wondering what he had done to deserve that.

"You're probably wondering what I did to deserve this," he said, reading my mind.

I flipped out my hands and sighed.

"If you ask Sadie, she would say I deserved it and probably more."

"Is that right?"

"I lived in Buenos Aires. That's in Argentina."

"Yeah, I know," I said, rolling my eyes.

"My profession sent me regularly to Poland, where I sought out young Jewish women and girls in small villages and shtetls, with promises to find them rich husbands if they moved to Argentina. The parents, desperate for their daughters to have a future out of poverty and a nice payoff, readily agreed. I then escorted the girls back to Buenos Aires, where they were sold as sex slaves at auction to one of the thousands of brothels in the city."

"Are you serious?" I said with a puckered grimace.

Ezra shifted his eyes up and down, displaying a disgusting sense of pride.

"No wonder you're down here," I said, waving him off.

"Oh," he continued, gazing upwards, "you should have seen her. Sadie Wollman was the most beautiful *Polaca* in all of Buenos Aires, and she was mine."

"Polaca?" I repeated the foreign word.

"Yeah," Ezra said, flipping a hand toward me. "That's what we called the girls."

I pointed at him and asked, "Were you a Jew?"

"I certainly was. What about you?"

"And you had no qualms about taking innocent Jewish girls from their homes and selling them as sex slaves?"

Ezra thought about it briefly, then shrugged and said, "It was a living and a good one at that."

"But look at you now," I said, holding my arms. "Don't you have any regrets?"

Ezra ran his fingers through his slicked-back hair and said, "What good would feeling sorry for myself help me now?"

"You're pitiful," I said.

"Hey, you're no one to talk to either," he said. "Talk to the others," he added, sweeping a hand. "That guy over there was a serial killer, and that one murdered thirteen children in a school. They're rapists, terrorists, and—"

"Stop! I get the idea."

"So now it's your turn," Ezra said, cocking his chin toward me. "What hideous sin are you guilty of?"

"It's not what you think."

"Ah, it's that bad? Now you piqued my interest."

I showed him my palm. "That's enough for now," I said, gazing down at the ice-glazed surface I remained encased within.

"Maybe later, Sam, when you get bored," Ezra said, twisting his body back around. "And trust me, you'll experience such dullness sooner than later; your mind will explode."

I imagined that the realm's monotony and emptiness fueled this desolate boredom he referred to. A future filled with a meaningless existence, accompanied by experiences of apathy, helplessness, and despair. I closed my eyes and released an exasperated sigh as my sanity descended into the desperate void.

*

The drone of cries, shouts, and moans never ceased, not even for a moment. My only distraction was watching the pained, contorted faces of my neighbors. There were all types; old and young, male and female, attractive and hideous. But the one thing we all had in common was our utterly helpless entanglement.

Occasionally, the steps reappeared, a sign Oriphiel was about to usher down a new wicked soul. Of course, this was an event of great interest, and we all gawked as the dark angel buried the newly condemned waist-deep alongside the rest of us.

Depending on the whim of the dark angel, the appearance of the steps occurred either nearby or at other times at a great distance. Amid the vastness of the Frozen Wasteland, there were instances when it was so far away, we could not witness the deposit of the new soul. We only knew it occurred because of the communication network of souls, which reminded me of the game telephone. By the time the information about who was buried reached us, it was twisted, distorted, and demented, which is what one would expect of despicable riffraff.

Between these arrivals, my thoughts drifted back to that decisive moment when I chose death rather than continuing my life. In retrospect, I wish I hadn't succumbed to the misguided allure of the peace offering, as nothing of my journey had been easy. And now it appeared I'd screwed up my death and eventual birth due to my circumstance. Though this depressing thought did little to quash my fantasies of what a new life would be like. I imagined reuniting with my wife and family and having a second chance to make things right. But at this point, as I was stuck in the fifth realm of Gehenna, moving on was no longer possible.

The steps appeared during one of my many musings about my hopeless existence. This was the only time the voices, cries, and moans all ceased in delightful anticipation. Within that brief silence, I saw Moshe cupping his hand behind his ear as if waiting for me to call him.

Then, just as quickly, the image vanished and was replaced with the sight of the dark angel spreading his enormous black wings and, with one mighty flap, rising from the staircase and taking flight. The angel soared in great sweeping circles over his kingdom of the fallen. The infinite number of heads turned round and round, tracking Oriphiel. Once satisfied he had gathered the flock's attention, he landed near where Pincus, Gray, and I were plotted.

"Greetings, residents of Tohu," he began as he withdrew his wings.

"Residents?" I repeated with a grimace.

"I'm aware of your distress. But I want you to know that your presence within this realm, your sacrifice, will do much for the betterment of humanity. Though this may be hard to accept, you all possess a powerful spiritual drive that can fuel the creative process and inspire new ideas and innovations to benefit humanity."

With those words, and for the first time since my arrival, the community of souls exploded in uncontrollable laughter.

Visibly angered at the public mocking, Oriphiel raised his wings and shouted, "Silence!"

Then once more, all was quiet, except for the ice cracking.

"I understand your feelings of abandonment and hopelessness, which, by the way, you all deserve," he said, pointing at the vista. "For these crimes you've committed are the most egregious against humanity. But within the chaotic nature of your deeds, you have provided an impetus for positive change by forcing those who dwell within this realm to confront their limitations. This, in turn, opens doors to new avenues for spiritual development and the advancement of human consciousness."

"What a bunch of crap," shouted a bitter soul from somewhere far off.

"It's hard to comprehend how all of you, the worst of the worst of humanity, have played an integral role in the larger spiritual process of human evolution," Oriphiel said, ignoring the insult. "Even during the earth's darkest moments, this process has led to a deeper understanding of the human condition, and ultimately a greater appreciation for the interconnectedness of all beings."

I shared a look with Gray and Pincus and said, "Is he serious?"

Gray shook his head and held out his hands, expressing our collective helplessness.

CHAPTER THIRTY-EIGHT
THE *TZADDIK*

We'd seen Oriphiel several more times since his sermon. During those subsequent appearances, he focused on planting fresh souls in his vast frozen soul garden rather than educating us about his lofty aspirations, at least for now.

After a while, we figured out how to use these visits to measure the passage of time by devising a system of tapping out a steady beat on the ice. Pincus, Gray, and I would take turns, one of us knocking our knuckles while the other counted the regular taps. This not only kept us amused, but after numerous attempts, we could anticipate the approximate arrival of the next soul. Lately, we figured it to be between 2,000 and 2,200 taps.

It was during one of these calculations, when we calculated with surprising accuracy at 2,030 taps, the portal appeared. We laughed and slapped each other's backs. But instead of seeing Oriphiel arriving with another undesirable, we saw Moshe grasping Solomon by his neck and shoving him down the staircase.

I nearly popped myself free from my bondage and shouted, "Moshe!"

The *tzaddik* pushed the *rasha* down to the tundra. Solomon, visibly distressed, collapsed onto all fours, cowering from Moshe. "Please don't do this," Solomon pleaded, holding up a crooked arm.

I couldn't believe my eyes. My great-grandfather stood just a few feet away, towering over the groveling gangster.

"Oriphiel," Moshe called out. "Take this evil being and plant him among his peers. In exchange, I demand the release of Samuel, Pincus, and Gray. Do this now."

This ruckus invigorated the population, who adored Moshe's audacity, cheering him on.

As I wondered if Oriphiel was even aware of the intrusion, the dark angel appeared.

"How dare you violate my realm, *tzaddik*," Oriphiel said, settling down alongside the commotion.

"I am here by the will of Michael!"

"The archangel," I said, raising my eyebrows.

"Ha," Oriphiel said. "The mighty one holds no sway here."

"Nonsense," Moshe said, his grip tightening around Solomon's skinny neck.

"I will prove it to you," Oriphiel said, spreading his wings and bringing them together swiftly, forming a canopy of darkness. Then a sudden blast of an icy breeze smacked me across my face, forcing me to shut my eyes.

"Argh!" Moshe called out.

When I opened them, to my horror, I saw my great-grandfather buried waist-deep between me and Pincus. "Oh, no!" I cried out.

"So once again, *tzaddik*, you've failed," Solomon said, back on his feet and towering over our half-height size.

"You underestimate me, Oriphiel," Moshe said, pointing the finger at the dark angel.

"Well, this should put an end to you, *tzaddik*, along with the rest of you misfits," Solomon said with a satisfied smirk.

I looked over to Moshe, who seemed surprisingly calm, considering our predicament. "What are we going to do?" I asked.

Moshe shut his eyes, clasped his hands together, rocked them back and forth, and said, "Michael is victorious before me, and the angels of Hashem sing praise. Michael is a mighty warrior before me, and the angels of Hashem sing praise. Michael is of great stature before me, and the angels of Hashem sing praise."

After several repetitions of this chant, the ground shook violently, cracking the ice around us. Then a bright blue light shone above, and the golden archangel emerged with a sword. Michael settled his presence just above us, though still hovering. Then he reared back his sword of fire and swung it down, striking the surface of the Frozen Wasteland, and spoke these words:

"By the power of the Divine, and as a protector against wickedness, I strike you down, *rasha*, and condemn you to an eternity within this icy realm of the Frozen Wasteland."

Within an instant, I was freed from my bondage and rushed upwards. As if in a wind tunnel, I passed swiftly through all the realms, catching only a glimpse of each one. Once again, I stood alongside Moshe, Pincus, and Gray in the Valley of the Shadow of Death.

"What just happened?" I said, looking around for the archangel.

"You've completed your quest, Samuel," Moshe said.

"I have?" I asked.

Moshe rubbed a hand on my back and said, "You've accomplished a great deed. The soul world is celebrating. You've seen the last of Valley of the Shadow of Death, at least in your beforelife."

"Beforelife?"

"The word *afterlife* no longer seems appropriate," Moshe said, wagging a finger. "You've been purified and ready to move on, readying yourself for the next part of your journey toward birth."

"I better be," I said. "I've been through all five realms of Gehenna."

"So have we," Gray said, patting Pincus's shoulder.

"That's true. We're the three purified amigos!" I said as our group of unlikely heroes broke out into belly laughs.

"That's funny," Pincus said, still chuckling.

I sighed and asked, "So what now?"

Moshe held out his hands and said, "You'll leave this place and move on to the planetary spheres."

"Will I see any of you again?" I asked, looking at Moshe, Pincus, and Gray.

"You may see me while you're still in the soul world, but not again on Earth," Moshe said.

"That's because you're *tzaddik*," I said, remembering my great-grandfather's elevated status among the souls.

Moshe nodded. "You may have some future connection with Pincus, as you're from the same soul family."

"But what about Gray?" I asked.

"That's hard to say, as you met in the soul world. But it's possible."

I flipped a hand toward Pincus and said, "But we also met here."

"It's because you and Pincus share a portion of your genetic code, which connects you two based on our spiritual memory."

"Well, anyway, it's been good knowing you, Gray. Thank you for looking out for my great-grandfather."

"I'm glad it worked out for all of us," Gray said.

I then turned to Pincus. "It's been an honor meeting you, and I hope we cross paths again in our future lives."

"Samuel," Pincus said, stepping forward and wrapping his skinny arms around me. "I'm proud of you. Our soul family is proud of you; you bring me such *nachas*."

"That word I know," I said. "My father used it in his speech at my wedding; it means you're proud of me."

"We all are," Moshe said.

"Thank you," I said. "But it was you who rescued us."

"If you hadn't dared to push through to the Frozen Wasteland, I would have never had the chance."

"Are you saying you were waiting for me?" I asked.

Moshe smiled. "It was all part of the plan."

"Plan?" I said with a grimace. "What do you mean?"

"This quest of yours; everything occurred as it was intended."

"You knew what was going to happen?"

Moshe smiled, put a hand on my shoulder, and said, "Remember, time in the soul world is not linear. Think of it as being within the eternal present, where all events and experiences are accessible at any moment."

I closed my eyes and shook my head. "That's hard to imagine."

"Where you are going, Samuel, you won't need to imagine it," Moshe said with a warm smile.

CHAPTER THIRTY-NINE
MOTHER OF *TZADDIK*

"Come with me, Samuel," Moshe said, summoning me with a wave. "I want to show you something."

"What about Gray and Pincus?" I asked, turning back to look for them. But they had already vanished. "Where'd they go?"

"Oh, they've begun their journey among the planets, as you will now," Moshe said, taking long strides and gazing straight ahead.

"But I didn't get a chance to say goodbye."

"There's no need; you can reach out to them anytime in the soul world. As souls, we are composed of finer substances, allowing us to communicate and interact with each other through thought forms. It's like some form of spiritual perception."

"Does that mean I'll finally be done with my body?"

Moshe nodded. "In some spheres, you may still need the illusion."

"There were times, in the Clay of Yaven and especially in the Frozen Wasteland, when my body nearly caused my demise. I'll be relieved when it is totally gone."

"Hold up," Moshe said, stopping short. "We'll wait for her here."

"Wait for who?" I asked, looking out onto a vast silver plain.

I didn't realize the change in the surroundings as we walked away from the Valley of the Shadow of Death. No longer were we in the passageway between the two towers of the black stone mountains. Instead, we stood upon a flat landscape, stretching out to the horizon far in all directions, the sky donned in the same silver as the soil beneath our feet.

"Just a moment; she's coming," Moshe said, pointing ahead.

Off into the distance, there was a disturbance. First, it seemed to be nothing more than shimmering vapors. But as I started, it transformed into the shape of a female body. She had a pale round face with large brown eyes and brown hair that reached to her shoulders. She wore a tattered and faded blue and pink floral dress, reminding me of an outfit from an old Western movie. With each step closer, her form solidified.

"Samuel, this is Clara, my mother," Moshe said.

I stared at the woman, who looked about the same age as Moshe.

"It's good to meet you, Samuel," Clara said, kissing my cheek gently. "I've been looking forward to this moment."

"I was just with your husband, Pincus," I said, jerking my thumb behind me.

Clara wagged a finger. "Oh, he's no longer my husband."

"But what about this whole thing I heard about soulmates?"

"Sadly," Clara said, shaking her head, "I've decided to move on."

"You can do that?" I asked, looking over to Moshe.

"Of course," Clara said with a chuckle. "Pincus waited too long to come for us due to his greed and inflated ego, and I can never forgive him after what happened to my children and me."

"But he was purified in Gehenna five times," I said, pointing off into the distance. "Isn't that worthy of spiritual forgiveness?"

Clara sighed and nodded. "The soul world may have forgiven Pincus, but I have not."

"Wow," I said.

"Mother is here to escort you to the next stage of your journey. To the remaining six planetary spheres, leading to your rebirth."

"But you're so much older than I am," I said, gesturing to Clara. "Shouldn't you have been reborn by now?"

"Our soul family is most interested in your journey. I've decided to stay longer to see you through," Clara said.

"Clara also can protect you," Moshe said.

"But I thought we were done with the *rasha*."

"Yes, that's true. Solomon won't be a bother to us any longer. But there are other dangers in the soul world, all looking to get their hands on someone like you," Moshe said.

"This is why we mustn't delay seeing you through the spheres. Moshe was able to rescue you from Gehenna, but things get more challenging among the planets. But don't worry," Clara said, placing her hand on my shoulder. "I promise to keep you safe."

"But you're not *tzaddik*," I said. What if I needed Moshe's protection, not his mother's?

"Ah, Samuel," Clara said, holding out her arms. "As a mother of a *tzaddik*, I come from a spiritual lineage tracing back to the biblical matriarchs of Sarah, Rebecca, Rachel, and Leah. These were powerful women whose prayers and spiritual merit had a tremendous impact on humanity. And most importantly, as the mother of the *tzaddik*, I birthed the light of the Divine presence into the world."

I swallowed hard, pointed to Moshe, and observed him in awe for the first time as I would an archangel.

"That's right."

"How did you learn this about yourself?"

Clara pointed into the silver sky and said, "On a similar journey you're about to embark upon. Who knows, Samuel, what you may discover about yourself."

Before I could say goodbye, Moshe vanished, leaving me and Clara alone on the expansive landscape. "He's gone," I said, holding up my arms. "It's going to take a while to get used to this."

"You are no longer of body, Samuel," Clara said.

I waved a hand to Clara and asked, "Then why do I still see you?"

"I see you too," Clara said, offering a similar gesture. "It's called spiritual sight."

"Which is?"

"Spiritual sight enables us to interact, and our thoughts are the engine that brings us together."

"I don't understand."

"If I want to interact with you, my desire alerts you. If you agree, we're together, and when our business is done, we're done."

"Where do I go?"

"Onward and upward," she said, pointing into the clouds.

I puckered my mouth, trying to comprehend.

Clara smiled. "You'll see soon enough."

Unsure, I bit my lower lip and nodded.

"Would you like a vision of what's to come?"

"Aren't I going to the planets?"

"That's right, and at each of these spheres, you'll study the karmic patterns from your previous lives and learn how to transform them to achieve your spiritual growth and evolution."

I blinked. "All that's possible?"

Clara placed her warm hand against my cheek and said, "It is, and rest assured, you won't do this alone. Throughout your journey, you'll be guided by many types of beings, including angels, archangels, and the Divine source of all existence."

"Oh no," I said, holding up my hands. "I've had enough of the angels."

Clara laughed. "You're funny, Samuel. It's such a joy having you here."

"Thank you," I said, taking a breath. "So what's next?"

"You need to move on to Mercury."

"What's it like?"

Clara wagged her head back and forth. "As you know, these planets can be tricky after passing through the Moon sphere."

"What are you saying?" I asked, wide-eyed.

"I wouldn't worry," Clara said, hearing my thoughts. "You've done well so far."

I sighed. "I thought the worst was behind me."

"Oh, what's to come is not bad," Clara said. "Though it will take the best of your wits to maneuver through it. But you'll do fine if you stay focused on your goal."

"My goal?" I said, looking into her blue eyes. "You mean my rebirth?"

Clara shrugged. "Isn't that what you're working toward?"

"Yes, but I never considered it a goal." I squinted.

"That's what this is all about. Moving you through the soul world, preparing you for your next incarnation."

"I understand."

"Good," she said, patting my back. "Would you like to see where you'll be going? A glimpse into the cosmos."

My eyes widened. "Sure, I'd like that."

~ ACT III ~

CHAPTER FORTY
THE COSMOS

Clara shut her eyes, clasped her hands, and brought them to her chest. She paused a moment, then opened them and looked upwards. I followed her gaze to what looked like a rip in the silver sky, offering a glimpse of the star-lit galaxy beyond. As I gawked, the tear widened, growing larger and larger until there was no silver sky left, just the infinite depth of the cosmos. A canvas of stunning, brilliant colors featuring mesmerizing blood-red swirls mingling with indigo blotches. Beyond that were bright pinpoints of sparkling lights populating the depths.

"It's breathtaking," I said, tilting my head back and my jaw hanging open.

"Do you see that?" Clara asked.

I shifted my eyes to follow Clara's outstretched arm. "See what?"

"The blue star?"

"That one there?" I asked, pointing.

"It's the closest one," she said.

"Yes, I see it."

"That's Mercury, where you'll move on to next. And that green star over there," she said, swinging her arm. "That's Venus."

"Oh, right."

"The sun is easy to find," she said, jerking a hand at the golden glow directly overhead.

"How's it possible to visit the sun?" I asked.

"Oh, you won't be on the sun as you know it," Clara said.

"Then where will I be?"

"You'll be where you need to be. Right now, you're in the Moon sphere. While this appears real to you," Clara said, tapping her foot on the gravel surface, "it's a creation of our soul's collective imagination. Useful for your journey."

"So it's the same for all souls?"

"Oh no. Though the planet's purpose remains similar, our visits differ, depending on our karmic patterns and the transformation we require."

"How is all of this possible?"

"The planetary spheres exist because of the interplay of cosmic forces, Divine wisdom, and the harmonious order of the universe."

"*Mmm,*" I murmured, trying to comprehend the scope of her words.

"Let me show you the rest," Clara said. "Though they're a little harder to make out, as they're great distances from here."

"Please, show me."

"Well, you see that red star there? That's Mars. And that lovely violet-colored one, nestled among the white ones, it's Jupiter. Lastly, there's Saturn. It's like a hidden gem with its deep indigo hue, almost blending into the sky."

I couldn't help but return my gaze to the sun, feeling an undeniable pull.

Noticing this magnetic connection, Clara said, "Souls are drawn to the sun because it's our ultimate source of energy and vitality."

"Just like on Earth," I remarked and thought a moment. "Except the living don't seem to have the same experiences with the planets as souls do."

"Excellent observation," Clara said. "The living experience the planets primarily through their life body, in a physical way. Many see them as nothing more than objects in the sky. But these planets have unique qualities for the souls, which are important to our karmic paths, each of which you will soon experience."

I wagged a finger. "But what about those who have a strong belief in astrology? Doesn't that mean the planets influence the living, more than just objects to observe in the sky?"

"I stand corrected, Samuel. Yes, the planets can significantly affect human consciousness and spiritual development. Astrology, used as a tool, can assist in understanding the living's association and personnel effects emanating from certain planets. Yet, it must be tempered with discernment, as some get carried away with its perceived influence."

"My sign was Sagittarius," I said. "Which planet is that related to?"

"Jupiter," Clara said, pointing to the violet star.

"That's a long way off," I said.

"Jupiter is where you'll achieve your spiritual awakening. A key stage before your birth."

"How long will it take to get there?"

"As you should know by now, nothing is measured by time or distance. Rather, we measure by the soul's acquisition of knowledge and wisdom. Here in the moon stage, you focus on the emotional aspects of your existence. Keeping you deeply rooted in the physical and material dimensions of reality."

"Oh, you mean like my visit to the realms of Gehenna?"

"Exactly!" Clara said. "Though once you reach Jupiter and eventually Saturn, you will have developed your intuition, wisdom, and spiritual vision."

I furrowed my brow and asked, "What's spiritual vision?"

Clara furrowed her brow for a moment, then said, "Spiritual vision is how souls perceive reality in a more comprehensive way than what's possible during our earthly life."

"Is that because souls are not limited by time and space constraints?"

Clara's eyes bulged, followed by a huge smile. "That's wonderful, Sam. You're one hundred percent correct. A soul's spiritual vision allows us to perceive the realities underlying all of creation and, in turn, connect more deeply with the Divine."

I took a breath and slowly exhaled. "Well, I guess I'm ready to move on. How do souls travel to Mercury?"

Clara held out her hands, smiled, and said, "I think you know by now."

CHAPTER FORTY-ONE
MERCURY

I found the blue star, and following Clara's instructions, I expressed my desire to transport myself to the distant planet. Then, before I could turn back toward my great-great-granny, I was perched upon a rocky cliffside, overlooking the tops of pine trees and a magnificent lake far below. Above me, capping this mountain, was a fresh coating of pure white snow, even though the warmth from the sun shining down upon me felt as if it was midsummer.

My first thought was that I had transported myself to the wrong place. In the soul world, the mountains on Mercury appeared similar to the magnificent peaks of Alaska. But as Clara said, visiting the planets was more about developing my intuition, wisdom, and spiritual vision than its perceived appearance.

Since I was put on a mountaintop, I assumed my purpose was to descend. I searched for a trail, but the foliage was too thick to see beyond the trees. The only way to find my way down was to explore. So I turned from the cliffside and headed downhill.

My first impression of the planet was a pleasant one. A cool breeze rustled through the trees, offering comfort from the brilliant sunshine breaking through the gaps of the evergreens. The air smelled of dirt and pine, an earthly reminder of what I avoided during my lifetime and a practice I planned to remediate in my next incarnation.

I continued what seemed to be the only pathway down the mountain, skirting around large rocky outcroppings and across an open plateau that offered an expansive and breathtaking view of the lake. Still trying to figure out my purpose, I decided to pause here and contemplate.

A large boulder offered shade from the midday sun and a comfortable backrest to lean against. While I sat comfortably, trying to drum up scenarios of what could lie ahead, I heard gravel scattering behind me. I scrambled to my feet, and just as I did, the deep rumbling of a growl penetrated through my bones. Cautiously, I peeked around the boulder and saw, poised a few feet away, an enormous lion with shapely, golden eyes locked onto mine.

But nothing happened as I stood there, my arms limp by my side. The ferocious creature did not viciously attack me. Instead, the lion cautiously crept closer and, from its height, gazed down upon me, my eyes barely reaching its brown and golden striped neck. I tilted my face upwards until my nose met its black snout and two long, yellowed fangs overlapping its lower jaw. I could smell its sweet breath. While I remained frozen in fear, the lion sniffed.

As my legs wobbled, the large cat lost interest and turned away. I watched its backside and the joyful swaying of its long tail disappear into the shadows of the trees.

Relieved from whatever harm was possible by confronting a lion in the soul world, I scrambled and charged down the trail. I scampered over protruding stones, exposed thick tree roots, and patches of green and yellow moss. I stopped when I came to a rock scramble along the mountain's ledge.

I knew it wasn't possible to feel exhaustion or to be hampered by any other physical limitations, but I did find myself being challenged. Could the purpose of this planet be one of evaluating my problem-solving ability? I have always had a keen sense of thinking logically and systematically about complex issues, thereby arriving at well-reasoned conclusions based on sound evidence and reasoning. But I had never faced dilemmas at the scale I did in Gehenna and now on Mercury.

Unsure of how to proceed, I continued my downhill journey, hoping to come up with an idea of what to do next. I noticed no bird songs or other sounds typically heard in the mountains. As I pondered the eerie silence, a vibrating growl filled the void. Swiftly I spun around and saw the lion again staring at me off in the distance.

I swallowed hard and took several steps backward. Though with each stride, the beast also advanced. Allowing fear to take control, I turned and ran without knowing if I was vulnerable to a vicious attack.

I dodged trees and bushes while the lion pursued. Just as I felt its hot breath burning the back of my neck, the ground gave way, and I plummeted into a hole. I fell hard into the dugout and spun around, waiting for the lion to pounce on me. But the big cat remained safely above, gazing down, its glistening tongue swinging from its open jaws.

The lion paced along the perimeter, seemingly contemplating ways of reaching me without trapping itself. Realizing there was no chance of having me as its next meal, the man-eater gave up and let me be.

I exhaled, relieved I no longer had a wild mountain lion interested in me. But I was still stuck in a ten-foot-deep hole with no apparent way out. But then I remembered I could beckon another soul. All I had to do was to express the desire, and if the other party agreed, we would meet.

Not sure how this was done, I closed my eyes and said, "Clara, I need to speak with you."

Now on my feet, I paced the circular ten-foot round hole, waiting for something to happen. But nothing did. "Clara," I tried again, "I'm not sure how this works." And it didn't work. Maybe she declined my invitation. Moshe said the meeting would only take place if the other party accepted. "Moshe, can you hear me?" Again, nothing. I tried Gray and then Pincus. No reply.

I knew no one else except a few poor souls trapped in Gehenna. Then it occurred to me—Poppy. I closed my eyes, held my hands together, and rather than speaking it aloud, I thought of my grandfather. *Poppy, I have a desire to talk with you.*

"Sam," Poppy said as I spun around, seeing my grandfather poised before me.

"You're here," I said, reaching out and clutching him.

"It seems you got yourself into a bind," Poppy said, returning the embrace.

"I'm so glad you heard me. I tried Clara, Moshe, Gray, and even Pincus, and no one wanted to speak with me."

Poppy shook his head. "They probably never heard your call."

"But why not?"

"On this planet, there are beings who control things," Poppy said, lifting his brow. "They can block desires."

"Beings?" I asked. "What sort of beings?"

"They are known as the Spirits of Mercury."

"Are these Spirits of Mercury souls?" I asked, shaking my head.

"Oh no, they're more like the angels. They're part of the hierarchies of beings."

"What do they do?"

"Their purpose is to inspire and guide souls that visit this sphere by helping them understand complex ideas and concepts." Poppy then took a moment to glance upwards to the top of the hole we remained stuck in and said, "There's been talk that these spirits are involved with the development of the human nervous system, which is essential for the processing of thoughts and ideas."

I grimaced. "How's that possible?"

"I don't know," Poppy said with a shrug. "But they've been at it for a long while, helping humans develop greater mental clarity, creativity, and intelligence."

"That's what happens to the souls coming to Mercury?"

"That's right," Poppy said. "Now, let's see how we can get ourselves out of this hole."

"One second," I said. "Why would they allow me to call out to you, not the others?"

"I'm not sure. But I know that the Spirits of Mercury don't do anything without a good reason. Are you ready to meet them?"

I nodded.

"Let's do this—"

"One last question," I said, interrupting my grandfather. "The last time I saw you was before I entered Gehenna. Why are you back?"

"You required my presence," Poppy said, sweeping his arms. "Do you want me to go?"

"Oh no," I said, wrapping my arms around my grandfather. "I was just surprised. I'm thrilled you're here."

"Me too," Poppy said. "Now, let's close our eyes and make our desires known to the Spirits of Mercury."

CHAPTER FORTY-TWO
THE LIBRARY

When I opened my eyes, I stood in a massive library, surrounded by tall towers of wooden bookshelves that vanished into a sky filled with purple and yellow pulsating stars.

"Where are we?" I asked.

Poppy gestured to the innumerable volumes of books and said, "This is the Spirits of Mercury's archives."

"I've never seen so many books," I said, tilting my head back, gawking at the massive display of row upon row of bookshelves.

"All of the universal knowledge is stored within these volumes," Poppy said, sweeping an arm across the vast walls.

"Do souls come here to learn?"

Poppy nodded, wide-eyed. "Mercury is where souls enhance their intellectual skills."

"Intellectual skills?" I asked with a furrowed brow. "Then why did that lion chase me? That hardly felt like a lesson in intellectual skills."

"Oh, I disagree," Poppy said, holding a finger. "Your smarts are most necessary when being chased by a voracious beast. You needed to think and reason effectively and keep mental clarity and focus. If you panicked, you wouldn't have escaped."

"But I fell into a hole," I said, cocking my chin forward. "Trust me; there was nothing calm about it."

"Survival is a cherished instinct ingrained within our essence, here in the soul world and on Earth. Never diminish its importance."

I looked around and saw no one. "So when do I meet these Spirits of Mercury?"

"They'll appear when they see fit."

I gazed at the leather-bound books, all neatly arranged, and asked, "Am I supposed to study?"

"A soul's education is unlike what you remember on Earth. You won't need to read or take tests; instead, you'll absorb the required knowledge."

"Oh," I said, glancing. "That sounds much easier than sitting in a classroom and doing homework."

"All right, Sam. I'm going to leave you now. You know how to reach out if you find yourself in need."

I nodded. "Yes, I do. Thank you, Poppy," I said, giving him one last hug before his image vanished.

Truthfully, I still had a hard time accepting the reality of my imagined body. If I understood fully, I should have been able to avoid being chased by a lion. Hopefully, by the time I've reached Saturn, I will have figured it out.

While waiting on the Spirits of Mercury, I wandered around the library. Huge, thick wooden tables were arranged in a particular order, reminding me of the New York Public Library on Fifth Avenue. These tables were twice as long and accompanied by oversized matching chairs.

I approached one of the bookshelves and saw a three-volume set. Each book was bound in a different leather color; its titles were embossed with gold-leaf letters. The first one read—THE IMPORTANCE OF INNER TRANSFORMATION, and the next one was—THE POWER OF SPIRITUAL KNOWLEDGE. And the last one's title was—THE VALUE OF SPIRITUAL DISCIPLINE.

I removed *The Importance of Inner Transformation* and brought it to the oak table. I sat down, lifted the sturdy brown leather cover, and as I thumb-flipped the pages, I saw they were all blank. Curious, I did the same with the remaining two volumes and found similar empty pages.

"I suppose you're wondering why there are no words," a voice said behind me.

I twisted around and saw a tall figure crowned with a halo of woven golden branches, carrying a long staff embellished with a carving of two entwined serpents and featuring a pair of golden angel wings at its top.

"Greetings, Samuel," the figure said, donned in a shimmering navy-blue robe cinched at its waist with an emerald green belt.

I quickly pushed back the chair and got to my feet. "Who are you?" I asked.

The being, at least a full head taller than me, said. "My name is Raphael. I've come to teach you the three lessons."

"Are you a Spirit of Mercury?" I asked.

Raphael laughed. "Oh, no. The Spirits of Mercury are shy beings who hardly ever make their presence known, though they like to play pranks on the souls passing through."

"You can say that again. A ferocious lion chased me."

"I saw that," Raphael said. "My apologies."

I ran my fingers through my hair and sighed. "Oh, it's fine," I said.

"I understand you had quite an adventure in Gehenna."

"You know about that too?" I asked.

"Of course. As an archangel, I see all."

"You're an archangel like Michael?" I asked, wide-eyed.

"I am, Samuel."

"So Mercury is your place?" I said, spreading out my arms.

Raphael nodded. "I provide souls with guidance and inspiration to awaken their higher spiritual nature and make them aware of the interconnectedness of all things."

"But what about these books?" I asked, gesturing to the three heavy volumes lying on the table.

"Let's sit," the archangel said. "And I'll explain each one."

"Before you do that," I said, sitting across from Raphael. "Can you tell me where archangels come from?"

Raphael smiled, which caused his eyes to sparkle. "You are, as your reputation precedes you, an interesting soul."

I put my hand over my chest and said, "I have a reputation?"

"Oh, indeed you do!" Raphael said with glee. "You're the talk among the hierarchies. You and your cohorts are the first souls ever to make it through all five realms of Gehenna. Quite an accomplishment, especially after you escaped from the Frozen Wasteland."

"No one has ever freed themselves from the Frozen Wasteland?" I asked, wide-eyed.

Raphael nodded and said, "Now, let me answer your question. Where do archangels come from?"

I leaned forward and rested my elbows on the table.

"The universe is composed of hierarchies; these beings are involved with the ongoing spiritual evolution of the universe, including the earthly ones and their souls," he said, pointing at me.

"Okay," I said, cupping my hands under my chin.

"Archangels, angels, the Spirits of Mercury, and the others have emerged from the Divine realms at the beginning of creation, and since then, we've developed our abilities throughout cosmic history. Our purpose is to support the ongoing evolution of the universe."

"Wow, that's quite a responsibility," I said.

Raphael wagged his head. "There's much at stake."

"What does that mean?" I asked with a furrowed brow. "Do archangels have enemies?"

"Occasionally, we encounter the adversarial spiritual beings known as the *asuras*."

"Who are they?" I asked.

"The *asuras* are entities opposed to our work of advancing the progress of human spiritual development, and they're negative forces influencing and manipulating human consciousness. While the archangels strive to uplift humanity and foster spiritual development, the *asuras* try to divert souls from their spiritual path by hindering their connection with higher realms of consciousness."

"How do you stop them?"

"Oh," Raphael said with a shifting brow. "By wielding the forces of wisdom, love, and truth."

"Ah," I said, wondering how effective such weapons were.

"That's enough about the *asuras*. Would you like to learn what's in these volumes?"

"Yes," I said, patting my palm on one of the books before me. "Teach me what I need to know."

Raphael reached out with his long, slender fingers and picked up the first one. He spun it around and read its title, "The Importance of Inner Transformation. The lessons within here are associated with the soul's need to rid itself of *negative karma*."

"Negative karma?" I said with a grimace. "What's that?"

Raphael leaned back, crossed his arms over his slender chest, and said, "Negative karma is the result of one's actions, thoughts, or words that generate negative energy, resulting in unfortunate consequences in a soul's previous lifetimes."

"Lifetimes? You mean I need to deal with actions not only from this past lifetime?" I said, pointing behind me.

Raphael nodded. "Your karmic patterns go back many lifetimes, and you will confront them again if you don't deal with them in the soul world."

"Like what? What are examples of negative karma?"

Raphael held out his clenched hand and unrolled his fingers one at a time with each word. "Lying, stealing, jealousy, anger, engaging in unethical behavior. You get the idea."

I nodded. "Yeah, I get it."

"Your visit here is a process of what I like to call inner alchemy. It's a way to burn away your negative karma, and you want to ensure you're clean before moving on. The Spirits of Mercury guide and support this by navigating the complex energies of this planet to gain greater insight and understanding."

"All right," I said, taking a breath. "What about this one—*The Power of Spiritual Knowledge*?"

"Mercury is the sphere associated with higher knowledge and understanding. Within this volume," Raphael said, tapping the book, "you'll learn the workings of the universe and the nature of the Divine. It's how you'll gain a deeper appreciation for the mysteries of existence and the potential of the human spirit."

I shook my head. "This all sounds amazing. But does any of this information stay with me upon my birth?"

"That depends. For most souls, little of it remains. Hopefully, you'll carry some of it forward. Maybe the next book will help," Raphael said, flipping open *The Value of Spiritual Discipline*.

As I watched, the archangel slid his fingertips across the blank page as if reading the words. "Here, you'll learn how Mercury's forces support the soul's development through discipline and focus and how to overcome the obstacles that prevent you from achieving your spiritual goals."

"How long does all of this take?"

Raphael shook his head. "You should realize by now that time has no meaning."

I nodded with a sigh. "Yes, this is what I keep being told. But I still don't understand how to get beyond my perception."

"It will happen for you, that I can promise."

"So, am I done here? On Mercury. Can I move on to Venus?"

Raphael wagged a finger and smiled. "Not until you do your work with the Spirits of Mercury."

I pointed to the three books and said, "I thought we did that here."

Raphael laughed. "All I did was place the knowledge within you, and it's up to the spirits to ensure you burn away your negative karma."

"But what about my purification in Gehenna? What was that?"

Raphael rocked his head sideways a few times, considering the question, then said, "Let me put it in an earthly way to help you understand. It's like going to the car wash. They wash the outside; maybe if you pay more, they vacuum the inside. A good cleaning, but not a great one. Unless, of course, you want to get your car professionally detailed. Then your car is not only washed, your engine is cleaned, a protective wax is applied, and all the crumbs are—"

"I get the idea," I said, holding up my hands. "So should I think of the five levels of Gehenna like a car wash and what's about to happen to me with the Spirits of Mercury as being detailed?"

"Exactly," Raphael said, clapping his hands together.

CHAPTER FORTY-THREE
HERMES

Massive weight machines, each the size of a car, along with hundreds of racks of dumbbells and barbells, row upon row of treadmills and bikes, filled an enormous gym, which felt even more significant with the reflections from the mirrored walls encircling it. I smiled, reminiscing about my visits to the fitness center, where I spent almost two hours daily.

"Ah, there you are, Sam," a young man said, tilting his head around a lat pull-down machine. "Are you ready for your workout?"

"Workout?"

"Sure, why not," he said, getting to his feet and approaching. "My name is Hermes."

I shook the man's hand, noticing his firm grip and muscular upper body. He wore a tight-fitting tank top that said PAIN IS WEAKNESS LEAVING THE BODY.

"Why would I work out when my body no longer exists?" I asked.

"Oh, it's just a way to pass the time while we chat."

"Are you one of the Spirits of Mercury?" I asked, watching him strolling over to the flat bench and placing forty-five-pound weights on each end of the barbell.

"Some say I'm the original one."

I wagged a finger and said, "Are you the same Hermes I learned about in school?"

Hermes lifted his brow and nodded. "You mean in your ancient Greek mythology class? Yes, that's me."

"Oh, I didn't realize your connection to Mercury," I said, sitting on the end of the bench while Hermes took a position behind the bar.

"It's because of my role as messenger. I meet many souls passing through Mercury," Hermes said. "Go on, Sam, lift it, and I'll spot you."

I lay back on the bench and reached up to the bar. "Messenger?" I said. "For who?"

"Oh, between souls like you and the Divine."

"Does the Divine have a message for me?"

Hermes shook his head. "No, but I was hoping you had one."

"What message would I have?"

"I don't know." Hermes shrugged. "Go ahead, give it a lift."

I gripped the bar, closed my eyes, breathed, and pushed. As the force of the weight engaged my arms and chest, I let loose a flood of emotion. "Oh," I moaned. "This feels so good."

"You know, Sam," Hermes said, as I pumped out ten reps. "When you were working out was when you were most healthy. Your body, mind, and soul were in a good place."

"This was my happy place," I said.

"That's what I want you to remember."

"Remember what?" I asked.

"How this feels for the next time."

"Do you mean my next life?"

Hermes nodded.

I swung my legs around and sat up. "I thought this was going to be about addressing my problems, and Raphael said something about how the Spirits will burn away my negative karma."

"That's exactly what we're doing, by focusing on the positive."

"But I can't work out all day, every day."

"No, no," Hermes said, shaking his head. "You must learn balance, Samuel. It's the key. This means integrating all aspects of the spiritual, intellectual, and physical, and it's the three-legged stool of life. Neglecting anyone leads to imbalances and disharmony."

I put my hand to my mouth and sighed. "I've neglected nature," I confessed.

Hermes nodded. "That's spiritual."

"So much to know," I said, exhaling a deep sigh.

"Just wait," Hermes said, pointing at me. "The best is yet to come."

I held my hands to my head and said, "How am I supposed to remember all of this?"

"These lessons learned are stored within your spiritual body, and they'll be there for you in your new incarnation."

"Spiritual body?" I said, jerking my head back. "There's another body?"

"Oh, it's the most important one. The spiritual body moves you beyond the physical world's limitations by connecting you with higher spiritual realities."

"Such as?"

"The higher spiritual realities refer to the dimensions of reality that are not accessible through one's rational mind. They exist beyond the physical world and are only accessible through direct spiritual experience."

"Which I can access in my next life," I said. "How's that possible?"

"I didn't say it was easy. You'll need to work on those aspects of your life to call upon your fourth body."

"My spiritual body."

"That's right," Hermes said with a bright-eyed smile.

Considering his words, I pursed my lips and said, "I've certainly had good teachers."

"Perfect," he said, slapping my back. "Interactions like ours will instill the lessons into your consciousness."

"I imagine there's more to learn," I said.

"You're going to like where you're going next. The planet Venus is one of my favorites. It's the cosmos's center of emotional intelligence, empathy, and compassion."

CHAPTER FORTY-FOUR
THE TEMPLE OF VENUS

I stood upon a wide promenade lined with rows of sculpted cypress trees, reaching at least twenty feet into the brilliant blue sky. Up ahead stood a magnificent Romanesque temple featuring a prominent pediment decorated with painted human figures in lively colors. Supporting it were columns crowned with Ionic-style capitals. The structure behind the elaborate entrance was spread wide, its roof covered with overlapping terracotta tiles. Inside, I saw a shadowed image of a giant statue.

I climbed the steps and passed through the immense, reeded marble columns into an open-air inner sanctuary. In its center stood a statue of a bronze-colored woman, at least twice my height. She had smooth-as-glass skin, full black lips, a perfectly shaped nose, and yellow eyes that sparkled like two sun stars.

Adding to her allure was a delicate headband of gold jewels that dangled at the edge of her pulled-back hairline. She wore iris-shaped earrings and an elaborate neckless collar crafted from bronze and gold metals. Her black dress glittered, seeming to exude light.

I remained in awe, observing the great deity, until I broke off my gaze and decided to explore the sanctuary. As I stepped away, a woman called, "Where are you going, Samuel?"

I turned and saw no one. "Who's there?"

"Up here," the voice said.

I looked up and saw the bronze figure staring back at me. "I thought you were a statue."

She turned to face me and held out her arms. "This was a statue until your arrival, and then I assumed its body and thought it would help your interaction with me."

"Who are you?" I asked, absorbed by her engaging, stunning face.

"My name is Haniel; welcome to the Temple of Venus," she said, spreading out her long, slender, bronze arms.

I looked around. "Are you here alone?"

"Samuel," she said, placing her hands on her hips. "You should know by now how things work."

I grimaced. "I guess I'm still a work in progress."

"Come, let's walk the garden. It's a lovely place," she said, taking long strides down the corridor.

I followed, nearly jogging to keep up.

We approached an archway that opened onto the greenest, lush garden I'd ever seen. Arrangements of colorful flowers in terraced beds surrounded fabulous fountains, spewing streams of turquoise water in interlocking arches.

"This is incredible," I said, as delightful bird songs provided a musical backdrop.

"Do you like it?" Haniel said.

"Oh yes, very much."

"That makes me happy," she said. "Come, let's sit by the waterfalls."

"Waterfalls?" I said, picking up my pace.

I followed Haniel through a field of cheerful sunflowers that soared several feet above my head. We passed bushes choked with roses the size of softballs. Farther ahead, we walked between fertile fields of lilacs until we arrived at the side of a cliff, where multiple streams of water rushed downward, crashing into a froth of a large lake.

"Let's sit here," she said, gesturing to a moss-covered embankment.

"Amazing," I said, sitting alongside her, bringing my knees to my chest.

"Welcome to Venus, Samuel."

"Thank you," I said, tilting my head to observe the majestic woman. "Are you an angel?"

"I'm an archangel," she said, gazing outwards.

"Oh, you're the third one I've met."

Haniel nodded. "I'm aware of your interactions with all the higher beings, and you've created quite a stir in the soul world since your arrival. We'll be sorry to see you go."

"Where am I going?"

Haniel looked at me with a squint. "Back home, eventually," she said.

"Home?"

"Yes, Samuel. Your home is on the Earth."

"Oh," I said with a squint. "I didn't know Earth was considered home."

Haniel nodded. "Earth is home for all living beings, and it's what orients your soul on your eternal spiritual journey. Staying connected to the earthly realm, and maintaining a deep reverence and respect for the natural world, allows you to move through the afterlife with greater clarity, purpose, and spiritual insight."

"Okay, that makes sense," I said.

"Good," she said. "What do you know about Venus?"

I shrugged and shook my head. "Nothing."

"Well," she began spreading her arms, "as you can see, Venus is the realm of beauty, harmony, and creativity."

"That's evident," I said.

"But besides the obvious, it's where souls are inspired to enhance their creativity, sensitivity, and emotional intelligence. A powerful force for one's healing and transformation."

"Mmm," I murmured.

"Was this an area where you were lacking?"

Impressed with her perception, I nodded. "Maybe in my creativity."

Haniel lay down, cupped her hands behind her head, and gazed upwards at the waterworks. "I don't want you to panic, Samuel. Because in a moment, you'll be taken by the Devas into their underground labyrinth."

I looked around, twisting my head back and forth, and asked wide-eyed, "Who will be taking me?"

No sooner had the last word left my mouth than the moss beneath me split open and I was swallowed into an abyss.

CHAPTER FORTY-FIVE
THE FAIRIES OF DEVAS

I landed on my back with a thud. Looking up, I watched the crevice I had fallen through close up like a clamshell, leaving in its place unruly tangled roots, crawling creatures, and edges of stones impacted within hardened dirt. I tried getting my feet but couldn't stand upright due to the low overhang.

Hunched way over, I looked around, and it appeared I was in what could best be described as a tunnel dug out by prairie dogs. I once saw an animal show about how these small, social rodents lived in large colonies in the grasslands, where they dug complex burrowed systems covering vast areas of multiple tunnels, chambers, and entrances.

"We're not prairie dogs," a high-pitched voice said.

"Excuse me?" I said, peering down the long tunnel for the source.

"Down here," the voice redirected me.

I lowered my eyes and saw a tiny person, no more than a few inches tall. "Who are you?"

The figure, dressed in a belted, hooded brown cloak, pointed to itself, and said, "Who me?"

I looked around, wondering if there were others, and said, "I don't see anyone else."

"Oh," the little man said, "you just need to look harder."

Then, dozens and dozens of similar-sized beings emerged from the tangled web of roots and networks of tendrils beneath my feet.

"Are you the Devas?" I asked.

"We are!" announced the greeter. "My name is Shee. Welcome to our underworld."

"Are you some sort of gnome?" I asked.

"Gnome?" Shee laughed, followed by the others, nearly falling hysterically at my absurd assumption.

"We're not gnomes," Shee said, wagging a finger. "We're fairies."

"Fairies?" I said with a smile.

"That's right," Shee said, flipping his beckoning hand. "We're the Fairies of Devas. Now, why don't you get closer so we can get a better look at you."

I dropped to my hands and knees.

"Closer," Shee demanded.

I lowered my head, bringing my nose inches away from the fairy.

"That's better," he said.

Not only could Shee see me better, but now I could observe this tiny person no taller than one of my fingers. Dressed in roughly textured garments of earthly, muddy colors, they were adorned with tiny bits of flowers and leaves, seemingly damp with shimmering dewdrops. Though their attire looked drab, their faces projected luminous, glowing features. Their skin and eyes emitted a subtle light, illuminating a magical presence.

"Why am I here?" I asked.

He raised a finger and said, "To help you remedy your broken connection with the natural world."

I scanned my eyes to the other fairies; all focused on me. "But aren't I too big to be down here?"

Shee wagged his itsy bitsy head and said, "I would have hoped you have figured that part out by now."

"Umm, should I become your size?" I said, waving a finger toward Shee and the others.

Shee nodded. "It's the only way we can move on."

I shrugged and said, "I'm not sure I know how."

"It's simple. Just express your desire, and it will be so. You've done this before."

"Yes," I said. "Clara taught me how."

Shee spread his tiny arms and said, "So what are you waiting for?"

While still on my hands and knees, I shut my eyes and said, "I desire to be the size of the Fairies of Devas."

When I opened them, I was still down on all fours, but now I needed to look up to see Shee's face.

"You did it," Shee said, gazing down at me. "Now, get up and follow me."

I got to my feet and looked around at the fairies, no longer looking like children's toys. They all wore brown hooded gowns, seemingly woven from some course straw. Though their attire was plain, their faces, like Shee's, exuded an illuminating glow, perhaps an expression of the universal wisdom they were about to impart.

"What are you waiting for?" Shee said, already walking ahead.

What was not visible before my resizing were dozens of burrowed-out tunnels in the walls surrounding us. One of which Shee had already vanished into. Assuming I was to follow, I stepped gingerly around the roots and rocks. It didn't take long to realize that the others were following me. One of the fairies caught up, touched my heart, and smiled. Assuming this was their greeting, I reciprocated, touching its heart, causing it to giggle like a small child, delighted at my endearing gesture.

The labyrinth wound up, down, and around in the underground habitat until we arrived at some earthen chamber. Besides its enormity, I took notice of its unique composition and formation. Instead of the familiar embrace of solid rock, typically found in a cavern, this space was enveloped in hardened earth.

As the fairies gathered around, I noticed a sense of tranquility enveloping me. The air smelled cool and fresh, with a hint of dampness and faint whispers of an ancient subterranean breeze, evoking a connection to the immortal age of this underground abode. Organically formed walls rose, their curves composed of compacted soil, clay, rocks, and roots. At the very top, beyond my reach, were crevices that allowed soft light to enter from the surface, creating shadows that danced upon the earthen walls, revealing intricate patterns and textures of lush vegetation, its roots interwoven with the soil.

"Gather close, everyone," Shee announced, standing upon an elevated mound of twisted sturdy roots.

The Fairies of Devas pushed forward, squeezing themselves closer and tighter.

"Samuel," Shee called out. "Come up here and join me."

Dozens of hands pushed me along, and before I knew it, I stood alongside Shee, the apparent leader of these fairies, overlooking the flock.

"This soul," Shee began wrapping an arm around my shoulder, "has come to us for a healing."

A buzz of hundreds of conversations ensued.

"As the Devas," Shee continued while holding up his arms to silence the assembly, "our realm oversees the growth and vitality of the plants, animals, and other living beings. Our efforts work in concert with nature's elementals and other spirits to maintain balance and harmony in the natural world. For over the past two hundred and sixty years, since the dawning of the Industrial Revolution, our work has been thrown into disarray, with humanity's devolving connection from the spiritual dimensions of existence. Through the exploitation of the Earth's natural resources, disruption of its ecosystems, fueled by the pursuit of personal gain, the accumulation of material wealth, unquenchable consumption, and immediate gratification at the expense of nature, we are witnessing the collapse of the natural world."

Shouts of agitated fairies shook the underground sanctuary, causing bits of the less-packed dirt to loosen from the canopy and rain down upon the congregants.

"Nevertheless, as Devas, we remain committed to seeking Earth's restoration, even if that means re-educating each soul, one by one, as they pass through our sphere."

Then, without warning, I was grabbed by several of the fairies and hustled off the stage.

"Where are you taking me?" I called out as I was carried through the crowd and ushered into an adjoining burrow.

I struggled to break free, but the grips of the fairies proved too strong.

"Let me go," I pleaded.

They ignored me as they bound my arms and legs to a dirt wall with thick roots the size of heavy rope. Then one of the fairies, perhaps a female, though it was hard to distinguish, placed a palm against my cheek and said, "There's no need to be afraid, Samuel."

Shee, with the others, left me behind. I continued to tug on my arms and legs, but the bindings wouldn't budge. I heard what sounded like whispers, but the words were foreign. I paused, trying to understand. Then, as if the roots awakened with an ancient hunger, I was sucked inside the earthen wall. The forest tendrils encircled me, slithering and writhing, coiling like wild serpents around my entire body.

Unusual insect-like creatures crawled on my skin, disappearing into my ears, nose, and mouth. I tried screaming but choked on some fuzzy, multi-legged bug sliding down my throat. I heard the buzzing of wings and rocks scraping as the earth around me shifted.

Then it stopped, leaving me trapped, like a prehistoric bug frozen in amber. *Will this be where my journey ends? Is this my punishment for disconnecting myself from the natural world?*

While I pondered my misfortune, a chorus of buzzing insects engulfed me, their relentless hum resonating in my ears. At first, I felt overwhelmed as the annoying things accosted my senses. But then something shifted. It was as if the roots that had captured me in their web let loose their grip, allowing me to calm myself and join them in a symbiotic bond.

In that transformative moment, the insects, once hideous, took on a newfound significance. Their delicate wings fluttered in harmony, their movements becoming an extension of my thoughts. They intertwined with my consciousness, merging with the forest web. I experienced a profound connection to the intricate dance of life unfolding around me.

The roots offered a newfound energy coursing within my being. The insect's melody filled my thoughts, their delicate wings carrying me deeper into their wonders. Thoughts flowed through my mind like whispers of ancient wisdom. I became a vessel of the forest's collective consciousness, embracing its secrets and wisdom.

In that extraordinary moment, I realized I was not merely an observer, but an integral part of the natural world. With a profound sense of unity and purpose, I understood the inherent harmony permeating all creation. A fantastical fusion connecting me to the Earth's eternal rhythms. Through this remarkable metamorphosis, I transcended the boundaries of my soulful form, embodying the essence of nature itself. With this epiphany, the earthly womb birthed me out into the burrow.

CHAPTER FORTY-SIX
THE GARDENS OF VENUS

"Ah, Samuel, you've returned," Haniel said as we stood within a lush garden designed in geometric patterns behind the temple.

"That was something," I said, brushing off remnants of dirt, twigs, and pebbles stuck in the creases of my shirt.

"Tell me, how do things look now," she said, sweeping her arm toward the serene landscape teeming with lush vegetation.

I breathed, taking in the vibrant colored flowers swaying in the soft breeze and towering, mighty trees soaring toward the cosmos-filled sky. "I have a new sense of curiosity," I said. "It's as if I'm in tune with the natural world's rhythms."

"That's because your spirit body has been realigned," Haniel said, entering a circle of ancient-looking trees.

"When I merged from the root system, I became aware of the life forces permeating the web of plants and organisms. I even understand how they speak with each other and the delicate balance of their vibrant ecosystem."

Haniel smiled. Her black lips glistened. "With your embrace of the root system, you've experienced a profound unity with the broader web of life. You've become a conduit for energy flow, nourishing the plants and the surrounding organisms."

I nodded. "I also noticed how, during that state of a merged existence, time lost its meaning and was replaced with the cycles of growth, decay, and renewal, as it unfolded with its natural rhythms."

"You've witnessed the wisdom inherent within the interconnected web of life. I'm pleased with your transformation, Samuel, and I hope you can carry such knowledge into your next incarnation."

"This has been remarkable," I said. "Am I ready to move on?"

Haniel wagged a finger and said, "Not quite yet. The lessons learned beneath only address your relationship with the natural world. As archangel of Venus, I instill your love for the natural world and your potential for romantic relationships."

"You mean like me with a wife?"

Haniel nodded. "Finding a partner to raise a family with is where many fall into a trap. Making the wrong decision can devastate one's life. In your search, finding a balance between connection and love is important. This involves mutual respect, compassion, and an understanding in fostering healthy and nurturing relationships."

I shook my head. "What does all that mean?"

"I'm referring to maintaining a healthy, harmonious, and honest relationship while navigating the challenges of being connected to another person."

"Are you saying my marriage with Meghan was lacking?"

"The secret to creating harmonious relationships is embracing unconditional love, emotional intimacy, mutual respect, and equality. If you can cultivate and practice this, these qualities will contribute to a deep and lasting connection between you and your partner."

"That's quite the ideal," I said, wondering how close I came to it in my time with Meghan.

Haniel nodded. "It's all about the transformative power of love, be it with a wife, a child, a parent, or a friend."

"There's so much to consider," I said, scratching the back of my neck.

"This is certain," Haniel said. "I hope you've developed a heightened spiritual perception and attunement from your visit to this sphere of Venus."

"What I've noticed about absorbing spiritual wisdom is it's not like sitting in a classroom."

"That's right. Knowledge flows in the soul world through energetic resonance, symbolic imagery, and intuitive insights."

"Energetic resonance?" I asked.

"It's the phenomenon where two or more energy fields interact. It's based upon the understanding that everything in the universe, even thoughts, emits and vibrates at a specific frequency."

"That's interesting," I said, nodding. "I used to think, when walking by strangers on a busy street, that if I made eye contact with them, that would somehow affect them."

"Exactly!" Haniel said. "Your openness to these frequencies allows for the integration of wisdom, acceptance, and an awakening. You're not just an individual soul but part of the collective consciousness. Those who understand this phenomenon do well during their lives on Earth. This shift in thinking expands your perspective, deepens your relationships, and, of course, your spiritual growth."

"Did I learn these things during my previous in-between time?"

Haniel held her hands and said, "Yes, you've been here before."

"I was here?" I asked, pointing to the ground.

"Yes, you have. This is your third visit."

"Third visit? Do you remember me?"

"Would you expect anything less of an archangel?"

I chuckled. "I suppose not," I said and thought a while. "Did I not learn from my past mistakes?"

"You will understand, as you continue to the remaining spheres, that each of your lives had a purpose of moving you toward your evolution. Often karmic debts need to be settled, which you may have done. Allowing you to move on."

"What are karmic debts?"

"Karmic debts are unresolved consequences of past actions, requiring balancing in subsequent lives. Your early death may be such rectification."

"That's some serious payback. What did I do in a previous life to deserve such punishment?"

"It may not be a punishment from a past life, and there's also the possibility of your actions affecting your future karma."

"Future karma?" I repeated another new unknown phrase.

"Future karma is the idea that thoughts, intentions, and actions can potentially create karmic effects that manifest themselves in subsequent lives. Choices one makes in the present life contribute to forming a soul's destiny."

I pinched my forehead, trying to absorb what this meant.

"Don't worry, Samuel," Haniel said. "All will become evident once you complete your journey of the planetary spheres."

I raised my eyes, gazing at the fabulously wise figure, and nodded.

"I'll be sad to see you go, Samuel. Until next time," the archangel said, and with that, I vanished.

CHAPTER FORTY-SEVEN
THE SUN BEING

As I approached the boundary of the sun sphere, I crossed what felt like a gateway. Shimmering with vibrant hues of golden radiant energy, it drew me gently into a luminous realm where my anticipation and reverence heightened.

Unlike the previous spheres, where entry was like arriving on a distant island, this time, I was enveloped by a wave of warmth and brilliance—not an actual increase in the physical temperature but rather a warmth nurtured by an embodiment of love, an abundance of compassion, and limitless life-giving forces.

I felt a profound sense of tranquility, with an invigorating light holding me in a gentle caress. I entered this realm seemingly untouched by the troubles and limitations of my previous earthly existence.

The luminosity of the sun's sphere appeared as a garment woven with threads of shimmering light. It embraced me into this harmonic realm, where what seemed like radiant beings of light and celestial energies danced before me. Vibrant, vivid colors seeped within, along with delightful fragrances permeating the air, igniting me with awe and wonder.

I became aware of a gentle hum and a symphony of vibrations, offering a sense of interconnectedness. I felt like I was part of some grand symphony of life.

I wanted to explore and delve deeper into the mysteries of the sun realm. With this thought, I sensed the presence of spiritual beings wishing to offer me guidance and support. Their voices resonated as whispers of wisdom and guidance, their energy a gentle breeze that caressed my skin. There was trust in knowing I was in the hands of benevolent forces seeking to nurture and assist me in this next leg of my journey.

A physical orb of light about the size of a basketball appeared. As it hovered over me, an iris-shaped shadow formed within its core. Slowly, the image morphed into an expanding figure, pushing itself beyond the limits of its capsule. Then a majestic figure appeared, emanating a brilliant, warm light. Though still unformed, its presence exuded serenity, love, and Divine knowledge.

In its essence, the Sun Being was pure consciousness, transcending the limits of the physical. It held a deep understanding of all beings' universal truths and interconnectedness, and its wisdom encompassed all knowledge and the evolutionary processes of the spiritual realms.

Bypassing the limitations of human language, the Sun Being spoke. Its ethereal utterances, a symphony of cosmic vibrations, touched the depths of my being. Each note carried profound significance, unraveling mysteries within me. Through wordless exchange, I was immersed in the essence of light and love. The unspoken melody harmonized with my soul, unlocking hidden chambers and revealing the boundless potential that lay dormant within me.

As my knowledge began to flow, I understood that the Sun Being was to help by discerning my purpose, assisting me with a recognition of my unique gifts, and teaching me how to navigate the complexities of the remainder of my spiritual journey. It was as if the Sun Being reminded me of the universal truths etched into my very essence. Truths that transcended intellectual concepts and the limitations of both space and time—such as the interconnectedness of all beings; the transformative power of love and compassion; the eternal cycle of birth, growth, and transformation; and the inherent worth and value of every life form.

Amid my sudden awareness of clarity, I asked, "What is my purpose?"

"Ah, Samuel, you prefer the making of words," the Sun Being replied, its voice possessing a depth and richness transcending human speech. Countless harmonies resonated, and each word seemed imbued with a vibration that touched my core.

"Would that be all right?" I asked rather timidly.

"You ask about your purpose?"

I nodded.

"This question of purpose will be evident once your planetary journey to the spheres has concluded. While here in this sphere, you first must consider discerning your purpose."

"Discerning?" I asked, trying to understand its meaning.

"Discerning a purpose means gaining clarity, an understanding of your unique mission in your next life. This is achieved by uncovering the significance of your existence."

I gazed into the Sun Being's shimmering embodiment. While I could not make out anything close to a human-like image, as I had with my previous encounters, I did feel a significant presence poised before me.

"To discern your purpose, Samuel," the Sun Being continued, "you need to gaze into your authentic self and recognize the gifts and talents you possess and how they can contribute to humankind."

"Humankind?" I repeated with a chuckle. "I doubt I have such a grand purpose."

The Sun Being didn't answer right away. Instead, vibration and warmth cascaded through me as if my essence were being examined.

Once it subsided, the Sun Being said, "A soul's purpose and its effect on humankind can be understood by doing what you've done so far. Connecting to your spiritual growth with the collective evolution of human consciousness."

I nodded, pleased knowing my accomplishments had an effect beyond my existence.

"Do you understand why?"

I shrugged and shook my head.

"It's the cosmic law of cause and effect and its influence upon your soul's purpose. All of your choices, actions, and intentions have created karmic imprints and need to be addressed and resolved, both for yourself and for the collective karma of humanity."

"*Mmm,*" I murmured, thinking of my responsibility to make things right. "That seems like a lot to consider for just one soul."

"The fulfillment of your purpose is not a solo act, and it involves interactions and shared experiences with other souls, all contributing to this collective evolution of consciousness. It's your purpose intertwined with the others that creates a collective web of learning and development."

I held my hands and asked, "It sounds like there's some grand plan."

The sun's brightening caused me to avert my eyes. Then a warmth encompassed me, and the light and heat intensified until I felt as if I embodied the elements of the Sun Being.

"You've learned a great deal, Samuel. A soul's purpose is a unique thread woven into the grand tapestry of existence. By fulfilling your purpose, you will participate in co-creating the Divine plan, playing a part in the unfolding of the spiritual evolution of humankind."

With those words, the Sun Being vanished, leaving me in a void.

CHAPTER FORTY-EIGHT
THE ARCHAI

I remained in the void, dwelling upon the imparted wisdom and wondering if my interaction with the Sun Being had concluded. Unlike the previous ones, this visit offered less physically challenging lessons.

Just as I contemplated the ease of passing through the sun's sphere and imagining how I would advance to Mars, I remained floating in a black sea of stars. No longer of body, I had no sense of my existence. With at least the illusion of a physical body, I had a familiar way of judging myself. Though my state initially amused me, I soon drifted toward worry. While I had been told this would be a significant milestone in my journey toward my birth, I was disoriented. *Was this supposed to happen to me, or has something gone wrong?*

All around me was infinite space filled with glittering stars too far away to touch—that is, if I had had hands. *Have I shed the last remnants of my life body?*

While I contemplated my current state of existence, the figure of a woman—tall, slender, and delicate—appeared, floating before me in the cosmic expanse.

"Who are you?" I asked.

"I am Aurelia, of the Archai of Wisdom," she said gently.

"Where am I?" I asked.

"You remain in the sun sphere, Samuel."

"This hardly feels like it."

Aurelia smiled and said, "Yes, it's different from what you've experienced."

"Why do you have a body?" I asked, observing her wrapped in a robe-like garment that shimmered with celestial hues and undulated perfectly with the cosmic winds. Unusual symbols and ancient patterns danced across the fabric.

"It's useful for our interaction," Aurelia said.

"Who are the Archai of Wisdom?"

"We are hierarchical beings who influence the collective consciousness of humanity. We do this through encouraging the emergence of new ideas, artistic expressions, social movements, and cultural shifts."

"And what is the purpose of our meeting?" I asked.

"You have an invention the Archai would like to help you develop."

"An invention?" I said. "I have no invention."

"During your remaining time, before your ensoulment, you will create an exciting product. From what we can understand, this invention will be able to use thought-energy generated by the human mind, which is then transferred through a clear cube, to affect sedentary objects'"

"Affect them how?"

"We are unsure, but we imagined it could move them."

"You mean like telekinesis?"

Aurelia pointed a long, slender finger at me and said, "Exactly."

"And I am supposed to invent this?" I said, doubting the validity of this being's assertation.

"Yes, this will occur," Aurelia said, nodding. "Though you'll need the technology on Earth to be ready for this before birth."

"*Um*, that sounds preposterous," I said, dismissing the possibility.

"Oh no," Aurelia said, shaking her head. "We have seen it."

"I don't understand. How's this possible? How do I create anything in the soul world that I can bring into a new life?"

"It happens all the time. I can assure you. I assume you've heard of Mozart?"

"Of course," I said.

"Did you know that by the age of eight, Mozart composed his first symphony, and by the time he was a teenager, he had written numerous operas, symphonies, and chamber music?"

"Are you saying Mozart learned this in his beforelife?"

Aurelia nodded. "Indeed, and I was the one who helped him."

"Were there others?"

"There were many," she said. "Let's see. There was Pablo Picasso, who completed his first painting, *Le Picador,* at nine. Louis Braille created the Braille system of reading and writing for the blind when he was fifteen."

"Let me see if I understand this. All these people who saw great success at a young age have the Archai to thank?"

Aurelia nodded and grinned. "In a way, yes. However, the ideas were their own. We just helped facilitate the idea" advancement before their birth. We have done so millions of times"

While Aurelia spoke, the idea of a cube began to take form. In my mind's eye, I saw it laid out before me. It's called the Cerebro-Cube Transducer or the CCT. It's a device that harnesses the power of the human mind to manipulate physical objects. The CCT is a small, transparent, lightweight cube, maybe four inches square, constructed of a substance known as a psychoactive crystal. This solid crystal can respond to human thought waves, similar to how a radio antenna responds to radio waves. The psychoactive crystal forms a three-dimensional matrix of nanoscale transducers, each capable of detecting and reacting to the minute electrical signals human thought produces.

"Impressive," Aurelia said, hearing my thoughts. "You have it all worked out."

"How's this possible?" I asked. "I've no such knowledge of any of this."

"You've done your research at the library on Mercury."

"No, I didn't," I said. "I just remember those three books, but nothing like this."

"That's because, according to linear time, you have not yet done your research."

I thought for a while and said, "I'm having a hard time coming to terms with this concept of time."

"As you've been told, time does not follow the progression you were accustomed to during your earthly existence. Here, moments from the past, present, and future coexist and intertwine. It's not a river flowing in one direction; it's an ocean with currents moving in all directions. Some call this understanding of time eternalism, meaning that past, present, and future exist equally and are equally real."

"Well, I do like my idea. But it's impossible to invent, as such advanced technology doesn't exist."

Aurelia wagged a finger and said, "Not yet. But upon your birth, it can certainly be possible."

"What do you mean?"

"What if your birth is fifty years after your passing?"

"Mmm," I murmured, considering the possibilities.

"I believe you've just discovered your purpose, Samuel."

CHAPTER FORTY-NINE
THE VEIL OF FORGETFULNESS

I returned to my presence before the Sun Being. While sudden, it didn't surprise me, especially after my enlightening interaction with Aurelia. At last, I was getting a grasp on the concept of eternalism.

"You've come up with an interesting idea for your purpose," said the Sun Being. "I'm impressed."

"But how can I remember my purpose after I'm born?"

"This depends upon your ability to pierce through the veil of forgetfulness."

"Veil of forgetfulness?" I repeated with a raised brow. "What's that?"

"It's what happens when souls descend into the earthly realm, and their memories and conscious connection to their spiritual origin are forgotten."

"After all I've learned," I said, spreading my hands.

"The veil allows souls to fully engage in the experiences and lessons of the physical world without being overwhelmed or distracted by memories of previous lives or the higher spiritual realms."

"So then, how will I remember my purpose?"

"By being aware, you can pierce the veil."

"What do you mean?"

"You'll need to be in tune with your feelings and desires. Perhaps, when you're in college, you'll feel drawn toward certain areas of study or have a strong sense of mission but will be unsure of where these feelings come from. Hopefully, you'll follow your calling and fulfill your purpose."

"I hope so, too," I said.

"Perhaps I can assist you with this," the Sun Being said.

"How would you do that?"

"I'm going to offer you three symbols. They are unrelated, but any of them will trigger something within your subconsciousness. When you're born, it will be up to you to recognize and act upon them."

"Okay, what are they?"

The Sun Being vanished, and a large, majestic tree with thick roots clinging to a large boulder stood before me. "This, Samuel, is the tree of life," the Sun Being said. "Its roots symbolize a connection to the physical world, while its branches represent the aspirations and upward growth toward the spiritual realms. The trunk symbolizes the integration of both realms, serving as a conduit between the earthly and the Divine dimensions."

While the Sun Being spoke, I observed the tree of life and the red fruit hanging off its branches. "Are those pomegranates?" I asked.

"They are pomegranates," the Sun Being said. "Each fruit represents six hundred and thirteen new souls yet to be born."

"There are new souls?" I said.

"Yes, there are new souls. Did you think all souls were reborn?"

I shrugged. "I guess I never considered the possibility."

"This is where they're created. Ready to enter the earthly realm with a clean slate of karma."

"But why six hundred and thirteen?"

"Because that's how many seeds there are in each pomegranate."

I stared at the unusual fruit, considering what life would be like without the burdens of karmic history.

"That's a good observation, Samuel," the Sun Being said. "A new soul's life would offer a clean slate, an untouched canvas ready to be painted upon with their choices, actions, and experiences. They would not carry any karmic debts that need balancing, nor any predetermined relationships or challenges born from past lives."

"That sounds great," I said with a chuckle.

"That doesn't mean that life would be smooth. Because, for a new soul, challenges would arise from the circumstances of their present life and not from a distant past. Leaving the individual without a spiritual road map to call upon."

"I would like to learn about my first life," I said.

"Such knowledge is possible. Before completing the planetary spheres, you will learn of all your previous lives."

"That would be wonderful," I said, returning my focus to the pomegranate tree and wondering where such trees grew and the likelihood of ever seeing one.

"They grow in the Middle East. But you don't need to see the tree; the fruit alone will cause the trigger."

"You mean like finding them in the produce section?"

"That's right. Seeing the pomegranate at the market will cause a tickle deep within the recesses of your mind."

Before I could reply, the tree of life vanished, and a muddy pond surrounded by tall pines took its place. Floating upon its surface were dozens of bright pink lotus flowers.

"Notice how the lotus floats," the Sun Being began. "It rises to the surface to bloom, unspoiled by the mud it dwells within. This represents the journey of the soul, which, like the lotus, emerges from the murkiness of physical existence to the pure consciousness of spiritual enlightenment."

"Would you say I was spiritually enlightened?"

"Not yet, Samuel," the Sun Being said. "Enlightenment is not a singular event, but a continuous journey of spiritual evolution that unfolds over multiple lifetimes."

"How will I know when I'm enlightened?"

"When you have balanced off your karmic debts."

"Like my great-grandfather Moshe."

"Moshe was a *tzaddik*, the righteous one. He not only resolved his karmic obligations, but he also served as a conduit between the Divine and the earthly realms."

"You mean like a hand of God?" I asked.

"Moshe was a vessel through which the Divine interacted as a way to guide humanity. The lotus, too, symbolizes your great-grandfather's journey."

My eyes widened. "In what way?"

"The lotus flower blooms under the sun, drawing sustenance from the light, just as Moshe also thrived on the light of spiritual wisdom. Despite being rooted in the mud, the lotus is not tainted, just as the *tzaddik* strived to maintain his purity amidst earthly challenges."

I stared at the population of lotuses choking the pond's surface, then said, "Even within the muddy waters of existence, we can transcend our shortcomings."

"Oh, Samuel, that's impressive. You've learned a great deal since you passed through the gate."

"Gate?" I asked. "What gate?"

"There are two gates," the Sun Being said. "The gate of death, which you know, and the gate of birth, which you will eventually pass through."

"So I'm between two gates," I said.

"Marvelous," the Sun Being exclaimed. "That's exactly right."

"But what about this lotus flower? I don't ever remember seeing one in my past life."

"That's fine, and you may not be in your next life. But if you do…"

"I'll take notice," I said with a smile.

"Exactly!" the Sun Being exclaimed.

"Where to next?" I asked in anticipation of the third symbol.

"This time, there's nowhere to go. The next symbol is a number."

"A number?" I asked. "What number?"

"*444,*" the Sun Being said. "In the sun sphere, 444 represents perfect alignment, and it's a celestial signature, symbolizing the unity of time, space, and energy."

"How would I use that as a trigger?"

"Imagine in your next life, during the ebb and flow of a normal day, you glance at the time, and it's 4:44. Or maybe you drive past a mailbox with the house number 444, or perhaps you notice an event on the news, like a volcano in Hawaii erupting at 4:44 in the morning. Whatever it is, at that moment, a strange familiarity will stir something deep within you, like a whisper from a forgotten realm. It's as if a veil was lifted, revealing fragments of a memory from a distant past."

"The veil of forgetfulness?" I asked.

"That's right, and hopefully, you'll use these inklings to drive you toward your purpose."

"The Cerebro-Cube Transducer," I said.

CHAPTER FIFTY
THE SPIRITS OF MOTION

I stood upon the landscape of Mars. Not unlike the Valley of the Shadow of Death, except upon this terrain, its rocky trail and jagged mountains off in the distance were all brick red. Even the sky, heavy with clouds, seemed composed of ruddy clay.

With no one to greet me, I wandered along the pathway. I took no more than a step before realizing I was once again of body, which provided a modicum of relief. Figuring there must be a reason, I continued onward.

I kicked at a stone and watched it skip across the surface, popping puffs of red dust along its trajectory. I bent over to pick up another stone and held it in my hand, caressing its dense weight and rough coarseness. Wondering how far I could toss it with this phantom body, I reared back and flung the stone.

It traveled in a great arc, vanishing into the low-hanging clouds. Where it landed, I was unable to see. But a moment later, I heard a distinctive cry of "oof." Then a distant voice called out, "Who threw that?"

I ran over, and upon my approach, I saw a shimmering, heat-induced vapor dancing, reminding me of the undulating heat rising off the blacktop on scorching summer days.

As I peered closer, I realized this wasn't a common earthly phenomenon caused by intense thermal energy. Instead, I observed some beings moving about with an aura of fluidity and grace; their forms were blurry waves in constant motion.

There also seemed to be some sort of dome enclosing this ethereal gathering. Once close enough, I reached out and tested its surface by passing my hand through it, and like everything else under this dome, my hand became translucent.

Curiously, I reached my arm in, up to my elbow. That was when someone grabbed my hand and yanked, and before I could resist, I stumbled into the bubble.

"Did you throw this?" a luminous figure asked, displaying the evidence.

"Oh, I'm sorry. Are you hurt?" I asked, having trouble finding the being's eyes.

"No, of course not. The *dynamis* are pure etheric; we have no substance to strike."

I squinted. "What does that mean? Pure etheric?"

"It means we're closely connected to the energetic aspects of existence."

"I see," I said, trying to focus on the shimmering image, unsure where to look.

"Don't worry about finding my eyes. We don't have any."

"Oh, but why did you cry out if the stone didn't strike you?"

"It seemed like a good way to get your attention."

"All right," I said, trying to look beyond the being. "But who are the *dynamis*?"

"We're the ones concerned with the harmonization of the cosmic forces."

"I'm sorry, but I don't know what that means," I said.

"We provide the energy and rhythm that give motion to the universe, not unlike how the life body serves as a bridge, enabling the living to perceive between the physical and spiritual dimensions."

"Ah," I said with a nod.

"Do you have a name?" I asked.

"I am called Lumisvel," said the radiant being.

I looked around at the undulating images and said, "Are there others?"

"Of course, don't you see?"

"I just wasn't sure…" I said, my voice trailing off.

"That's Vortekin, and over there is Eneriax, and this here is Pulseon," Lumisvel said, seeming to wrap a wavering arm around a being.

"Okay," I said, trying to differentiate between them.

"Do you know why you are here?" Lumisvel asked.

"I'm passing through the spheres toward my birth," I said.

"But do you know why you are with us, the *dynamis*?"

I shook my head.

"Besides guiding the universe, we're also entrusted with the sacred education of souls on the intricacies of the living body."

"The living body?" I asked. "Is that anything like the physical body?"

"The physical body is composed of physical matter, like organs, tissues, bones, and fluids. The living body, however, encompasses the vital energies that animate and sustain our physical existence," Lumisvel said. "Allow us to demonstrate."

I stood speechless as the figures took on shapes that were closer to recognizable human forms and began moving in an ethereal dance punctuated by energetic gestures. I understood they were offering me an interpretation of a living body in motion. First, they moved in geometric unison; then, the dancers split into groups. Some formed wide circles, while others glided in straight lines.

"Notice," Lumisvel said, "how the living body acts as a conduit, orchestrating the vital energies that sustain and animate the physical organism."

I watched the dance of delicate movements, following the flow of the beings emulating the motion of the life forces within the living body.

"That's a good observation, Samuel," Lumisvel said, following my thoughts. "The dancers demonstrate how the *dynamis* infuse the life body with a vibrant energy that permeates every aspect of the physical form. This energetic infusion imbues the living body with its vitality."

"What is the connection between the living and physical bodies?" I asked.

"The well-being of the physical body is intimately tied to the vitality and balance of the living body. Any imbalances or disturbances in the living body can manifest as disharmonies in the physical body, affecting its functioning and overall state of wellness."

"I see," I said, as I heard the faint sound of music, unlike anything I remembered from my past life. Rather than an external sound, it reverberated within me as shimmering, exquisite tones and melodies.

As this inner symphony played on, the dancers moved in harmony, their forms becoming vessels for the interplay of movement and sound. With fluid gestures, the beings translated the melodies into motion, weaving a story of beauty and meaning, causing me to wonder if they were the instruments creating the sounds.

"Does this help you understand why the *dynamis* are known as the spirits of motion?" Lumisvel said.

"Indeed it does," I said as the dancers vanished.

"Take this wisdom with you, Samuel, as you continue with your journey within the sphere of Mars," Lumisvel said.

CHAPTER FIFTY-ONE
THE SPIRITS OF WISDOM

Once again, I was poised upon the expansive, desolate sphere of the vast Martian landscape—a land dominated by rugged, rocky terrain and jagged cliffs far off. The ground, as before, was coarse and uneven, bearing the markings of ancient turbulent forces. The soil was tinted with hues of rusty reds, while the sky was bathed in deep crimsons and burnt oranges.

I wandered toward the mountains, searching for my subsequent encounter. Taking no more than a few steps, I sensed a presence.

"Welcome, Samuel. We are the *kyriotetes*, the Spirits of Wisdom," a bodiless voice called out.

"Show yourself," I demanded.

"Ah, you're finding your confidence," the voice said mockingly.

I held my arms, twisting my head back and forth, searching for the source.

"The *kyriotetes* are formless beings, transcending the boundaries of conventional perception."

"All right," I said. "Do you at least have a name?"

"You can call me Orionis if that helps."

"It would help more if I could see you," I said.

"That's not a problem," Orionis said. "Here I am."

With a grace that defied physicality, the space before me shimmered and transformed, and a radiant presence emerged, emanating a celestial glow. It was as if a thousand stars had converged into a single, ever-shifting form, offering a dance of light and energy.

"Would you like to learn our story?" Orionis asked while I remained in awe.

"Sure," I said with a nod.

"Come, Samuel, the circle has formed."

I followed the shimmering being toward where the granulated soil had formed into a delicate series of concentric circles. I stood along the edge of the outermost one and observed how the *kyriotetes* created a harmonious symphony of light and sound.

As a stillness and silence encompassed me, I experienced a telepathic transfer of thoughts and emotions. The *kyriotetes* showed me glimpses of the timeless origins of their spirit. Through their collective consciousness, they unveiled the inherent divinity stored within my soul, communicating that I was a unique manifestation of universal wisdom. I understood that the vast tapestry of existence was where each thread represented a unique soul, revealing the intricate web of interconnected relationships. The Spirits of Wisdom demonstrated how every thought, action, and intention ripple throughout the cosmos, influencing shared awareness and shaping evolution.

Then they revealed how my past incarnations served as stepping stones for my growth and self-realization, allowing my soul body to expand my understanding of my Divine nature.

An unexpected flood of emotions cascaded through me, and tears flowed for the first time since passing through the gate. I wept in body-convulsing heaves.

"Love, compassion, and unity are the guiding principles of your journey, Samuel," the voice of Orionis said.

"But there's so much to know. How do I remember all these lessons?" I asked in between my blubbering.

"Wisdom is not the accumulation of knowledge, but rather a deep connection to the universal consciousness and recognizing the inherent worth and dignity of all beings."

"I don't know," I said, wiping away my imaginary tears. "I never realized what was within me came from elsewhere."

"Your gifts and talents are expressions of Divine wisdom. Your soul body delivers your contributions to the greater good."

"But I'm just one man. How can I be so important?"

"Within the universe, every soul, no matter how seemingly small, plays an integral role in the grand symphony of creation. Think of yourself as a precious gem within a vast mosaic, bringing a distinct energy, purpose, and contribution to the collective whole. Your smallest actions, thoughts, and intentions can transform the cosmos. The ripple effect of love, compassion, and acts of kindness are inspirations to others and the further development of human evolution."

"How's that possible?" I asked. "Are you saying if I say something nasty to a stranger, that will harm humanity?"

"The journey of the soul," Orionis said slowly, "is not meant to be experienced in isolation. All beings are connected, and each soul has the power to inspire others, catalyzing positive or negative change in the world. You must recognize and cultivate your innate potential with love and purpose."

"I think I understand," I said, trying to settle my emotions. "What you're saying is that the guidance of my soul body is not a solitary endeavor, but a forever journey of awakening that permeates all creation."

"That's a wonderful explanation," Orionis said.

While I stood among the *kyriotetes*, a pattern of interwoven geometric shapes appeared in the center of the smallest circle.

"What you're seeing, Samuel, is a symbol of the interconnectedness of all knowledge."

I stared at the complex design on the scrolls and books suspended in mid-air before me. Its covers were adorned with ornate symbols and intricate calligraphy.

These sacred texts were not mere static objects, like those in a library. But instead, they appeared to be alive, pulsating with vibrant energy and emanating a gentle glow. Even the symbols etched upon the surfaces shifted about, forming a language transcending human words.

I understood that what I witnessed expressed the vast wisdom and cosmic understanding of the *kyriotetes*. Their symbols were gateways to profound insights and transformative knowledge.

"You will carry forth imprints of these symbols forever upon your consciousness. They will constantly remind you of your inherent connection to the Divine and the limitless potential of your soul body as it manifests through the Spirits of Wisdom."

CHAPTER FIFTY-TWO
THE SPIRITS OF WILL

Seated before me, on an outcropping of blood-colored stone, was a being resembling human form, yet dressed in a radiant light. As I dwelled upon this image, I realized it was my reflection.

"Greetings, Samuel," it said. Its voice sounded eerily like mine. "I'm of the Exusiai."

"The Exusiai?" I asked.

"Yes."

I pointed a finger and asked, "Are you me?"

"No, I am a being of the spirits of will."

"But why do you look and sound like me?"

"The Exusiai find it's best to mirror one's soul to explain its purpose."

"My purpose?" I asked with a furrowed brow.

"To reveal the true nature of your ego. The singular aspect of self that often stirs up internal conflicts, hindering a soul's connection to the Divine will."

"Is there something wrong with my ego?"

"Nothing that can't be corrected."

"Corrected how?" I asked.

"Before we get into that," the Exusiai said, "let me first explain. Despite its disruptive nature, the ego plays a vital role in your soul's evolution, catalyzing personal growth and transformation. Your ego, while in pursuit of your desires, creates a contrast push against what the soul requires in its quest toward enlightenment."

"You mean I can't have it all."

"That all depends on your desires. If they align with the will of the Divine, then you should be able to. But sadly, most often, it's not."

"Are you a reflection of my soul?" I asked, trying to gaze into the being's eyes.

"I am," the Exusiai said.

I nodded, absorbing the presence before me. "So what desires are creating barriers toward my evolution?"

My reflection shrugged and said, "There are a few. Let's begin with materialistic desires. Excessive attachment to possessions, such as wealth and sensory pleasures, distracts a soul from its path. When the focus of one's life is accumulating money or indulging in sensory gratification, a barrier is erected, hampering the soul's evolution."

I sighed, thinking about my attachment to money. "How do I manage this next time?"

"By learning from the consequences. Look at what happened to you. Your desire for debilitating drugs certainly blocked your growth. Hopefully, in your next life, you'll allow your soul to blossom during your time on Earth."

I lowered my eyes and nodded. "I understand."

"There are also egotistical desires," the Exusiai said. "These desires are driven by personal gain and the fulfillment of ambitions that can impede one's growth. When the individual is primarily concerned with success, power, or reputation, these desires create barriers that limit the expansion of the consciousness and the ability to develop higher values."

I shook my head and said, "But I thought the ego was the source of a soul's consciousness, willpower, and creativity."

"That's right, it is! As the soul's fourth body, the ego is the vessel through which inspiration, imagination, and artistic impulses flow."

I squinted and said, "It seems like there's a good and bad ego."

The Exusiai shrugged. "Yes, if you allow these doomed desires to control you. The goal, however, is to align your ego with higher spiritual principles and virtues."

"Are there other doomed desires?" I asked.

"There are, though I don't think you dabbled much in any of them."

I spread my hands and asked, "But what are they?"

The Exusiai held up a finger and said, "There are unbridled sexual desires, which need no further explanation." He then showed a second finger. "Some get caught up with destructive desires. These are the expressions of negative emotions, such as anger, hatred, envy, or revenge."

The Exusiai held a third finger and said, "Lastly, there's an attachment to illusions. Such as desires rooted in false beliefs, rigid ideologies, or distorted world views. These delusions prevent an individual from seeking higher truths, hindering the expansion of their consciousness."

"I see your point about how such desires keep a soul from evolving, but they seem normal behaviors. It's like you're asking me to be a saint."

"Ah, what a great insight. But living a life while striving for personal growth, spiritual development, and a deep sense of integrity doesn't mean being a saint. Remember that the soul's journey is an eternal process, and it's natural to experience challenges or mistakes. But by cultivating self-awareness, discernment, and a commitment to growth, one can lead a meaningful and purposeful life without needing to be without sinful type behavior. It's about embracing the human experience while continually seeking higher ideals and striving for personal transformation."

As my reflective soul spirit spoke, I understood that the ego could be harnessed to strengthen my willpower when approached with awareness and understanding. By navigating the complexities and conflicts arising from my ego, I could develop resilience and determination, which would help me distinguish between my ego's desires and the higher calling of the Divine will.

*

In the vast expanse of the cosmos, I embarked upon a transformative journey, venturing to the realm of Mars. There, the spirits propelled me further toward my evolution. I met the enigmatic spirits of motion who, with their dance, ignited the fires of inspiration and creative expression.

With newfound grace and fluidity, I encountered the luminous Spirits of Wisdom, who unveiled the depths of cosmic knowledge and the secrets of the universe. I drank from the wellspring of wisdom, expanding and embracing my understanding of the interconnectedness of all existence.

Lastly, guided by the spirits of the will, I unraveled the layers of desire and how to reconcile them with the Divine.

Gazing back at the celestial sphere of Mars, I felt gratitude for the profound lessons learned and the spiritual gifts received. I assimilated these lessons by facing challenges and embracing the teachings offered by the three spirits. I integrated them into my being while preparing for the next phase of my cosmic journey—an onward odyssey of growth, exploration, and spiritual evolution.

CHAPTER FIFTY-THREE
THE ZEPHYRATH

Vast open plains, bathed in swirling mists of a violet-colored fog, stretched endlessly in all directions. Like Mars, Jupiter's air felt charged with energy, inviting me to explore this unique realm.

As I ventured across the terrain, I saw an image shimmering in the same purple hue as the fog hanging above my head. At first, I thought three identical beings were coming to greet me. But upon my approach, I understood the vision before me was instead the shape of three numbers—444. Before I could focus on or question, the image vanished.

I paused to reflect. *Why would the Sun Being's trigger appear here and not in my next life as a reminder of my purpose?*

Then a thought occurred. *If the number 444 is a way to contact the earthly realm from the soul world, then why can't I use it now as a way for me to connect to someone living?*

The Sun Being suggested that I would take notice after experiencing random sightings of 444. *Why can't I do the same? But who would be so observant to realize the messages were coming from me?*

I didn't need to dwell on this question for long before coming to the obvious conclusion—Dad. A surge of anticipation coursed through me as I envisioned a series of events where I could ignite Dad's curiosity, leading him to witness the repetitive occurrence of 444.

After seeing this combination frequently, all by chance, he might realize this was something to consider coming from the soul world and, most importantly, from me.

So, without further consideration, I made my intention known to him. Pleased with my brilliant idea, I continued searching for the beings in this sphere and the education they were to provide.

I walked on, and while seeing no more illusions of numbers, I noticed a disturbance. It looked like a funnel cloud stretching from the ground and vanishing overhead into the purple fog.

As I approached, I saw within the turbulence tiny beings, each about the size of a child, fluttering about. Confused, I took another step, and that was when about six of them grabbed me. I was lifted into the air and carried into the swirling funnel cloud, which, upon my entry, collapsed, dropping me into a hole in the ground below.

Quickly, I got to my feet and saw hundreds of these childlike figures buzzing about like hummingbirds. Their slender bodies were adorned with luminescent patterns that shimmered like stardust against their pale, translucent skin. Delicate wings, reminiscent of gossamer, sprouted from their backs.

"Where am I?" I asked, twisting back and forth.

One of the beings hovered before me and said high-pitched, "We are the *zephyrath*, and this is our abode. Welcome, Samuel."

"The *zephyrath*?" I said, mangling the pronunciation. "Are you the protectors of Jupiter?"

The beings, seemingly amused by my question, flapped their wings faster, creating a loud buzz.

"You can say that we're the guardians of these depths. Upon the surface, we rarely venture."

"But you came for me," I said.

"Oh, that's because your thoughts reached the earthly realm, alerting us of your presence."

I squinted while darting my eyes back and forth at the energetic beings. "You mean when I signaled 444 to my father?"

The high-pitched buzzing once again became loud, vibrating the cavern floor and forcing me to cover my ears. While I waited for the agitated *zephyrath* to settle, I noticed the cavern walls were packed with pulsating purple crystals. Further beyond, into the depths, I observed a series of subterranean tunnels leading into darkness.

Sensing trouble, I said, "I'm sorry to have disturbed you, but is it possible that I can be on my way?"

"No, no," the *zephyrath* said. "You will remain here; a traveling soul hasn't visited us in a long time. You will provide us with much curiosity."

"You mean to keep me here?" I asked, wide-eyed.

Again, the loud buzzing answered my question.

"But I must move on. I'll take whatever lessons I need from this planet, then onto Saturn and, eventually, my birth."

Without a reply, six of the *zephyrath* flew over, grabbed my arms and legs, lifted me in the air, and brought me into one of the tunnels.

"Hey, let go," I demanded, trying to squirm free. But their grip tightened, forcing me to comply.

I was taken into the narrowed passageway, where the light traveled along with us, leaving where we came from in total darkness.

The tunnel led into a large cavern. Surrounding us, growing on the stone walls, were lush growths of luminescent flora intermixed with thatches of glowing amethyst-type crystals. A soft, radiant light bathed the space, casting an enchanting glow. The air was filled with a delicate, earthy fragrance, a testament to the symbiotic relationship the *zephyrath* shared with the underground growth of plants and crystals.

The leader once again approached. Though I wasn't sure it was the same being, as they all appeared identical. "The *zephyrath* are the guardians of this realm, entrusted with its preservation and harmony. You will remain here with us."

"But why? I'm destined to be born. Not stay here among you winged beings."

"Oh, but you will become like us. Though that may take a while, especially for someone your size."

I pointed a shaky hand at the *zephyrath* and said, "You mean for me to grow wings?"

"Oh, you'll find them a necessity," it said, and with that, I was lifted into the air and brought to a small alcove high above the sanctuary floor. "Once your wings grow large enough, you can free yourself and join the flock."

Then they all vanished, leaving me alone, waiting for my wings to sprout.

CHAPTER FIFTY-FOUR
ZADKIEL

While languishing in captivity, I repeatedly tried to reach around to touch my back, wondering if wings were about to emerge. Not since I was trapped in the Frozen Wasteland of Gehenna had I felt so helpless. Though now, I doubted the *tzaddik* or any archangel would come to my rescue. *On this distant planet, can anyone hear my desperate cries?*

As I sat with my back against the crystal-encrusted wall, wallowing in despair, a bright light suddenly appeared. It was coming from the sanctuary below. I got to my feet, hurried over to the edge, and looked down. There, to my astonishment, rising upwards, was a significant being. Certainly grander in size than any of my winged jailers.

This being also had wings, though these were tremendous due to its magnificent height and shimmered with soft iridescent colors of violet and indigo.

"Who are you?" I asked, peering into the being's eyes.

"I'm the archangel Zadkiel," he said, holding out a hand. "I've come to take you from here."

Without hesitation, I reached out for the archangel's hand and, upon its grasp, transferred from the *zephyraths'* prison to the safety of the archangel's embrace.

"Thank you for saving me," I said. "I don't know how I ended up in their clutches."

The archangel grimaced. "That should be evident."

"What do you mean?" I asked.

"When you shared your trigger number with the earthly realm, the *zephyrath* were aware of your presence and set the trap."

I stared at the Zadkiel, then realized. "Oh, you mean the number 444?"

"You've allowed the veil of separation to be pierced. Your father now knows the number, which is highly frowned upon by the hierarchical beings."

I squinted and thought: there's another veil? "What's the veil of separation?"

"Its purpose is seen as a means to protect humanity from being overwhelmed by Divine energy. If the veil is breached, it can disrupt the natural order and the balance between the soul world and the living. It may lead to disturbances, confusion, or chaos, as the energies and dynamics between these realms collide."

I swallowed hard. "I'm sorry, but the Sun Being—"

"You are well aware that was not the intent," he said, cutting me short. "Those signs were meant for you and you alone. You must have learned by now the interconnectedness of any action, no matter how small, and its effect on the cosmic tapestry. Even the slightest tear can cause it all to unravel."

I stared into the archangel's eyes, and unlike Michael and Raphael before him, he offered no expressions of love or compassion but rather a disappointment, perhaps even bordering upon anger. "I'm sorry," I said with a puckered brow.

"Well, since I am here to illuminate your path forward with insights and teachings, illustrating the power of forgiveness and mercy, I will accept your apology."

"Thank you," I said, still wondering what harm I had caused.

"Ah, that's interesting," Zadkiel said. "Have you ever heard of the phrase *unintended consequences*?"

I nodded. "Of course. Unintended consequences are unexpected or surprising outcomes of decisions or events."

"That's right. Let me give you a famous example from human history. You've heard of Mao Zedong?"

I nodded. "Yes, he was the leader of the Communist Party in China."

"During his rule, Chairman Mao was intent on taking action to alleviate severe food shortages by instituting a campaign to eliminate the entire sparrow population of his country. These birds were considered pests, causing massive damage to the farmer's grain crops, and Mao believed that yields would thrive by getting rid of those birds.

"However, the unintended consequences of this decision were severe. Without the natural predator of the sparrows, the population of locusts thrived, decimating the crops the policy was supposed to preserve."

"I didn't know that story," I said.

"Take note, Samuel. Because the choices you make can have far-reaching, unanticipated effects."

"But that can't be a realistic approach. If I'm constantly worried about what may go wrong, I'll never make a decision."

"It's true, most decisions or choices don't have cosmic-altering consequences, and not all consequences are negative. Sometimes there are good surprises. For example, when the Scottish scientist Alexander Fleming noticed a mold inhabiting a growth of bacteria on a petri dish, he left it inadvertently."

"Oh," I said, interrupting by wagging a finger. "That was how penicillin was discovered."

"That's right," Zadkiel said. "My point is, there are times when to consider the possibility of a positive unintended consequence."

"What do you think will happen now that my dad knows my trigger number?"

"That's hard to say, and it all depends on how far he intends to pursue it."

"But maybe," I said, pointing a finger in the air. "It will have a positive unintended consequence."

"Let's hope so, for your sake," Zadkiel said.

"I never thought how my decisions in the afterlife had consequences on the earthly realm."

"You should know that karma is not a concept delegated to the living alone. Decisions and actions made by souls can have far-reaching consequences upon their next incarnation. Just think about what you've already been through. The choices you made. Remember being lured by the *rasha* and how you decided to stay on the righteous path?"

"Yes, of course, I remember."

"What if you decided to give in to the allure of the Roman gladiator Crixus? Would you be here on the precipice of your birth?"

"I doubt it," I said, shaking my head.

"The choices you make here in the soul world will shape the circumstances, challenges, and opportunities you'll eventually encounter in your future lifetimes."

"Like my Cerebro-Cube Transducer."

"Exactly!" the archangel said. "The importance of conscious awareness and responsible decision-making, both in the soul and physical realms, cannot be dismissed."

I sighed, taking in the significance of Zadkiel's words.

"Now, we must get on with your lessons. But to do that, I must rest. You've stirred my anger, and that's not good when I'm about to teach you about the power of forgiveness, mercy, and the profound effects it will have upon your spiritual growth."

And with those words, the archangel Zadkiel vanished.

CHAPTER FIFTY-FIVE
ZADKIEL'S GARDEN

I was left alone within the bosom of Zadkiel's exquisite garden, a delight to my imaginary senses, filled with a medley of colors, fragrances, and textures. Blossoms of various hues abounded while delicate petals unfurled. A symphony of roses, orchids, and lilies intermingled their scents, permeating the air with sweet fragrances. Bird-sized butterflies fluttered about gracefully.

At the heart of the garden stood a pavilion dressed with cascading vines and delicate ivy, weaving and wrapping its way around posts and beams. The structure, adorned with intricate carvings, depicted scenes of human acts of forgiveness, compassion, and spiritual awakenings.

There was no doubt that this was a sacred space meant for contemplation, introspection, and communion—a place where one could find solace and renewal. The only thing missing was the presence of the archangel Zadkiel, and with that thought, the being appeared.

"You're back," I said. "Are you feeling better?"

"Isn't that ironic," Zadkiel said with a chuckle. "The soul consoling the archangel. Yes, thank you, Samuel, I am better."

With its wings withdrawn, the archangel stood before me and said, "I understand that in your past life, you had issues with your anger."

"At times," I said, offering a tempered confession.

"There are ways to release the shackles of resentment by allowing the light of forgiveness to dissolve dark thoughts."

"The light of forgiveness?" I shrugged and said, "How do I do that?"

"I'll show you," Zadkiel said, gesturing for me to follow him.

He brought me to a magnificent fountain in the heart of the celestial garden. Slender pillars ascended gracefully from their circular base, intertwining and branching into delicate vines. Where the posts peaked, a series of descending-tiered basins began, each larger than the previous. From its edges, cascading waters overflowed, creating a mesmerizing display of fluid motion.

I stood by the lowest and largest basin and gazed into the still pool. As expected, I saw my reflection, but it seemed distorted. My forehead was furrowed, my eyes squinted, and my jaw clenched. There was no doubt my image was burdened with anger.

I jerked my head back, and as I did, Zadkiel grabbed my hands and slowly guided them into the fountain. As I dipped them in, the waters settled and turned warm at my touch. Immediately, I experienced a massive shift. It was as if barred rooms hidden within the deepest recesses of my mind had opened up, releasing whatever pent-up negative emotions were stored there. Repressed memories, evil thoughts, and my deepest fears all gushed out.

When I gazed again into the pool, my reflection appeared at ease. The flushing away of my anger transformed me, providing a deep sense of peace.

"Remember, Samuel, that this healing energy is always available for you to call upon in your next incarnation. Use it while in meditation, and its imagery to unshackle yourself from the burdens of life."

Zadkiel next led me over to a grand hall adorned with reflective surfaces of various shapes and sizes. Each mirror displayed tragic scenes from my past life, causing me to cringe at the images I preferred to forget. In one, I saw Dad in the emergency room, narrowly surviving a heart attack. Another was hearing the sad news of when Poppy died. I saw an image of when I refused to offer forgiveness for what was later considered a minor insult.

"This, Samuel, is the hall of harmonious reflections."

I averted my eyes and said, "I'd prefer not to look."

"That's okay. I'm sure you remember those times. But I want you to fully feel the weight of your actions and how they've hindered your soul's evolution."

I looked up and saw several exchanges when I lost my temper, acted foolishly, or took offense to an insignificant or misread slight. "These were not my finest moments," I said, waving a finger at the array of mirrors.

"Let me show you something else," Zadkiel said, guiding me to a mirror that stood apart from the collection. "When you gaze into this reflection, you'll see a vision of your next life. Someone unshackled, an individual embracing forgiveness, offering abundant compassion, and experiencing a life of inner peace."

I swallowed hard, glanced at Zadkiel, and observed myself in the last mirror.

As I stood there, gazing at my reflection, I saw a radiant and luminous version of myself—someone who embodied a life freed from negative emotions. The glow from my being enveloped me in a warm, Divine light. My eyes, clear and vibrant, sparkled with compassion and understanding, reflecting the profound depths of wisdom I acquired along my journey. The peace and serenity on my face mirrored my sense of harmony and contentment.

As I continued to admire this new me, Zadkiel patted my shoulder and said, "Do you like what you see?"

"Very much. I hope I can live up to such an ideal."

"You will not be alone in your next life; those you met in the soul world will accompany you always, reminding you of what's possible."

I smiled while admiring the joyful version of myself in the reflection. "Thank you."

"There's something else I want to show you."

Once again, I followed the towering figure. The feathers of its wings rippled with each step. He led me under a trellis, heavy with large red roses, and into a walled garden.

"This, Samuel, is known as the garden of change," Zadkiel said, gesturing to the tall, expansive wall of climbing roses.

I'd never seen such beauty. Accompanying the large red roses, each the size of a melon, was the delightful aroma of its soft petals. "It's stunning," I said, leaning in close to inhale its intoxicating scent.

"Why don't you sit over there," Zadkiel said, pointing to a soft bed of rose petals.

I nodded and settled comfortably into the flowers.

"You are to be only of thought, Samuel," Zadkiel began. "Discard your imaginary body."

I gathered myself, allowing the roses to infuse their essence into my soul body.

Zadkiel spoke softly. "Let these roses remind you of your commitment to your emotional liberation. You're to carry this experience into your next incarnation to symbolize your dedication to releasing your anger and replacing it with forgiveness and compassion."

With each passing moment, my capacity for such sensitivity toward others expanded. I could see beyond the surface of the menial and perceive the inherent goodness in all beings, understanding that everyone carries unique burdens and struggles.

"Forgiveness and mercy are not signs of weakness," Zadkiel whispered. "But rather expressions of Divine strength and wisdom."

With gratitude, I ventured forth from Jupiter, forever imbued with the transformative teachings of the archangel. I'd become a vessel for kindness, radiating light and healing for all I would encounter. Guided by the archangel Zadkiel, I had embraced the role of an agent of spiritual change, offering the gifts of mercy and forgiveness to a world in desperate need.

CHAPTER FIFTY-SIX
THE DIVINE ORACLE

I stood at the base of a majestic mountain, its peak swallowed by hungry cosmic clouds. Assuming I arrived on Saturn, the last planetary sphere on my journey toward birth, I gazed upwards and thought my purpose for being here must reside at the top.

Unlike my previous encounters with the mountains in Gehenna and throughout several of the planetary spheres I've since visited, this one appeared, at least from the outset, to be the most challenging. My concern proved to be the case as I began my venture upward. Its pathways were rugged, strewn with large rocky outcroppings that I had to climb over, crawl under, or squeeze in between. Large, intertwined roots created impenetrable barriers, forcing me to find alternate pathways. Yet, an inner strength, plus the idea that a finish line lay ahead, propelled me to conquer the obstacles with determination and resilience.

Undeterred by my struggles, I climbed until I reached the summit, where a startling vision of a lustrous temple stood before me. Unlike any of the impressive structures I visited in the previous realms, this one radiated a light outwards, illuminating the sky above as if it was the sun itself.

The temple, round in design, was built with a series of heavy marble columns that encircled an inner chamber. Surrounding the structure was a babbling stream of clear water that meandered around the perimeter. Though gentle in its appearance, I was reminded of an ancient moat protecting its castle. Except this one was not meant to keep out invading marauders; this gentle brook offered itself as an invitation. So I hopped across the convenient flat stone cresting above the waterline and quickly reached the other side.

With trepidation, I entered this mysterious shrine. Once within the inner chamber, I noticed hundreds of ancient scrolls neatly stacked on marble shelves. The walls featured celestial-type symbols, expressing the relationships between geometry, mathematical ratios, and the spiritual realm, causing me to wonder if this was what was called sacred geometry.

"Welcome, Samuel," a deep voice said, resonating with a celestial timbre.

I turned and saw, seated upon a throne of light, a being. "Hello," I whispered. "What is this place?"

"This is the Temple of the Divine Oracle," the radiant being said, looking back at me with eyes that mirrored the cosmos and sparkled with hints of the secrets of the universe.

"Are you the Divine Oracle?" I asked, though it was apparent.

The Oracle's face held an expression of serene understanding and compassion. "I'm pleased to see you, Samuel. You've accomplished a great deal," the Oracle said, running a hand down his leg to smooth out a crease on his sheer robe.

"Am I on Saturn?" I asked and noticed a radiant halo of light above the Oracle's head.

"This is your final sphere, Samuel, before preparing for birth."

"This has been quite a journey."

The Oracle looked at me and said, "Before I allow you to move on, there are four questions you must answer, each carrying the weight of universal truths."

"Four questions," I said. "Do I need to answer all four?"

The Oracle's eyes brightened. "You are amusing, Samuel, asking me a question."

I held out my hands and smiled. "My apologies, Oracle. Please ask your questions."

The Oracle paused while I shuffled my feet, worried about what would happen if I stumbled with any of my answers.

Then, an utter stillness fell upon the temple as the Oracle spoke. "Tell me, Samuel, since passing through the gate of death, you've been exposed to many universal truths; how have you absorbed this incredible knowledge?"

I took a deep breath and let it release slowly. "Wow, that's quite a question. Well, I've been told that wisdom is not acquired by simply accumulating knowledge; it has more to do with a thirst for the truth. True wisdom," I said, holding a finger into the air to make my point, "arises from being in a state of openness, expressing humility, and being receptive to higher sources of knowledge."

The Oracle nodded and rolled his hand, expecting me to continue.

"Um," I said, taking a deep breath. "Wisdom can be found in many forms and from many diverse sources. In my time in the soul world, I've called upon various spiritual practices, learned from sacred texts, explored ancient teachings, and reached out for guidance from enlightened beings. These avenues have offered me insights into universal principles, Divine laws, and the interconnectedness of all existence."

"That's very good," the Oracle said. "How do you look within yourself when seeking answers to such challenging questions?"

"Is that the second question?" I asked with a raised brow.

"No, no, Samuel," the Oracle said, laughing. "It's still part of the first question."

"Oh, okay," I said, smiling at the Oracle's amusement. "To draw upon the wisdom within, I've realized the importance of inner reflection. By exploring the realms of my consciousness, seeking to unravel its mysteries through self-awareness, introspection, and meditation."

"Now, tell me more about your learning from others," the Oracle said. "And yes, you're still on the first question."

"Okay," I said with a warm smile. "I've acknowledged the importance of absorbing experiences from powerful teachers. After all, soul life has been a classroom for me, presenting lessons and opportunities for growth and understanding. I've tried embracing the challenges and triumphs that have come my way, recognizing them as catalysts for expansion and learning. It's how I've gained a deeper comprehension of the universal truths."

The Oracle nodded and asked, "Can you explain how you've acquired wisdom through compassion?"

"All right," I said, nodding. "I understand the importance of embodying humility, compassion, and love, and by cultivating these virtues, I've created an inner space allowing for the unobstructed flow of Divine wisdom and cosmic insight."

"And you realize, Samuel, that this process is ongoing?"

I nodded. "I do. My birth is not my destination but a continuously unfolding journey through multiple dimensions and many realms of existence. Each step delivers deeper layers of understanding, expanding awareness, and a broader perspective of universal truths."

The Oracle nodded as its presence took on a brighter glow. "You've done well with your first question, Samuel. But before I ask you the second question, I want you to remember that spiritual wisdom is a sacred partnership between the soul and the Divine. It requires a willingness to explore, question, and seek out truths while at the same time surrendering to the guidance and illumination of the cosmic forces as you orchestrate the universal dance of wisdom and understanding."

CHAPTER FIFTY-SEVEN
AMENHOTEP

Seemingly satisfied with my answer to the first question, the Oracle vanished, leaving me alone within the great temple. With one last look around, I wandered over to the shelves where the ancient scrolls lay and picked one up. Carefully, I slid off a brown ribbon tied around it and unrolled the delicate parchment.

There, in words I could read, was the story of a young man living in ancient Egypt during the time of the great pharaohs. An era of both grandeur and oppression. This man in question was a Hebrew slave, toiling under the scorching sun, enduring the hardships of a lifetime of bondage.

Though no name was given to this Hebrew, he was strong in body and mind and determined to fight against the repression imposed on his people. Even against the brutal taskmasters, this rebellious Hebrew found ways to frustrate and humiliate the Egyptians.

That was until Amenhotep determined to teach this upstart a lesson. He devised a contest of strength, proving once and for all who was a superior man. Word spread throughout the slave quarters of this battle, stirring a mix of excitement, trepidation, and hope for a measure of redemption among the Hebrews.

On the event day, a massive crowd of slaves gathered on one side of a vast sandy arena. At the same time, the Egyptian elite, including the Pharoah himself, sat under a series of fabric canopies protecting themselves from the oppressive sun.

Amenhotep, adorned in elaborate battle garments, was escorted into the arena by an entourage of his fellow Egyptian soldiers. He exuded an air of arrogance and superiority. On the other hand, the Hebrew was dressed in his sweat-stained shirt, torn pants, and worn sandals. Regardless, he stood tall with quiet confidence. His eyes filled with determination and steadfast resolve.

As agreed, neither man would carry a weapon. The fight would be a bare-knuckle brawl, and the winner would be declared when the defeated man raised a hand. After a swift display of brute strength, quickness, and agility by the Hebrew, Amenhotep, his face covered in sweat and sand, appeared beaten. The Hebrew had him on the ground, his arm cinched around his neck in a choking headlock. Assuming that the Egyptian would raise his hand, signaling his defeat, the Hebrew released his grip. Then before he realized it, Amenhotep pulled a knife hidden within his boot and, with a swift lunge, stabbed the Hebrew in his heart, instantly killing him.

"Ah, Samuel," the Oracle said, interrupting the story. "Did you find that interesting?"

"I'm sorry," I said, quickly rolling up the parchment and placing it back on the shelf.

"That's fine," the Oracle said. "You were supposed to read it."

I scratched the back of my head and said, "Why's that?"

"Because the Hebrew slave in that story was you in a past life."

"I was a Hebrew slave in Egypt?" I said, placing a hand on my chest. The Oracle nodded.

"And I was killed by that Egyptian?"

"That's right."

"Wow," I said, thinking of life over three thousand years ago. "Are there more stories about my other lives?" I asked, pointing to the scrolls.

"There could be, but for now, you must answer my second question."

I stared at the scrolls, more interested in learning about my past lives than amusing the Oracle with my wisdom.

"Do you think you're here for my enjoyment, Samuel?" the Oracle said, reminding me how my thoughts were as transparent as my words.

"I'm sorry," I said, bowing my head.

"I don't blame you for being curious. But it would be best if you remained focused. There will be time for you to examine your past incarnations."

I nodded while shifting my eyes for one last look.

The Oracle clasped his hands together and said, "Tell me, Samuel, with all that's been presented to you in the soul world, how have you been able to distinguish between what's genuine and what's illusory?"

I nodded a moment, giving myself to dwell upon the question. "Well, here in the soul world, it's different than it was on Earth," I said. "On Earth, I could interpret someone's body language, tone of voice, facial expressions, and overall demeanor to determine if their words were truthful. But here in the soul world, the best way to discern between what's truthful and what's not is more of an intuitive perception. Trusting my instincts, which often bypasses the limitations of the conscious mind and taps into the intuitive faculties of the soul."

The Oracle nodded. "But how do you know to trust your instincts?"

"By creating a sacred space where I perceive the nuances, the hidden truths, and the authentic essence of who I am. In a way, it's more of a form of self-mastery. Being able to govern my thoughts, emotions, and actions with conscious intent and alignment with higher principles."

"Tell me more about this concept of self-mastery."

"Mmm," I said, mulling this over. "It's not about suppressing or denying my authentic nature, but rather about harmonizing the different aspects of myself. They're my beliefs, my way of doing things and avoiding things that don't serve or support my soul's growth. Self-mastery empowers my soul to shape my reality by making choices that align with my higher purpose and embodying my Divine essence," I said, wondering how I became so eloquent.

"That's excellent, Samuel," the Oracle said. "You've been blessed with an abundance of insights from your journey. You're an instrument of the Divine will; your thoughts, emotions, and actions are aligned with the higher truths of the universe. You've become a vessel for which wisdom and love flow, becoming a beacon of light, illuminating the path for others."

CHAPTER FIFTY-EIGHT
THE FINAL QUESTION

Unlike his sudden disappearance last time, the Oracle remained poised upon his throne of light. Though I took advantage of moments to steal curious looks at the stack of scrolls. I couldn't help but wonder if one of my past lives was indeed that of a Hebrew slave in the times of the ancient Egyptians; how did that profound life shape my karma and its effect upon my subsequent lives?

Seemingly unperturbed by my distraction, the Oracle said, "Samuel, can you explain how you've achieved your spiritual transformation during your time in the soul world?"

"Is that the third question?" I asked with a raised brow.

The Oracle nodded.

"Spiritual transformation?" I said with a grimace. "What do you mean?"

"Since your arrival, and until this very moment as you stand here before the Oracle, how have you embraced the extraordinary changes you've experienced, and how have these changes contributed toward your subsequent awakening?"

"Ah," I said, nodding. "Well, I suppose it's about understanding the need to be connected to a force greater than myself, and that's what set me on the path toward my spiritual transformation."

"That's a good beginning," the Oracle said. "But a spiritual transformation also calls for you to step beyond the limits of your pride, recognizing that your journey is not just for yourself, but is intricately woven into the fabric of the collective human experience."

"Yes, I understand that ideal," I said.

"Good," the Oracle said. "Tell me, how was this transformation achieved?"

"In the realms of Gehenna, I was purified five times," I said, holding up five fingers. "Throughout those realms, I was forced to confront old wounds, deal with my limited beliefs, and of course, my unhealthy behavioral patterns that no longer served me. My multiple purifications and visits to the planets have realigned my soul with the true essence of the natural world."

"This knowledge will serve you well, Samuel," the Oracle said. "But I also want you to know that when you accept your spiritual transformation, you're surrendering to the guidance of the Divine, trusting in the unfolding of your journey, and embracing the inherent wisdom and love within you. And most important, your spiritual growth is not an individual endeavor, but a co-creation with the Divine forces of the universe."

"That's quite a partnership," I said with a bright-eyed grin.

The Oracle laughed. "During your time in the soul world, you've provided great joy to the hierarchal beings with your humor."

"That's good to hear," I said, glancing over to the shelves. "Would it be okay, Oracle, if I browsed through the scrolls now?"

The Oracle wagged a finger. "Not yet, there's still one more question."

"The final question?"

"Yes, the final question," the Oracle said, tapping his fingertips together. "Once you move on into your next life, how will you call upon all you've learned here in the soul world?"

I shook my head and shrugged. "That's a question that I've been struggling with."

"Yes, it is a good question," the Oracle said, nodding. "What's your answer?"

I exhaled and said, "I'm not quite sure. I suppose remembering lessons learned in the soul world undergoes some process, like an unveiling. Similar to how we lock away bad memories in the recesses of our mind, our soul memories are also hidden from our conscious awareness, allowing us to focus on our new life."

"But are there ways to make these lessons accessible?" the Oracle asked.

I sighed, thinking about it. "I would say that the lessons and experiences from the soul world are not completely hidden. Because they've become imprinted into the deepest layers of our being. They may become evident in influencing my character or in my unique and quirky inclinations."

"That's a good explanation, Samuel."

I shook my head, confused at my expressed knowledge. "How do I know all these things?" I asked.

"It's not just you. Remember, Samuel, you're part of a collective consciousness. What you know is known by all, and all that you speak will be spoken by all."

"I wish I could take everyone with me when I'm reborn."

"You can," the Oracle said with a nod. "You just need to know how to nurture these connections."

"And how do I do that?"

"Developing spiritual practices will allow you to access the higher realms of consciousness. Gradually you'll be able to unveil deeper layers of your being, allowing for the remembrance and integration of your soul's acquired wisdom and experiences."

"I hope I can do that. I've learned so much. It would be a shame to forget it all."

"Ultimately, Samuel, remembering what you learned in the soul world is unique and may unfold over many years during your next life, as long as you engage in your quest for self-discovery."

I wagged my head back and forth and said, "I'll try my best."

"I'm going to leave you now, Samuel. You're welcome to stay and look through the scrolls. When you're done, walk back down the mountain."

"Then what will happen?" I asked.

"You'll make the final preparations for your birth," the Oracle said and vanished.

CHAPTER FIFTY-NINE
ROMAN GLADIATOR

With the Oracle gone, I remained alone in the temple, gawking slack-jawed at the hundreds of identical rolled-up scrolls, contemplating which one to choose. I rubbed my hands together, anticipating the excitement of learning about another of my past lives.

Without any particular reason, I reached for the very bottom of the pile and carefully pulled out a scroll. I looked at it momentarily before slipping off the brown ribbon and unrolling the parchment.

There, written in neat cursive script, I read the following story.

In the heart of the grand Roman Colosseum, a fierce battle unfolded between two gladiators, their weapons poised for combat and the air thick with anticipation. The sun beat down upon the sandy arena, casting long shadows as the spectators filled the stands, eagerly awaiting the spectacle about to unfold. The first gladiator and champion of Rome, Crixus, stood tall and imposing, his muscular frame glistening with sweat.

"Crixus," I said, putting a hand to my mouth. Could this be the same man tormenting me here in the soul world? Wasting no time, I returned to the narrative.

Adorned in shining armor, Crixus wielded a mighty gladius, a short sword honed through countless battles. His eyes burned with determination, his focus unwavering as he prepared for the clash.

Opposite him stood Dazas, a nimble and agile warrior known for his lightning-fast strikes. Dressed in lightweight armor that allowed for swift movement, he brandished a net in one hand and a trident in the other. His eyes glittered with a mix of excitement and steely resolve.

As the signal for battle sounded, the gladiators lunged forward, their movements fluid and calculated. Crixus launched a powerful strike, his gladius slicing through the air with precision. Dazas expertly evaded the blow, his lithe form gracefully sidestepping the attack.

Sparks flew with each clash of their weapons, and the crowd erupted in cheers and applause. Crixus, fueled by his strength and determination, delivered thunderous blows, his gladius meeting the trident in a shower of sparks. Dazas, relying on his agility and cunning, countered with quick jabs and entangled his opponent's maneuvers using his net.

Their battle was a dance of skill and strategy. Some would describe it as a symphony of grace and power. Crixus relied on his sheer might, while Dazas leveraged his speed and agility to outmaneuver his opponent. The intensity of the fight heightened as the gladiators circled one another, anticipating the next move, seeking an opening to strike.

Bloodied and bruised, their bodies became a canvas of scars and sweat. The clash of metal, the grunts of exertion, and the crowd's roars merged into a cacophony of excitement and primal energy. Each gladiator fought fervently, fueled by survival and the desire to entertain the masses.

The gladiators displayed their physical prowess, resilience, and endurance as the battle raged. Their faces etched with determination, they pushed through exhaustion, their spirits unyielding. They fought for their lives, honor, glory, and the fleeting chance of freedom.

Finally, after what seemed like an eternity, a decisive moment arrived. Dazas, summoning the last remnants of his strength, launched a devastating strike, breaching Crixus's defenses. The gladius slipped from his grasp, and Dazas wasted no time, lunging with his trident and piercing Crixus's right thigh. Blood spewed forth, and the crowd gasped in horror. The champion of Rome was wounded, down on one knee.

As the crowd held its collective breath, Dazas kicked Crixus hard in the chest, knocking him flat on his back.

Crixus looked up at Dazas and said, "Brother, spare me."

Though they were biological brothers, Dazas ignored his elder's plea and looked up to the Emperor's box, as was the custom upon deciding on the fate of the defeated. The Emperor waited and allowed a moment for the masses to voice their opinion. Dazas knew the crowd loved his brother and would give their thumbs up, wanting him to spare the champion's life. On the other hand, the Emperor was angry with Crixus, as his only daughter was caught speaking with the gladiator, raising suspicions of an illicit affair.

Dazas saw the Emperor glance over to his daughter, who had turned ashen, her hands cupping her face. Then he looked toward his wife, who was shaking her head, wanting her husband to spare Crixus's life and prevent their daughter's heartbreak.

The Emperor stood, holding a clenched fist with his thumb in the neutral, sideways position. As the audience held its breath, he twisted his wrist, pointing his thumb downward.

Dazas nodded. Lifting the trident above his head, its prongs dripping with Crixus's blood, he drove it deep into his brother's neck. Crixus's eyes bulged, and he coughed out a black glob. His body convulsed one last time before he lay still. Dead at the hands of his younger brother.

I let loose a long exhalation. *Was I Dazas? Was Crixus my brother? Did I kill my brother in a previous lifetime?* How could I have gotten this far in the soul world without knowing this?

While I pondered these disturbing questions, the Temple of the Divine Oracle began to shake. At first, it was just a minor vibration, but it didn't subside. Within moments, the marble floor shook violently. The hundreds of scrolls fell off the shelves, and the walls and columns began to crack. Large pieces of stone dislodged, crashing to the ground all around me. Clouds of dust filled the air, obscuring my sight. I dropped the scroll and ran toward the doorway.

I stumbled, but stayed upright and found my way outside. Far enough away, I turned and saw the temple collapsing upon itself into piles of rubble. However, this didn't stop the mountain from shaking. I'd never experienced an earthquake, but I imagined this was what it felt like.

I remembered the Oracle's words—*You should walk back down the mountain when you're done.* I decided to listen, except instead of walking, I ran.

With the ground shaking, branches falling, and the mountain appearing as if it was about to collapse, I found my way to the bottom. Just as I stepped beyond the tree line, the earthquake ceased, and all was quiet.

Taking a breath to gather my wits, I paused and observed what lay before me. It was a lovely open field of tall grasses, and off in the distance, shimmering in the sunlight, appeared to be a small village. I turned to take one last look at the mountain, which now seemed peaceful and undisturbed. With nowhere else to go, I proceeded toward the collection of small dwellings.

CHAPTER SIXTY
CLARA AND CRIXUS

As I approached the village, the sun's gentle rays illuminated humble wooden homes donned with thatched roofs, standing tight, shoulder to shoulder, forming harmonious rows along narrow cobblestone streets. Each house, adorned with brightly painted shutters, exuded a historical rustic charm.

At the heart of the village was a lively marketplace lined with stalls offering all sorts of foods and household goods. As I wandered beyond the busy market, I stumbled upon a synagogue featuring wooden posts inscribed with intricate carvings and a row of delicate stained-glass windows. A large Star of David painted blue and white was displayed above its front doors.

I entered the synagogue, and as I stepped into the sanctuary, I thought of Moshe's story of when he was a young boy and how the Russian soldiers barged in. I cringed, imagining how they forced the wounded Jewish fighters outside, lined them up against the synagogue wall, and shot them dead by firing squad. As I shook my head at the outright cruelty, I heard footsteps approaching. Quickly, I turned around and saw Clara.

"Welcome, Samuel," Clara said, her arms spread wide. "It's good to see you again."

"Oh, hi, Clara." I hugged my great-great-grandmother. "Was this your synagogue?"

"This was Krzywcza, the village my family came from, and yes, this was our synagogue."

"I thought so," I said. "Why am I here?"

Clara shrugged. "It seemed like a good place for us to talk."

I rubbed the back of my neck, thinking about where I just came from and what I learned about my past lives. "Talk about what?" I asked.

"Oh," Clara said, holding up a hand. "There's quite a bit to discuss. But I'm sure you want to ask me about your experience at the Temple of the Divine Oracle."

"You know about the scrolls?"

"Of course," Clara said, nodding. "Come, Samuel, let's sit and talk about what you've learned."

We sat side-by-side on one of the long wooden benches surrounding the elevated Bimah. Unlike the temples I'd been to during my lifetime, I figured this unusual layout was typical of synagogues in this era.

Once seated, I leaned forward, resting my elbows on my knees, and said, "I learned about two of my past lives."

"Those were the only two. Except, of course, your last one."

I tilted my head and squinted. "That's it? Three lives."

Clara shrugged. "How many were you expecting?"

"I don't know," I said, shaking my head. "How many did you have?"

Clara gazed upward toward the upper balcony of the synagogue, seeming to be giving my question some thought, then said, "Six lives so far."

"But you're the mother of the *tzaddik*. Do you still need to be reborn?"

Clara nodded slowly. "Indeed I do."

"Mmm," I said.

"Would you like to talk about what you read in the scrolls?"

I scratched my forehead and said, "About my life in Egypt?"

"You were killed in the arena by Amenhotep."

I bit my lower lip and nodded.

"Your family was devastated. No one wanted you to fight."

"How do you know all this?" I asked, fanning out my hands.

Clara grasped one of my hands, cupped it between hers, and said, "Because I was your mother."

I jerked my head back. "You were my mother! Is that true?"

"That's why I'm with you now."

"You've waited for me?"

"Time is of no consequence. But yes, I've stayed on."

I stared at Clara and said, "What was it like being my mother?"

"You were a good son, though your temper was short."

"Is that what got me into trouble with Amenhotep?"

"Yes, that's what got you into your fight. But the real reason had to do with Amenhotep and your sister."

"My sister?" I asked.

"The Egyptian had his eye on her for weeks, and we all saw it. She tried to avoid him, but he caught up with her one day when she filled the water jugs at the well. He tried pulling her into his wagon, tearing at her robe, and she resisted, broke free, and ran from him."

"What happened next?"

"She came to you, obviously upset and frightened. That's when you had enough and challenged Amenhotep."

"And he killed me," I said.

Clara furrowed her brow and said, "Yes, he killed you."

I got to my feet and paced around the sanctuary floor, trying to grasp the significance of this life from long ago.

"There's one more thing you should know," Clara said, standing up and grasping my arm.

"What's that?" I asked.

"It's about your sister. Do you know who she was?"

"My sister in Egypt?" I asked.

Clara nodded.

I shrugged, held my hands, and said, "Who was she?"

"Meghan."

I grimaced and closed my eyes. "My Meghan?" I asked, placing a hand on my chest.

"Your wife, Meghan, was your sister during your short lifetime in Egypt."

"And you were my mother?"

Clara nodded.

I rubbed my chin, trying to comprehend the significance. "But why was she my wife in my last life?"

"Because you promised to protect her, and what better way than to be her husband?"

"But I failed her again," I said, thinking of how I left her.

"Yes, you did. But there's a bigger picture that you need to understand."

"What's that?"

"Before I explain, let's review your second life as a Roman gladiator."

"Don't tell me," I said, holding out my hand. "Meghan was there too."

Clara nodded. "But this time, she was the daughter of the Emperor."

"The one whom my brother Crixus spoke with?" I said.

"It wasn't just words that passed between them. There were secret trysts."

"They were lovers?"

"And you were jealous," Clara said. "That's why you killed him."

"Because I wanted the Emperor's daughter for myself?" I asked.

"Yes, though that never happened. Once Crixus was killed, you were vanquished to Pompeii, where you were slain in the arena a few months later."

I sat on the wooden bench, trying to comprehend the revelations that Meghan was a significant presence in my three past lives. She was my sister in Egypt, and in Rome, we were entangled in a complex love triangle with Crixus. And after my last life, it was apparent that Meghan and I had unfinished business together, causing me to wonder how our relationship would resume in our next lifetimes. But one thing I knew for sure—there was no doubt about it in my mind—was that we were soulmates.

"One more thing to note: you died all three times at age thirty-two."

"What does that mean?"

"It's hard to say," Clara said with a squint. "Perhaps it refers to your life's unlearned lessons. Think of it as an opportunity for growth in your next incarnation."

"All right," I said, staying focused on my life as a gladiator. "Why has Crixus been taunting me since I arrived in the soul world? Who was he?"

"In Egypt, he was Amenhotep, your rival, and in Rome, he was Crixus, your brother."

"Was he reborn since?"

"No," Clara said, shaking her head. "He's been waiting for you in the spirit world."

I scratched the top of my head, trying to understand. "But would he do that?"

"Why don't you ask him yourself," Clara said, gesturing an arm toward the front of the sanctuary as doors swung open and in walked Crixus.

A young-looking man dressed in a Roman-style robe cinched at the waist with a brown belt walked toward me. He wore traditional leather strapped sandals that crisscrossed up his calves.

"It's good to see you, Dazas," Crixus said.

I stared at him, looking remarkably different than he did in his battle gear.

"Why have you been avoiding me?" Crixus said, now standing about a foot away.

"I was told you were my dark side, my inner *rasha*."

Crixus nodded. "I was during your last life."

I furrowed my brow, staring at him. "How could it be possible to influence me from the spirit world while I was in the earthly realm?"

"Through the help of the asuras," Crixus said.

"The asuras, yes," I said, wagging a finger. "I know about them. The archangel Raphael said they were negative forces influencing and manipulating human consciousness. Their purpose was to divert souls from their spiritual path by hindering their connection with higher realms of consciousness."

"I was approached by the asuras, who were most interested in you. They allowed me to strengthen your inner *rasha* during your last life, which weakened your resistance."

"And I, in turn, sought out the painkillers," I said.

Crixis nodded.

"But why would the asuras have interest in me?" I said, putting my hand on my chest.

"It's about your invention," Crixis said. "They were seeking ways to stop it."

"The CCT?" I said, flipping out my hands.

Crixus nodded.

"How can you affect my invention before it has occurred?"

"I can explain that," Clara interjected. "Future karma plays a role where intentions can manifest karmic effects in future lives."

"So it's true," I said, pointing at Crixus. "You lured me toward drugs as a way for your revenge?"

"I'm ashamed to say it," Crixus said, lowering his eyes.

I looked over to Clara, who remained silent. Then I returned to Crixus and said, "Why are you ashamed? You nearly got what you wanted."

"But it's not what I want anymore."

"Why, what happened?"

"After I immersed myself into the River of Fire, I was purified of my anger and the shackles chaining me to my dark thoughts. I was offered a chance for renewal, and I decided to treasure it."

"That's wonderful," I said.

"I also want to say that I am proud of you, brother, because of what you accomplished in Gehenna. By capturing the true *rasha*—Solomon— and rescuing Clara's husband, Pincus, you've done a great service to the collective of beings in the soul world. The angels and archangels are singing your praises."

"Is that right?" I said, though still unsure of Crixus's intentions.

"Brother," Crixus said, touching my shoulder. "I've come to ask for your forgiveness."

"My forgiveness? Shouldn't I be asking you for forgiveness? After all, I killed you."

Crixus puckered his mouth and said, "And in your last life, I had a hand in your doom."

While I stood there speechless, Crixus reached out and pulled me close, wrapping his muscular arms around me, and said, "I love you, brother. Please forgive me."

Wishing tears could flow, I wrapped my arms around my brother and whispered, "I love you too, and I forgive you. Will you forgive me?"

"Of course," Crixus said.

As we reconciled, I thought about my brother Max. While my previous relationship with Crixus was toxic, Max had positively influenced me as a source of solace and inspiration. He deeply understood the delicate balance of life, finding harmony by immersing himself in the natural world. I vowed that as I embarked on my new life,

I would hold onto the hope that Max and I would again cross paths, united as part of our soul family.

CHAPTER SIXTY-ONE
FINAL PREPARATIONS

I offered my fond farewell to Crixus, who assured me we would meet again in our next lives. "Though we may not be brothers," he added.

"Hopefully, we'll be at least good friends," I said as the former champion of Rome waved goodbye, exiting the synagogue.

"Are you ready for your final preparations?" Clara asked, standing beside me.

"Final preparations?" I asked.

"To make yourself ready for your birth. You'll be involved in reflection, evaluation, and decision-making."

"Okay," I said and took a breath. "What do I need to do?"

"There's no need to explain; just know that these final preparations will be important in shaping your next life."

"In what way?" I asked.

"By taking responsibility for the continuation of your karmic journey."

"All right," I said, nodding.

"Good," Clara said. "But not here."

Then, in the blink of an eye, I found myself in that same library that housed the Spirits of Mercury's archives. Surrounded by countless amounts of books, each containing the vast wisdom of the universe.

While standing there, I took notice of one book on the shelf that seemed to glow with a soft, radiant light. Curious about why I was drawn to this volume, I pulled it out and brought it to the table.

I sat down with the book lying before me. Gently, I ran my fingertips across the leather-bound, unmarked cover before opening it to the first page. As I gazed within, a cascade of images and emotions unfolded before my eyes. Animated scenes played out from my time as a Hebrew slave in Egypt. Page after page of my thirty-two years of life. How I protected my sister and defended my family and people, culminating with my death at the hand of the Egyptian soldier Amenhotep.

Following that life came my thirty-two-year life as a gladiator. I observed my disturbing interactions with Crixus, jealousy toward his relationship with the Emperor's daughter, and how I killed my brother in the arena to take revenge.

The last section of this book was about my recent thirty-two-year-old life. A combination of a joyful youth, a loving and supportive family, a cherished wife, and the personal struggles that forced me off the righteous path. I read about my many challenges and the subsequent karmic debt that resulted from each experience.

As I became immersed in these stories, I noticed patterns and recurring themes that emerged over my three-thousand-year journey. There were lessons of love and compassion, forgiveness and acceptance, all interwoven into the essence of my existence. I couldn't help but marvel at the opportunities I was presented with and how I learned and evolved from each of them. I also began to discern numerous threads that connected my past lives. I recognized how specific challenges and relationships were purposely woven into my path, all designed to facilitate my growth.

In ancient Egypt, I had struggled with my life as a slave. My overly strong ego had tormented me and ultimately brought on my demise. Then I had found myself confronted with intense jealousy issues as a Roman gladiator who caused my own brother's death. Lastly, I had lived a life that had to deal with the consequences of my past incarnations, or, as I had now learned to call it, my karmic footprint.

I observed the people I encountered and continued to meet from one life to the next. Testament to the lessons I was taught and how they were all connected. With each turn of the page, I gained clarity and insight, becoming aware of the themes that shaped each of my lives. Themes of courage, resilience, and the pursuit of truth, along with bursts of creativity, seeking to help others in need, and the power behind my human connections.

While I remained in this sacred library, I reflected upon the immense knowledge I acquired, realizing these lessons were not merely an intellectual exercise but a profound recognition of my spiritual essence. This understanding assured me that I would catalyze my continued growth into my next incarnation.

With newfound clarity, I closed the book and sighed, ready to step forward and embark on my new life.

"Not yet, Samuel," Clara said, appearing seated across from me. "There's more."

"All right," I said, sliding the book away. "What's next?"

"Based on the insights you've gained, you'll want to set forth your spiritual goals for your upcoming incarnation. You can choose the lessons or experiences you wish to engage with to facilitate your evolution. You'll align these goals with your purpose and how it contributes to your overall development of consciousness."

"Is there another book I need to read?" I asked, pointing to the shelves.

"No, this time, you will meet with the first soul that greeted you upon your passing through the gate."

"Oh, Poppy," I said, and in an instant, I found myself standing on a tropical beach.

CHAPTER SIXTY-TWO
GOALS AND RELATIONSHIPS

"Walk with me, Sam," Poppy said, gesturing to the desolate, pristine beach.

I looked about at the seabirds, swaying palm trees, and clear blue water lapping on the shore beneath our bare feet. "This reminds me of Florida," I said.

"That was my intention," Poppy said with a smile. "I thought it would be a good place for our last conversation before you move on."

I grabbed Poppy's arm, stopped him from walking, and said, "Will we be together again?"

"Since it's both our desire, then it will be so. Though there's no way of knowing when or in what capacity."

"I know," I said, realizing how the veil of forgetfulness works.

"But before you go, there's some goal setting we need to discuss."

"You mean besides the goal of us being in each other's future lives?" I said with a wide smile.

"Yes, besides that one," Poppy said, gently tapping my cheek.

We walked on for a while, accompanied by the natural sounds of a pleasant beach day, before Poppy said, "The preparation for setting your spiritual goals began that very first moment you passed. Since then, you've been surrounded by angels, archangels, and others who've provided guidance and support. A time when you've engaged in deep reflection, examining the lessons and challenges you faced in your previous lives. You've contemplated your spiritual progress and areas where you fell short, and you dealt with your unresolved karmic patterns. This introspection has provided you with a foundation for setting your goals."

"Yes, it has been quite an education. More than I ever received during any of my past lives."

"Looking forward, I want you to envision how to further develop the virtues of compassion, wisdom, love, and courage based upon the specific growth areas you wish to improve upon."

"*Mmm,*" I pondered. "Can you give me any examples?"

Poppy wagged his head a few times, then said, "You've struggled with such issues as a lack of patience, offering forgiveness to those who've offended you, or shying away from hard work. These are all areas you can focus on improving."

"Okay, I'll try," I said.

"Once you've formulated your goals, they'll imprint onto your consciousness, where you can act upon them, like a road map for your upcoming life."

"You make it sound so easy," I said.

"I know, it sounds easy," Poppy agreed. "But the exact unfolding of your experiences and your response to them are subjected to your free will, as are the choices you'll make during your new life. Your goals are only to provide you with a framework. But your decisions alone will ultimately shape your journey."

We came across some large boulders hugging the shoreline. "Can we continue our chat over here?" Poppy asked as he propped himself on a large stone, his bare feet dipping into the ocean water.

"Sure," I said, sitting next to my grandfather.

"This next idea is about seeking out potential karmic relationships with souls who can play significant roles in your upcoming life."

"You mean like me and you?"

"Sure," Poppy said. "But we'll always have an unbreakable bond. It would be best to examine the connections with other souls you'll encounter throughout your lifetime, even with adversaries. These connections can be characterized by love, friendship, or conflict as a way to resolve past karmic imbalances."

Poppy pointed a finger and said, "You may decide to be born into a family where you had previously experienced strained relationships, which is certainly an option for you. By doing this, you'll aim to heal these wounds, foster forgiveness, and promote growth for you and the other individuals involved. Or, you may seek new connections with people you have yet to encounter."

I furrowed and asked, "How do I reach out to unknown souls?"

"You can initiate an exchange through your thoughts. It's a way to connect while you're still in this unborn state."

"All right," I said.

"With the guidance of your spiritual mentors, you'll reenter the physical realm with individuals ready and eager to engage in karmic relationships with you."

"I've had quite a few of these spiritual mentors since I arrived in the soul world."

"Yes," Poppy said. "Especially now, during this preparatory phase, they're all engaged in providing you with insights, guidance, and assistance. Helping you make informed decisions about the karmic dynamics and life circumstances you'll encounter."

"Do I need to do something to acknowledge them?" I asked.

Poppy shook his head. "Just be open to the guidance of these elevated beings. Trust in their wisdom, and be accepting of their loving presence. As the time draws near for your departure, rest assured they will be ever-present, accompanying you as you navigate the challenges and triumphs of your upcoming life."

"But what about my karmic debt? Do I bring any of this into my next life?"

Poppy leaned forward, clapping my back. "That's a terrific insight. Yes, you must embrace a sense of responsibility for your past actions and the karmic imprints it carries forward."

"But I was purified in all five realms of Gehenna. How can there be any negative karma left?"

"There may not be, but while you're still in this realm of introspection and reflection, you should take advantage of deep self-examination, reviewing the experiences, relationships, and patterns that have shaped your previous lives. Acknowledge the consequences of your positive and negative actions, and accept the karmic debts you may have incurred. In other words, don't take for granted that you've cleaned the slate."

"Okay, Poppy. I'll do that."

"Your journey was not easy, but you've done remarkably well. I have tremendous pride in you. As you prepare to descend into the physical realm, I want you to take on your karmic responsibilities head-on. Trust in the inherent wisdom of the universe and the transformative power of accepting and learning from your past. Step forward with courage, knowing that accepting and addressing your karmic responsibilities can pave your way toward a future filled with great harmony, growth, and spiritual fulfillment."

We sat silently, watching the waves crashing and birds crossing overhead.

"Is this when we say goodbye?" I said, gazing outwards upon the distant horizon where the sea met the sky.

"It is, Sam," Poppy said, wrapping his arm around me, and like when I was a little boy, I rested my head upon his shoulder.

"I love you, Poppy. Thank you for being here for me. I don't know how I would have managed without you."

"I love you too, Sam. You bring me much joy and happiness."

"What's going to happen to me?"

"Once you've made your final decisions, you'll be ensouled into a fetus."

"A newly conceived one?"

"Oh no, you must wait until about the third or fourth month after conception."

"Why is that?" I said, lifting my head.

"It takes time for a sufficient physical foundation to be established before you can begin your ensoulment."

"It's hard imagining all of this," I said.

"Could you've imagined what you've just been through while still alive?"

I laughed. "No, of course not."

"Well, you need to go and make some big decisions," Poppy said, squeezing me.

"What about you? When will you return to Earth?"

"Soon," Poppy said, nodding. "Very soon."

CHAPTER SIXTY-THREE
AQUARIUS

I sat in a circle around a cosmic version of a campfire. But instead of the typical red and orange flames, a radiant glow of what could be best described as celestial energies danced and flickered about, casting a warm and inviting light.

Seated around the flame was a gathering of familiar hierarchal beings, the four archangels—Michael, Raphael, Zadkiel, and Haniel. Each entity in this sacred circle emanated a unique vibration, representing the different aspects of their Divine wisdom and compassion.

Looking through the flame, I saw Clara directly across from me. I was surrounded by a council of wise beings dedicated to the next stage of my spiritual journey. Clara spoke at ease and with a sense of calm enveloping the sacred space.

"Samuel has reflected upon his past life; he's gleaned insights and lessons and addressed unfinished business that required his attention before committing to his incarnation. He has acknowledged his growth areas, dealt with his karmic patterns, and taken advantage of the opportunities for spiritual development. It's with a deep yearning for evolution that Samuel shares these reflections with the spiritual hierarchy present."

I momentarily greeted each winged archangel seated around the circle with a warm smile and two hands over my heart.

"It is with great joy that we gather to discuss the circumstance of Samuel's birth," Clara continued. "Deliberation will begin on the geographic location, the cultural context of the era, and the familial environment that will best serve Samuel's soul evolution. Consider the dynamics of the potential parents, extended family, and friends, and the opportunities for growth and the healing these relationships will offer."

Then there was utter silence. Not a word was spoken. This continued long enough that I tilted my head around the flame to see Clara. When she looked back, I shrugged and held out my hands.

"They are discussing the circumstances of your birth now," she said.

I looked at the plain faces of the archangels, who all appeared quiet, saying nothing.

"They are conversing in sacred dialogue. Not meant for your ears. When they've decided, they will let us know."

"What will they say?" I asked.

"They will inform you of the optimal timing and circumstances of your incarnation and, of course, align these decisions with your intentions and purpose."

"My purpose?" I repeated. "You mean my invention?"

"That's right. The archangels have great interest in your Cerebro-Cube Transducer."

"Really?" I said with a squint of curiosity. "Can you tell me why?"

"It's believed that such an invention can revolutionize how people connect and share information globally. Such an advancement in technology has the potential to bridge gaps, promote understanding, and build more inclusive societies."

"All from my CCT?" I said, wide-eyed.

"According to what the beings are saying, the applications are numerous. Offering breakthroughs in healthcare technology resulting in saving lives, alleviating suffering, and enhancing the well-being of humanity."

I wagged a finger around at the sedentary, winged beings. "That's what they're discussing?"

Clara nodded.

"Why can you hear them, and I can't?"

"It seems to be the way they want it," Clara said with a shrug.

I looked around at their faces, but they continued staring straight ahead, expressionless.

"What are they saying now?" I asked.

"They're debating the karmic considerations related to the cosmic rhythms and the confluence of energies that will support your birth."

"Sounds complicated."

Clara raised a finger and said, "Now they're discussing your choice of parents and its significance in fulfilling your purpose. Your parents must possess specific qualities, strengths, and challenges that will mirror and evoke your growth."

I held my hands and said, "It sounds like perfect parents."

"It's the ideal," Clara said. "But I'm sure you've heard of the phrase—unintended consequences."

"Oh yes," I said, jerking a thumb over to the archangel sitting to my right. "Zadkiel had a lot to say about that."

"Even the archangels can't foresee the whims and foibles of humankind. But they try their best."

"Nobody's perfect," I said.

"They're now discussing the timing of the birth. It's critical that the positions of the celestial bodies and the corresponding astrological influences are being implemented to determine the specific timing of your earthly incarnation."

"Why is this so important?"

Clara flipped out her hands and said, "Because the positions of the planets create distinct patterns of cosmic forces which will impact your life's path."

"In what way?"

"The position of the sun at the time of your birth indicates the potential for your individuality, self-expression, and vitality. At the same time, the placement of the moon will determine your emotional tendencies and patterns. The positions of the other planets will reveal aspects of your temperament or how you handle challenges."

"Wow, I had no idea such thought went into a new life."

"You should know, Samuel," Clara said, waving a hand, "that this gathering of the archangels to oversee a birth hardly ever occurs. They only congregate when they believe the soul about to be born has something significant to offer humanity."

My jaw dropped. "You're not serious."

"You're indeed special, Samuel," Clara said, nodding. "I hope you've realized that by now."

I offered an uncomfortable, pained smile. "They have great expectations for my CCT."

Clara held up a finger and tilted her head. "They're discussing that now."

"What are they saying?" I said softly.

"They're exploring the timeline of future innovations, trying to find the moment when the CCT will reach its maturity and become accessible to humanity," she said, then paused to listen. "The archangels say it will be in 2075, just as new and appropriate technological advancements unfold."

"2075? I died in January 2021. That's fifty-four years later," I said, mulling over the period. "Did they discuss a date of birth?"

Clara smiled. "Your birth date will be the twenty-seventh of January, 2075."

"January twenty-seventh?" I asked, wide-eyed. "That's the same date of my death. Why would it be that day?"

"The archangels explain that you're being provided a bridge connecting your past and future."

"But why?"

"It's because that's when the archangels feel it's important for your birth to occur to fulfill your purpose," Clara said.

"But I thought I needed knowledge of the future, not the past, to create the CCT."

"By connecting with the past, you'll gain insights into the universe's workings, the mysteries of consciousness, and the dynamics of creativity. It's tapping into the collective wisdom of all souls that have journeyed before you, drawing from their innovations, breakthroughs, and discoveries."

"Is that the only reason?"

"No, it's also the time of Aquarius, and as an Aquarian, you'll be blessed with an independent and unconventional nature. You'll possess a strong sense of individuality and will be driven by a desire to impact the world positively. With a natural curiosity and affinity for abstract thought, the archangels believe that as a child, you'll likely exhibit a keen intellect and a knack for innovative ideas."

"My grandmother was Aquarius."

"Yes, your Nanny was my granddaughter. A woman embodied with a strong sense of kindness and compassion. Driven by a deep concern for humanity and social justice."

"I miss her," I said, thinking of our beautiful times together.

Clara held up a finger. "The archangels say it won't be until your thirty-third birthday before the CCT is introduced to the world."

"Why at thirty-three?"

"It's about breaking free from the repetitive patterns of your past lives."

"Because I died at thirty-two?"

"That's right," Clara said, nodding. "Your thirty-third birthday will culminate your karmic journey with the birth of your purpose."

"Really?" I said with a grimace. "I hope I make it."

"Hold on," Clara said. "The archangels have decided upon a specific place of birth, and it's in a city that does not yet exist. It's called NeoAurora."

"NeoAurora?" I repeated. "I've never heard of it. Where is it?"

"It's next to Boulder, Colorado, and this city will become a bustling metropolis at the forefront of scientific innovation and conscious exploration. NeoAurora will boast a vibrant community of forward-thinking individuals who will embrace the transformative potential of the CCT."

"I've always liked Boulder," I said.

"They also have recommendations for your parents," Clara said.

"Really?" I said, looking at the expressionless group. "Who are they saying?"

"Their names are Leah Silverman and Jonah Adler. They're both research doctors in neurotechnology and met at the Massachusetts Institute of Technology as students."

"MIT?" I said, gaping at her.

"They're both esteemed researchers in the field of neurotechnology and will play pivotal roles in the development of the CCT."

"Oh," I said, mulling it over. "It sounds like I need them to fulfill my purpose."

"It appears so."

"But besides their brilliance, will they be good parents?"

Clara nodded. "Both Leah and Jonah embody the perfect balance of wisdom, compassion, and intellectual curiosity that will nurture and guide your journey. They will not only be your parents but also your mentors and allies embracing the transformative potential of the CCT."

"All right," I said. "They sound perfect."

"Do you accept Leah Silverman and Jonah Adler as your parents?"

I took one last look at the archangels and nodded. "Yes, I do."

CHAPTER SIXTY-FOUR
BIRTH

"Your time has arrived," Clara said as we stood alone in the open field beyond the village of Krzywcza. "With the alignment of time, place, and parents, based upon your chosen purpose, you're ready to embark on an extraordinary journey of self-discovery, conscious expansion, and the exploration of a CCT-infused world."

"So this is it?" I said, staring at my great-great-grandmother. "I'm ready to be born."

Clara wrapped her arms around me and whispered, "We will meet again soon in the earthly realm."

"Thank you for everything," I said with a long sigh.

Clara released me, pointed off into the distance, and said, "Before you depart, a few souls would like to say their farewells."

Walking down the pathway between fields of tall grasses, I saw Poppy, Moshe, Pincus, and Gray approaching.

"Oh, look who's here," I said with a huge smile.

Gray was the first to extend a hand. We shook, and he said, "Congratulations, Samuel. This is a wonderful moment, and I wish you all the best with your new life."

"Thank you so much, Gray, for all your help and everything you did for Moshe and Pincus. You risked much, and you're not even family."

Gray shrugged and said, "We're soul family."

"Samuel!" Pincus shouted. "I'm so pleased with you, as we all are. You have done well and are our family's pride and joy."

The two men stepped aside, allowing Moshe to come forward. He put two hands on my shoulders, gazed into my eyes, and said, "My dear Samuel, you are about to embark upon a new chapter in your eternal dance of life. Remember, you carry forth the Divine sparks, giving you the power to create. Embrace the challenges that lie ahead, for they're the crucibles that will refine and shape your spirit."

I smiled and nodded.

"Remember, you will encounter both darkness and light," Moshe the *tzaddik* continued, his voice resonating profoundly. "In your moments of doubt, turn inward and connect with the eternal flame burning within your being. It will guide you through the labyrinth of your human experience, leading you back to the path of righteousness and compassion."

"Thank you, Moshe," I said as my great-grandfather backed away, allowing Poppy to approach.

"I've been with you from that very moment you passed through the gates of the soul world, and now I am here as you depart through the gates of the earthly world. During our time together, between these two gates, I've watched you transform from a frightened, beaten soul to one the spiritual beings are praising as the chosen one who can change humanity for the better. To say I'm proud would be a vast understatement. Let me acknowledge and express my profound gratitude for the privilege of witnessing your transformation to a soul of substance."

Then Moshe gathered us in close. Clara, Poppy, Pincus, and Gray each laid a hand on me as Moshe said, "May you be guided by the wisdom of the ages, and may the light of your soul illuminate the lives of those you will encounter. Go forth, dear soul, with courage, compassion, and unwavering faith."

With those words, I departed from their presence and found myself poised upon the threshold of a beautiful golden gateway. With one final breath of spiritual essence, I bade farewell to the soul world, ready to embrace what awaits me in the earthly world.

Slowly, I began my descent, carried by a warm, comforting light, guiding me through cosmic currents, resonating with celestial energies, and connecting me to the awaiting life.

At the precise moment of ensoulment, I merged with the four-month-old fetus. I was then ready to join the intricate web of life, intertwining my consciousness with the delicate framework of newly formed cells and tissues.

Within the sanctuary of the womb, my transformation commenced. I gradually adapted to the confines of my new home and became attuned to its life rhythms, the pulsations of Mother's heartbeat, and the nourishing flow of her vital energy.

As the fetus grew and developed, my presence became more pronounced. I started infusing it with my karmic-cleansed individuality and my intentions for growth and self-realization, imprinting my unique qualities, talents, and predispositions onto the growing body.

During this sacred period, I established a profound connection with my mother. We shared an intricate dance of energies, emotions, and experiences, contributing to our mutual growth. Mother, a vessel of love and nurturing, provided the necessary conditions for my physical incarnation.

As months passed, my consciousness expanded within the developing body. I dreamed of the experiences, relationships, and lessons I would encounter once in the earthly realm. I was prepared for the challenges and joys ahead, trusting in the Divine plan that had brought me to this moment.

With each passing day, I connected further to my physical body. I felt the first stirrings of life, the fluttering of my heartbeat, and the subtle movements heralding the awakening of my senses. I rejoiced in the unfolding miracle, eagerly anticipating when I would take my first breath of earthly air.

As I approached the threshold of my incarnation, I carried the wisdom of my three past lifetimes. I embraced the opportunities ahead, trusting in the guidance and support of the spiritual realm that had nurtured this journey, and eager to embark upon a new chapter of growth, discovery, and self-realization.

Finally, the moment of my birth arrived; an exquisite culmination of my journey within the womb. As Mother's labor pains surged and her efforts intensified, I sensed the impending departure from the nurturing confines of the womb to the vast expanse of the physical world.

With each contraction, I experienced mighty waves of energy propelling me forward. I recognized that the moment of my birth would signify the completion of my integration with the physical body and initiate my fourth earthly adventure.

And then, with a final surge of energy and a profound wave of love, I emerged from Mother's womb, crossing the threshold into the earthly realm. I took my first breath, filled my lungs with the fresh air of physical existence, and screamed.

Moments later, I was placed in Mother's arms. As we gazed at each other's eyes for the first time, I saw Clara's gentle brown eyes staring back, just as the veil of forgetfulness fell.

THE END

ABOUT THE AUTHOR

Neil Perry Gordon is a highly regarded and prolific novelist acclaimed for his historical and metaphysical fiction. With eleven novels and a novella to his name, his latest work, *"Between Two Gates – A Young Man's Quest Toward Birth,"* showcases his literary prowess. Gordon's writing has garnered commendation from esteemed publications like Kirkus, Midwest Book Review, and Book Viral. At the same time, his readers on platforms such as Amazon and Goodreads have praised his works with numerous positive reviews.

Neil's education at the Green Meadow Waldorf School significantly shaped his passion for writing. There, he imbibed the belief that music, dance, theater, writing, literature, legends, and myths were not mere subjects to be studied but experiences to be embraced and absorbed.

In terms of his writing process, Neil adopts an organic approach. Rather than relying on a detailed outline, he begins with a premise for his characters and allows the story to unfold naturally. This method gives rise to unforeseen twists and captivating outcomes that have captivated readers. His novels balance character development and exhilarating action, ensuring a dynamic pace that keeps readers engaged.

Neil Perry Gordon's dedication to his craft and ability to craft engaging narratives have firmly established him as an accomplished historical and metaphysical fiction author. With each new novel, he continues enthralling readers with his imaginative storytelling and insightful explorations of the human experience.

Linktree: https://linktr.ee/neilperrygordon